DEATH OF A MINISTER

' "So to sum up, sir," said Detective Superintendent
Stupples to Captain Detterling, "what we have is this:
Mr Somerset Lloyd-James, identified by your own good self,
dead in the bath of his own uncurtained bathroom and
naked except for his spectacles. His wrists have apparently
been slashed, a safety razor blade has been found at the
bottom of the bath, and the bathwater is coloured by a red
substance which we may assume to be Mr Lloyd-James's
blood. Nothing more can be said until the medical experts
have examined the body and given us the results of all the
appropriate tests. That's about it . . ." '

But that was just the beginning of Captain Detterling's
quest to discover the truth behind the mysterious death of
his former school and university friend, fellow-officer and
erstwhile Party colleague.

Bring Forth the Body is the ninth novel in Simon Raven's
outstanding 'Alms for Oblivion' sequence.

D1313156

Also by Simon Raven

Novels
The Feathers of Death
Brother Cain
Doctors Wear Scarlet
Close of Play

'Alms for Oblivion' Sequence
The Rich Pay Late
Friends in Low Places
The Sabre Squadron
Fielding Gray
The Judas Boy
Places Where They Sing
Sound the Retreat
Come Like Shadows

Essays
The English Gentleman
Boys Will Be Boys

Plays
Royal Foundation and other Plays

Simon Raven

Bring Forth the Body

Panther

Granada Publishing Limited
Published in 1977 by Panther Books Ltd
Frogmore, St Albans, Herts AL2 2NF

First published by Blond & Briggs Ltd 1974
Copyright © Simon Raven 1974
Made and printed in Great Britain by
Richard Clay (The Chaucer Press) Ltd
Bungay, Suffolk
Set in Linotype Pilgrim

Contents

Ulysses : Time hath, my lord, a wallet at his back,
Wherein he puts alms for oblivion ...

SHAKESPEARE : *Troilus and Cressida*
Act III, Scene iii

TABLEAU

In the bathroom of Somerset Lloyd-James's chambers in Albany the bathwater gradually lost its temperature, from hot to warm to tepid to cool. By the time the early sun first reached the window the water was quite cold; cold, and deep orange in the busy sun, placid and rather scurfy, drawn up, like a blanket, under Somerset Lloyd-James's chin.

Later on some letters pattered on to the floor of the hall a few yards away; and a little while after that the telephone rang in the drawing-room, was silent, rang again (thirteen times) and then again desisted. But Somerset Lloyd-James, who had so often answered that telephone with eagerness, listened into it with anger or relish, and spoken down it in command or prohibition – Somerset Lloyd-James stayed quiet beneath the waters, recking naught of the filth and the chill; for no telephone could summon him to bustle now, nor any bright morning quicken his stiff shanks.

PART ONE

*Matter for
a May
Morning*

At 10.30 a.m. on Wednesday, May 10 1972, Captain Detterling, M.P., decided to pay a morning call on his old friend, Somerset Lloyd-James, M.P. As both men lived in chambers in Albany, Detterling had not very far to walk; but he took his time over it, thinking, as he went, of what he would say when he arrived.

The object of his visit was to check up on an item of political gossip about the Ministry of Commerce, in which Lloyd-James had been Parliamentary Under-Secretary of State since the Conservative Party had been returned to power in June 1970. It was whispered that the Minister, a distant cousin of Detterling called the Marquis Canteloupe, was showing signs of cracking, and Detterling was anxious to ascertain what Lloyd-James opined in the matter. Everyone knew that pressure of business had been mounting at the Ministry ever since Canteloupe had assumed office there nearly two years before, and that these pressures were by now very tough indeed. So was it true that Canteloupe was no longer capable of coping, as rumour had it, and if so was this due to his health, his years, or his liberal use of alcohol? In particular, Detterling wished to know whether Canteloupe had managed to make adequate arrangements for the representation of Great Britain at an important Trade Convention which was to take place at Strasbourg at the beginning of June. For wishing to know all this Detterling had two reasons: first, it was the sort of thing which he enjoyed knowing; and secondly, he wanted to receive ample warning in advance if, as he suspected, his ageing relative was about to make a public fool of himself.

But the immediate problem, as Detterling reminded himself *en route*, was how to frame his questions. Somerset Lloyd-James did not give away information, even to old friends, for nothing. He would want his *quid pro quo* and, even if Detterling could meet him in this respect, he would also want to know the motives behind Detterling's enquiries. Mere curiosity he would certainly refuse to gratify, while a plea of family solicitude he would probably dismiss as irrelevant. For Detterling would not be enquiring into the health of his cousin Canteloupe (which he could perfectly well ask of elsewhere), he would in fact be enquiring into the competence of the Minister of Commerce, a very different and a very delicate matter, about which it would be naïf to expect candour.

And so what, thought Captain Detterling, am I to say to Somerset? Shall I try to provoke him? E.g., 'I hear the old boy's getting pissed too often', or, 'They say the P.M.'s very worried about the arrangements for Strasbourg'. But that kind of thing was too tentative; it would provoke Lloyd-James only to curt and simple denial, whereas what Detterling wanted was a full assessment of the factors *pro* and *con*. Well then: should he formulate a charge so definite and powerful that Lloyd-James would be bound to refute it in some detail? Such detail could then be checked, and would be almost as useful where found to be false as where found to be true; for falsehood detected would indicate those areas in which the Minister and the Ministry were vulnerable and, quite possibly, why. The only trouble with *this* plan, Detterling now thought, was that he had no really strong or definite charge which he could formulate – nothing that could not be dismissed in a dozen words at most.

By this time Detterling was standing in front of Somerset Lloyd-James's door, and was still no clearer how to proceed than he had been when he left his own. But he did not let this deter him. He knew of old that if one scripted one's conversation too carefully beforehand, if one prepared one's questions and effects too precisely, one was very easily put out of countenance: for one's opponent seldom spoke or behaved in accordance with the script, and this could be very awkward if one was too heavily committed to it. Far better to be flexible, as they used to say in the army, far better play it by ear and feel one's way gently in.

Captain Detterling considered himself rather a hand at feeling his way in, and he had good hope, now, that either luck or instinct would tell him what questions to ask and when. He had known Lloyd-James for over twenty-five years (off and on); after all that time he really ought to be capable of judging his friend's mood and teasing out the information he wanted. He smiled in self-encouragement and pressed Somerset Lloyd-James's bell.

The bell was answered, after an unusually long time, by Somerset's woman-of-all-work, Dolly, who looked rather glum.

''Morning, Dolly,' said Detterling. 'Mr Somerset here? Or has he gone to the Ministry?'

'Mr Somerset is inside, sir,' said Dolly. 'Please to come in and see him.'

When Dolly introduced Detterling to Lloyd-James's dead body in the bath (which she did in precisely the same manner as she would have used to show him into the drawing-room) Detterling's first reaction was one of disapproval (how very *infra dig.* of Somerset to let himself be found in such a state), his second reaction one of sorrow, and his third one of pleasurable curiosity. Somerset had sprung a few surprises in his day but this beat everything. For some three or four minutes Detterling looked down at Somerset's face, almost as if he hoped it might still be able to open its mouth and tell him something. Then he made a noise between a sigh and a whistle, and went to find Dolly, who had discreetly withdrawn to the kitchen.

'Have you sent for the police?' he said.

'No, sir.'

'How long have you known about it?'

'Since I came.'

'Since *seven*?' (Detterling knew all about Somerset's domestic routine.)

'Not quite then, sir. A while after – when I went to do the bathroom.'

'But my dear Dolly, it's now getting on for eleven. What

have you been doing all this time?'

'Sitting here in the kitchen,' Dolly said.

'I see,' said Detterling easily. 'But you really ought to have sent for the police. They've got to come, Dolly.'

'Not just yet. Once they've taken him away ... that's it, isn't it?'

'He can't stay here, my dear.'

'A little longer, sir?'

'Sorry. It's been far too long already. You'd like me to do the telephoning, I expect?'

'If you would, sir.'

So Detterling rang up the police and then sat down by Dolly at the kitchen table to wait. As they sat there together, he let her hold his hand and listened to her quiet talk of her Mr Somerset, who had never forgotten her birthday in all the years.

'So to sum up, sir,' said Detective Superintendent Stupples to Captain Detterling, 'what we have is this: Mr Somerset Lloyd-James, identified by your good self, dead in the bath of his own uncurtained bathroom and naked except for his spectacles. His wrists have apparently been slashed, a safety razor blade has been found at the bottom of the bath, and the bathwater is coloured by a red substance which we may assume to be Mr Lloyd-James's blood. Nothing more can be said until the medical experts have examined the body and given us the results of all the appropriate tests. That's about it ... eh, Sergeant Pulcher?'

'That's about it, sir,' Sergeant Pulcher said.

Detective Superintendent Stupples was long, thin and fibrous, with a small oval head and very bright eyes which were protected by mathematically circular spectacles. Detective Sergeant Pulcher was round yet hard, like a jacketed barrel. Both men wore plain clothes, Pulcher a blue double-breasted suit, Stupples a tweed coat and mustard-coloured corduroy trousers.

'But tests or no tests,' Stupples now continued, 'there can only be one solution.'

'Suicide,' said Pulcher. 'Stands to reason. No evidence of intruders, nothing been pinched or damaged – not if we're to believe the char, that is.'

'Dolly,' said Detterling, 'is not "the char". She is a valued servant who enjoys Mr Lloyd-James's affection and trust. If she says nothing has been interfered with, then nothing has been interfered with.'

'Except for Mr Lloyd-James,' said Stupples, 'who must have interfered with himself. Slit his veins in the bath. The old Roman way.'

'Why?' said Detterling.

'You claim to be an old friend of his,' said Stupples. 'Why ask *us*?'

'I was asking myself, Superintendent.'

'And what's the answer, sir?'

'That,' said Captain Detterling, 'I should very much like to know.'

'Anything been troubling him lately?'

'Not that I heard of. He was always well off, and since his father died some years ago he's been rich. He's always had interesting work – and done it well – and recently he's been highly successful as a politician. He has ... he had ... a wide social acquaintance among the very best people in every sense of the expression. His relations with women ...'

'... He wasn't married?' put in Pulcher.

'... And didn't miss it. His relations with women, as I was about to remark, were always ... sensibly regulated.'

Superintendent Stupples glinted through his spectacles at this information, while Sergeant Pulcher nodded with conscious sophistication.

'In short,' Detterling concluded, 'so far from having reason to commit suicide, he had just about every reason not to.'

'And yet,' said Stupples, 'suicide it must be.'

'I suppose so,' said Detterling, remembering the tableau in the bathroom.

'Beyond any possible doubt,' corrected Stupples.

'Very rum,' grunted Sergeant Pulcher.

'And even rummer,' said Detterling, 'as Mr Lloyd-James was a Catholic. They don't usually go in for that kind of thing.'

'Perhaps he wasn't a very serious Catholic,' Stupples said mildly.

'As to his private spiritual beliefs, it is hard to say. He was a worldly man, Superintendent, and not, on the face of it, much affected by religious or moral scruple. But he *did* set great store by formal and well-mannered deference to all recognized rules and ordinances ... whether Catholic or other. That is not to say that he obeyed them, but it *is* to say that he would never willingly have allowed himself to be detected in their violation. It would have offended his sense of good order. But what more indecorous a violation could you have, *and what more certain of detection*, than an act of *felo de se*?'

'And such a very messy one too,' said Superintendent Stupples. And then to Pulcher, 'Get Dolly in here, would you, Sergeant? It's time we had a word with her.'

'Do you mind if I stay?' said Detterling as Pulcher went out. 'Dolly is an intelligent woman in her kind, but nervous of strangers. It might steady her to have someone she knew in the room.'

'Very considerate of you, sir.'

'Not really. As you may have gathered. I am rather curious about it all.'

'And you think that Dolly will say something of interest?'

'Quite possibly. Dolly, like her master, set a high value on routine. She will have noticed even the tiniest departure ...'

'... The last I seen of Mr Somerset – seen of him proper, I mean – was yesterday morning,' Dolly said. 'He was in his brown country suit and he said he was going out of London for the day. But he'd be back in the evening – after I'd gone, which is always five o'clock – and if anyone rang up I was to say so. He'll be back some time after five p.m., that's what I had to say.'

'He didn't tell you where he was going ... or why?' asked Superintendent Stupples.

'Oh no, sir, and of course I didn't enquire.'

'When did he leave?'

'About eleven o'clock, sir. So then I went on with my cleaning work, and answered the telephone...'

'... Did many people ring?'

'No, sir. His friends all know he's usually at the Ministry any time after eleven, so anyone who wanted him would have rung there.'

'But you answered the telephone, you say, so *somebody* must have rung here.'

'Yes, sir. Just the one time. It was Lord Canteloupe's secretary, Mr Carton Weir, from the Ministry. He knew Mr Somerset was away for the day, he said, because Mr Somerset had warned them he would be. But would I please tell Mr Somerset when he got back that the Minister particularly wanted to have dinner with him on Wednesday – meaning today, sir – and to cancel any other engagements he had, because there was going to be an important discussion about Strasbourg.'

'About the Trade Convention in June?' put in Detterling.

'I suppose so, sir. I know Mr Somerset's been doing a lot of work getting ready for that, because he told me something about it. "It's going to be make or break at Strasbourg, Dolly," he said – about a week ago it was – "make or break at Strasbourg, I can tell you. The work's just about killing me." But I knew he was enjoying it, really, because he had that look on his face.'

'And that was all he said about it?'

'Oh yes, sir. He never told me much – why should he? But every now and then he'd tell me something, just a little ... particularly if he was enjoying it himself ... to make me feel part of it all.'

'I see,' said Stupples. 'Let's get back to this telephone call. What time was it?'

'Around three o'clock, sir.'

'And you were to tell Mr Lloyd-James that he must cancel any other appointment in order to dine with Lord Canteloupe the next day – *i.e.* today, Wednesday?'

'That's right, sir.'

'But Mr Lloyd-James wouldn't be back until after you left at five. So what did you do about it?'

'I decided to tell him in the morning, sir. I could have left him a note, but he didn't care for that unless it was absolutely necessary. "Notes give things away, Dolly," he told me once: "they're always apt to be lost – or read by the wrong people. I'd sooner trust to your memory, Dolly – it's never let me down yet." So I thought to myself about this dinner, I'll tell him first thing in the morning, that'll leave time enough.'

'And then?'

'And then I left at five like I always do and came back this morning at seven.'

'And ... then?'

'I followed my usual programme, sir. Mr Somerset always dined out, but I checked the dining-room, in case he'd had a late-night snack in there or something.'

'And had he?'

'No, sir. So then I laid the breakfast things and went to call him. He liked to be called at a quarter past seven for breakfast at a quarter to eight – an early rising gentleman he was. So I'd call him at a quarter past seven, and he'd get shaved and that while I cooked his breakfast, which he never sat down to until he was all dressed and ready for the day. "It doesn't feel right, Dolly," he used to say, "flopping about at the breakfast table in slippers and pyjamas".'

'But what happened when you called him this morning?'

'He didn't answer when I knocked nor even when I'd knocked twice, so I opened the bedroom door and went in. Bed not slept in. "Oh dear," I thought, "he's decided to spend the night away after all. I hope he's coming back in time for me to tell him about this dinner." But meanwhile there was nothing for it except to carry on as usual, so I went and had the cup of tea which I always had while I was cooking his breakfast, and then, when it was his break-fast time at a quarter to eight, I went like I always do to clean out the bathroom, being as how he's a clumsy shaver and makes spots on the mirror and blood on the towels. Poor gentleman ... he suffers cruel from pimples, you see.'

'And when you went into the bathroom,' said Superin-tendent Stupples, 'you found ... what you found. Did you touch anything?'

'Oh no, sir.' Although Dolly's face crumpled slightly, she remained in control of herself. 'I said to myself, "So *that's* where you've been instead of your bed. No point in telling you about that dinner until you're in a fit state to listen." I didn't quite take it all in, you see, sir. I just went and sat in the kitchen ... hoping that things would somehow come right again and we could just go on as usual without men-tioning it. And there I sat until the letters came at nine ... I heard the noise of the flap. But I didn't go for them, nor I didn't answer the telephone, though it rang soon after the letters, because it seemed to me that if I didn't do things for him he might pull himself together and start doing for himself. He was always very fierce about answering the telephone, so perhaps, when he heard it ringing, it might *make* him get out of that bath.'

Dolly paused and shook her head slowly from side to side.

'Go on,' said Stupples briskly.

'So there I sat, quite still in the kitchen. And as time went on, the telephone began to ring more and more, and still I didn't answer it, hoping for what I told you to happen. But nothing did. And at last, much later, the door-bell rang; and I thought, "I'll give you one final chance, Mr Somerset. I'll leave you to answer that bell ... a whole minute I'll give you. And if you still don't answer it, I'll have to go myself ... and then whoever it is will have to know what you've been up to." Well the, minute went by, and I went

to the door myself ... and it was Mr Somerset's friend,
Captain Detterling ...'

'... A routine-minded lady, as you said,' remarked Stupples
to Detterling, while Sergeant Pulcher was seeing Dolly into
a police car to be driven home. 'The sort that's totally
reliable ... until something out of the ordinary happens.
Very weird, the way she seems to have behaved over this.'
He removed his glasses, blinked energetically, and then replaced them. 'Not,' he said, 'that it changes anything. Anything important, I mean.'

'Would it have helped if she'd called you in right away?'

'Not really ... though of course she should have. The
doctor's rough estimate is that Lloyd-James had been dead
between ten and twelve hours. If we'd been called in earlier,
he might have been able to be more exact. But what difference does it make whether Lloyd-James died at mid-
night or two a.m.? Suicide it must be.'

'I wonder where he went yesterday,' Detterling said. 'Out
of London for the day ... He went off absolutely calmly, it
seems, in one of his country suits; he gave Dolly some
simple instructions, and he'd warned them at the Ministry
that he wouldn't be coming in. All of it entirely sane and
sensible, nothing the least bit out of the way – *but then he
comes back and does this*.'

'It wasn't an official outing,' said Stupples casually, as if
the matter were of little moment. 'If it had been, he
wouldn't have needed to warn the Ministry about his absence. He must have been taking a day off, for private business or pleasure.'

'*What* business or pleasure? Where did he go and whom
did he see? It could explain everything.'

'It could.'

'You don't sound very interested.'

Stupples shrugged. 'Perhaps I am,' Stupples said, 'and perhaps I'm not. Either way, I shan't follow it up officially.'

'But damn it, man,' said Detterling, 'you *must*. You want
to know why he did it, and this outing of his—'

'—Ah,' interrupted Stupples, 'but *do* I want to know why he did it?'

'Of course you do. The coroner will want to know and it's your job to tell him.'

'The coroner will be told ... pressure of work,' said Stupples. 'The work is killing him – as Dolly says he told her himself.'

'But that was only humorous exaggeration – of the kind people make every day. Dolly said he was really enjoying his work, and from what I've seen of him lately I entirely agree with her.'

'Nevertheless, his actual words refute you, sir. "The work's just about killing me," he said. The coroner and his jury needn't know he was joking ... if we only take a little care with Dolly.'

'In which case,' said Detterling disingenuously, 'you'd be deliberately serving up lies.'

'Look, Captain Detterling. You've been a Member of Parliament for a very long time, and I have heard that you are a man of some experience in other fields. Do you really need me to spell it all out for you?'

'Yes, Superintendent. I wish to be sure that you've got your spelling correct.'

'Very well,' sighed Stupples. 'Here is a top man in the Ministry of Commerce – a man second only to the Minister himself – who would have had an important role to play at the forthcoming Convention in Strasbourg. Right so far?'

'Right so far.'

'Now, this man suddenly kills himself for no ostensible reason. That reason, when discovered, could be political dynamite. Still correct?'

'Yes, but you've given me an abbreviation. I want the spelling in full, please.'

'As you like. In most suicides,' Stupples pursued, 'the motives are just squalid or pitiful; but what is just squalid or pitiful in an ordinary case can start a national scandal in a case like this. Rows about politicians' morals, public hysteria about security, God knows what. And so we, the humble police, not wishing to embarrass our betters, we play the whole thing down. We do not look behind locked doors, we pretend we can't find the key. We do not rip away the arras because we do not want to discover the rats there – or rather, we don't want the Press and the public to discover them. What we do instead is to settle as quietly as we can for the least disturbing explanation : in this case for overwork, for temporary mental imbalance due to strain – one of the few plausible reasons which are also respectable. He was desperately tired and anxious, we say in the Coroner's Court for everyone to hear, he went for a day in the country to rest and calm himself down, it didn't help, he returned as depressed as he set out, and then he killed himself. So there we are; a verdict of suicide due to strain and overwork; official enquiry closed; public indifference at such a boring conclusion; and a grateful sigh of relief from our betters in Downing Street.'

'Very good, Superintendent. And I suppose that takes care of everything?'

'Except for the truth, sir. We still have to find that out. It could be dangerous, you see, not to know it.'

'Ah yes,' said Detterling, 'the truth. I'm glad we're getting round to that.'

'As soon as the official investigation is publicly completed by the police,' Stupples went on, 'and as soon as the coroner has recorded his tame and harmless verdict, the whole thing goes underground along with the body. But unlike the body it is still alive. I tell all I know to a little man in a scruffy office in Jermyn Street, and then *his* men take over. *They* nose through the dustbins and dig out all the dirt from the sewers. They discover whether there has been a breach of security or anything in that line to sort out. And at length the little man in Jermyn Street composes a very secret report—'

'—Top Copy to the P.M.—'

'—From whom he asks permission to take the necessary steps to repair any damage.'

'Permission granted, I take it.'

'As a rule, yes. And meanwhile Somerset Lloyd-James, *quondam* Under-Secretary at the Ministry of Commerce, lies in his grave, conveniently forgotten both by the newspapers and their readers—'

'—Who know as little of this second *post-mortem* as he does. A very ingenious system,' Captain Detterling commented, 'but not in the least original. Also expensive to operate and liable, I should have thought, to back-fire ... particularly at the early stages when you, Superintendent, must deliberately falsify police enquiries.'

'*Limit* police enquiries, sir. But you're right: the method does have its drawbacks, and ... er ... *they* ... are often reluctant to employ it.'

'Then why are you so sure that they'll instruct you to employ it here?'

'Because they already have instructed me, sir. You remember all those telephone calls Dolly talked of – the ones she didn't answer. Well, those – or most of 'em – were from the Ministry, it seems. Lord Canteloupe's secretary, Mr Carton Weir—'

'—Wanting to check up that Lloyd-James was all set for this dinner tonight?'

'I dare say. After he'd tried time after time and couldn't get through, Mr Weir got rattled. He knew Lloyd-James was due back in London last night and he knew that anyhow Dolly should have been here to answer. So at length he phoned our people, to ask us to come and check up just in case something was wrong here. As it happened, he came through to us just after your good self.'

'So you were able to tell him there was indeed something wrong here—'

'—And exactly what it was. Mr Weir gave a screech like a night-owl, and within three minutes, sir, my superiors were instructed by telephone from No. 10 that this case was to be treated as Category Sigma – that is, on the system I've just been outlining to you.'

'So clearly somebody regards it as being very sensitive.

I'm much obliged to you, Superintendent, for telling me all this so frankly. I had not expected your account to be quite so ... so comprehensive.'

'It's not only to oblige you, sir. I expect you, in return, to oblige us.'

'How can I do that?'

'By not ballsing us up, sir. As I've told you, we need an uncontroversial verdict from the coroner's inquest to douse the whole thing down before our friend in Jermyn Street can get properly started. Now, Dolly's evidence about Mr Lloyd-James telling her his work was killing him is going to be a godsend ... and we can present it so that the jury will think he really meant it. In fact, Sergeant Pulcher's squaring Dolly about that now – telling her that it will be the best way to preserve "Mr Somerset's" good reputation, all that kind of thing. But when it comes to you, sir ...'

'...I might not be so amenable a witness, you think. I might say that Lloyd-James was enjoying his job very much, and was right on top of it.'

'And you being you, they'd listen. Which wouldn't suit us at all. Because then they'd start looking in other directions—'

'—Much more interesting directions, like the direction he took into the country on the day before he died. Which would suit *me* very well, Stupples. Because I, as I have told you, am curious about the truth. I'm in no mind to help you suppress it.'

'It's your own party, sir – your own Ministers – who want it suppressed. Isn't it your duty to help them? Everyone else will go along with the theory that Mr Lloyd-James's suicide was due to overwork. Lord Canteloupe, Mr Weir – all of them. Why must you be so difficult?'

'Because I want to know what really happened.'

Sergeant Pulcher came in. 'Sorry I've been so long, sir,' he said to Stupples, 'but I thought I'd see Dolly right home.'

'And she appreciated your kindness?'

'She did. She understands that we mean everything for the best – and she realizes now that her poor gentleman *was* very tired these last weeks, and that's what she'll tell the coroner.'

'It's not what she told us in here,' said Detterling.

'No, sir,' said Pulcher, poker-faced. 'But she's remembered, you see, how kind and thoughtful her Mr Somerset was; and *now* she's sure that he meant what he said about his work killing him but was then suddenly afraid he might be upsetting her. So at the last moment, him being the gentleman he was, he tried to put on a cheerful face and turn it into a joke. She won't go into all that at the inquest, of course, because she agrees with me it might be rather muddling: she'll just say that he said it and he meant it.'

'You see, sir?' said Stupples to Detterling. 'Everyone else ... on reflection ... understands what will be the most fitting way to look at it all. Why do you want to spoil things?'

'I don't want to spoil anything. *I simply want to know what really happened.* For my own satisfaction.'

'Ah,' said Stupples, 'for *your own* satisfaction? Not because you think there is a duty to inform the coroner ... or the British people?'

'Be damned to the coroner and be damned to the people. I simply want to know for myself.'

Superintendent Stupples lifted his arms to heaven and gazed on Detterling, with condescending and unctuous charity, like a member of a religious order in the act of welcoming a novice.

'In that case, sir,' he intoned, 'we can surely come to an accommodation. If you will respect our wishes and support our line at the inquest, I for my part will guarantee that you shall be subsequently informed, by the Jermyn Street men themselves, of everything which they turn up in their investigation.'

'Why should they confide in me?'

'Because I shall ask them to. And because I shall tell them that you can be very helpful to them if they make themselves agreeable. In fact, sir, I'm going to propose you to them as a temporary assistant.'

'With what qualifications?'

'As an expert on the subject in hand. On Lloyd-James's past and present – past and recent, I should say. They will listen to my recommendation, I promise you that. So do you accept my terms?'

There was a knock at the door, and a uniformed constable appeared. Sergeant Pulcher went to him. There were whispers.

'The wagon's here, sir,' called Pulcher, turning back to Stupples.

'Then tell them to take him away, and then follow the usual procedure about this apartment.' Stupples turned to Detterling. 'Your friend must leave his home now,' he said, 'and I must go after him where he is taken. So before I go, do you accept my terms?' He pursed his mouth plummily and almost ogled. 'Your ... discreet co-operation with us now,' he purred, 'in return for full enlightenment later?'

Detterling nodded briefly. 'I accept,' he said.

When Captain Detterling was back in his chambers, he thought at some length of the deal he had done with Stupples. Although he disliked the man, he did not resent the bargain (he was no stranger to such agreements) and he was inclined to think he could have done no better. In return for his silence while the police proposed to the coroner a false motive for Somerset's suicide, he, Detterling, would later be made privy to – indeed party to – the investigation which would seek out the truth (never mind what others might believe); and since it was to be elicited by the secret processes which were directed by 'the little man in Jermyn Street', his only hope of learning it was to be accepted as an ally in that quarter. This he would now be, if he could trust Stupples to perform the offices promised, and on the whole he did trust him : disagreeable though Stupples might be, there was no reason to doubt his word – quite the reverse, in fact; for if Stupples were to renegue on his part of the deal, Detterling, knowing what he did about the conduct of the case, would still be in a position to make trouble for him.

Very well then, thought Detterling: as soon as the second and secret enquiry begins, I shall be in on it. But it would not begin for a little while yet, not (or so Stupples had stated) until the inquest was safety done with. If Detterling himself wished to make an immediate start (which he did), he must depend, for the next few days, on his own sources of information and his own unaided wits. These might not take him very far; but at least, he told himself, he could do some useful homework. There were several pertinent questions which lay, so to speak, in his own area; to some one or two of these at least he could probably find answers fairly quickly, and he could thus have some useful information with which to impress the representatives from Jermyn Street when they came knocking on his door. Jermyn Street must be made to realize that it was in truth getting an assistant and not just a privileged spectator.

The first person whom Detterling intended to approach was his own cousin and Somerset's immediate political superior, the Most Honourable the Marquis Canteloupe, Minister of Commerce. Although the cousinhood lay at several removes, Canteloupe had always acknowledged it, and was on personal grounds well-disposed towards Detterling; they had been mixed up in several intrigues together over the years, and Detterling was in no doubt that his noble relative both could and would tell him a great deal that he wished to know about Somerset's recent activities on behalf of the Ministry. An evening with Canteloupe (for an evening Detterling was decided it should be, the old man being always more amenable after the fall of darkness) would also give him the opportunity to examine the Minister's physique with some care, to assess his consumption of drink, and to determine whether or not the rumours of his deterioration were well founded. It was to check on these rumours that Detterling had originally sought out Somerset that morning; he was still without satisfaction on the topic, and he now had an additional reason for pursuing it. While the motives behind his abortive morning call – family *pietàs* and sheer inquisitiveness – were still as pressing as ever, he now, moreover, had an interesting conjecture which he wished to test: if the Minister were indeed deteriorating, and if this were proving deleterious to the running of his Ministry, might there not have been some muddle or mistake or even disaster which, having impinged on Somerset as second-in-command, had some connexion, indicative if not causative, with his death? It was, Detterling told himself, a long shot but just worth the cartridge; and if it went wide, well, there were other, nearer, and more definitive targets for his attention. For example, he was particularly anxious to learn from Canteloupe the nature and, if possible, the exact scope of the operations which Somerset was to have undertaken in three weeks' time at Strasbourg.

And so, after a restoring luncheon of gulls' eggs and stuffed quails, Detterling telephoned the Ministry of Commerce and was connected with the Minister's P.P.S., Carton Weir.

'Ghastly news about Somerset,' said Weir. 'I'm being tortured by the Press.'

'Well, don't tell 'em I was in on it. I don't want 'em round here.'

'But whatever *can* I tell them, my dear?'

'I thought the official line was quite clear. Suicide due to strain and overwork.'

'But that's so *boring*.'

'I gather it's meant to be.'

'Oh yes, dear, and we'll stick to it all right, but you can't expect the Press to find it madly amusing, and they keep nagging away trying to make me say it was something else.'

'Well, if it was, there's not the slightest clue anywhere, so you're batting on a pretty sound wicket.'

'Stonewalling. It makes them so nasty and cross. Like vampires, my dear, who have spotted someone full of lovely blood, only to find themselves sucking a waxwork ... Oh dear, there's more of them just arrived – panting with excitement, the doorman says. So what can I do for you before they tear me apart?'

'I gather my cousin is now free for dinner tonight?'

'That's right. It was to have been with poor, dear Somerset – not that I ever liked him much, he was a rotten, scheming old sod, but *de mortuis* and all that.'

'Where were they going?'

'The Ritz. So nice and empty, you see, if there's anything shady to talk about.'

'Had they got something shady to talk about?'

'I never knew them talk about anything that wasn't. And what with this great big conning match that's coming up at Strasbourg . . .'

'Well, look here, Carton. Tell Canteloupe that if he cares to dine with *me* at the Ritz tonight, I'll pay the bill.'

'Oh, he'll love that. Being paid for is his very best thing. But you must be nice to him, Detterling, in other ways, I mean. He really is cut up about that old bitch Somerset – about poor, dear Somerset, that is – and he needs taking out of himself.'

'How's his drinking form these days?'

'Same as ever. No less – but certainly no more. You mustn't listen to any of these tales about his boozing, Detterling. He's a lovely old darling, so he is, and in splendid shape all round. But he *is* sad about Somerset – though why he should bother about the stringy old cow is more than I can imagine – so you must be very sweet to him.'

'All right, Carton. Tell him eight-thirty for a drink at the table . . .'

This settled, Detterling decided on a little revision, to make quite sure he had the elementary background of his subject right. He took the latest volume of *Who's Who* from a shelf and turned to

LLOYD-JAMES, Somerset; MP (C) Bishop's Cross, Somersetshire, since Oct. 1959; Parliamentary Under-Secretary of State, Ministry of Commerce, since June, 1970 . . .

Funny, thought Detterling; it sometimes seems, when I

look back, as though he's been in the House at least as
long as I have; yet of course it was only in 1959 that he
came in, at the General Election, nearly ten years after I
did. But then he was up to his neck in politics long before
he became a Member of Parliament, so I suppose that
accounts for the illusion. It only goes to show the value of
revision ...

...*b* 11 Dec. 1927; *o s* of late Seamus Lloyd-James, and
of Peregrina Lennox Lloyd-James (*née* Forbes Eden), of
Chantry Marquess, near Bampton, Devonshire....

Peregrina Lennox Lloyd-James, thought Detterling: the
old mum. Still alive, it seems. I don't remember that he
ever spoke of her to anyone (nor of his father, except to
announce his death). I wonder how often he saw the old
lady. Perhaps it was her he went to see on the last day of
his life? Can one get to Devonshire and back inside the
same day? Hardly, unless one turns round as soon as one
gets there. Whether he went or not, however, old Peregrina
may know something to the point. But she'll need very
careful handling at her age; best leave her to the experts
from Jermyn Street.

...*Educ*: St Peter's Court, Crediton ...

How very odd. Never before, thought Detterling, have I
known anyone list his preparatory school in *Who's Who*.
But of course Somerset was always a cracking snob, and St
Peter's Court was once a very smart private school, much
patronized by the Royal Family. Now surely, Detterling
remembered, it was really situated at Broadstairs and was
evacuated to Crediton (Devon) for the duration of the war.
So that if, as this entry implies, Somerset attended it only
when it was at Crediton, he cannot have gone to it before
September of 1939, by which time he must have already
been eleven years and nine months old. Either, then, the
little Somerset was too delicate to go away to school until
he was nearly twelve, or he attended another prep. school
first – one which he doesn't deign to name here. Could he

have been expelled from it? Or did Seamus and Peregrina merely transfer him to St Peter's when it arrived in their own vicinity? And if so, were their motives primarily snobbish or educational? No doubt, thought Detterling, Peregrina Lennox will know the answer to that question, if anyone thinks it worth asking; but the important point is, as regards the adult Somerset and his character, that he wished the world to know that he had been to a preparatory school held fit for little princes ... and wished the world to know so imperatively that he risked making a fool of himself by ostentatiously recording it.

Compensation, thought Detterling, as he returned his eyes to *Who's Who*: compensation for the next place he went to, which was a decent enough school but middle-class to say the least of it. For as Detterling well knew and as *Who's Who* now confirmed, Somerset had attended, between 1941 and 1946, the same public school, one of the first six in the kingdom but definitely low in the category, as Detterling himself had attended in the 1930s. It was there, indeed, in the summer of 1945, that Detterling remembered he had first met Somerset. Detterling, the returning old boy, had been gorgeously got up in a Service dress jacket and the cherry trousers of his regiment, the 49th Earl Hamilton's Light Dragoons; Somerset had been scrofulous, sickly and underfed, in appearance a more than usually seedy schoolboy even for that more than usually seedy period, and Detterling had instantly written him off as of no account whatever. Wrongly, of course; for even then Somerset had been a power in the land – or at least in the school – though of this Detterling was only to learn years later.

For after that summer's day in 1945, he had scarcely set eyes on Somerset for a whole ten years. While Somerset Lloyd-James (according to *Who's Who*) was winning a scholarship to Cambridge, taking firsts in the History Tripos and potting the Lauderdale Essay Prize, Captain Detterling had been moving round the world in the last stages of his somewhat desultory career as a regular soldier; while Somerset had been struggling to prove himself as an apprentice journalist on an economic daily, Detterling had been moving comfortably into a safe Conservative seat and making prudent dispositions for his ample inheritance. Detterling, the Member of Parliament and the Member of Lloyd's, was worlds removed from Somerset, the toiler in Grub Street; and even when, as occasionally happened, they were asked to the same party, Detterling, who by this time hardly even recognized Somerset, saw no reason at all for renewing so slight and unattractive an acquaintance.

Only when Somerset, his apprenticeship conscientiously and profitably concluded, emerged as the Editor of a new weekly called *Strix* ('A Journal of Industry and Commerce', as he sub-titled it in *Who's Who*) and had made of it an organ powerful enough to win the attention of astute politicians, did Somerset and Detterling at last meet as equals. That would have been in 1955, Detterling thought now, when *Strix* had started to give valuable support to the so called 'Young England Group', a crusading movement of young Conservative M.P.s (clean-up-the-dirt-and-fling-wide-the-windows) to which Detterling himself had once briefly belonged. There had been a dinner party, given by Peter Morrison, the leader of the group, which Detterling and Somerset Lloyd-James had both attended. The object of the meeting had been to discuss unethical property deals, against which the Young England Group wished to legislate and on which Somerset was something of an expert. Even now, nearly seventeen years later, Detterling remembered the fluent and lucid exposition with which Somerset had both entertained and instructed Morrison and himself; remembered, too, how Somerset's pimples had flared as he warmed to his work and how his tongue had come coiling out through his teeth in a pronounced and slobbering lisp whenever he came to any passage in his discourse which particularly excited him. Nothing, of course, had come of the plans mooted at that dinner, nor had any of those present (Detterling now thought) really supposed that anything would; but for Detterling himself the evening had had a lasting importance, in that it had brought him once more into contact with Somerset Lloyd-James.

This time he did not make the mistake of writing Somerset off. Although the Editor of *Strix*, with his spots, his lisp and his shamble, bore a good deal of resemblance, in manner and physique, to the distasteful hobbledehoy first encountered in 1945, Detterling recognized from the tone of Somerset's exegesis that here was a man of good value – a man who might, over the years, provide him in ample measure with just that kind of corrupt and sophisticated amusement that was most to his liking. He had no thought at first of making a close friend of Somerset; he wanted him as a mere casual familiar whom he could watch and relish, whose intrigues and antics he could follow and annotate, upon whose sources of information he could occasionally draw. Somerset, he had told himself in 1955, was for enjoyment, not for intimacy. But as the years went on the enjoyment he derived from the connexion was of such quantity and quality that gratitude had brought him to regard Somerset with immense affection and at last almost with love.

But never with trust. The business of the Desmoulins letter, for example, which had led, in 1959, to Somerset's securing his seat in Parliament – no one who had observed *that* with any care, thought Detterling, could ever again look on Somerset with trust. For Somerset had always chosen the crooked way, even when the straight would have served as well and better. Possibly this was why his entry in *Who's Who*, while factually correct, was yet so unrepresentative of his career; all his most notable activities had been conducted in large part *sub rosa* (there was even a story that he had contrived to cheat in his Tripos examinations) and so it was impossible that *Who's Who* should convey the true flavour of the man and his achievements. 'Editor of *Strix*, A Journal of Industry and Commerce; personally edited the literary and artistic, etc., sections as well as the main text ...' While this was accurate enough, it suggested nothing of the whoredoms and imbroglios, the tortures by financial racking, the literary jobberies and the professional assassinations which were the real stuff of his ten years odd of editorship. 'Resigned in 1964 to devote his full time to politics...' Who could conceive, from reading those few innocent words, that Somerset had in truth resigned to become political and social hatchet-man for Lord Canteloupe. Canteloupe and Somerset had taken to each other right back in the spring of 1959, when Canteloupe had first joined the Tory Government and while Somerset was still worming his way towards Parliament. From that time on Somerset had begun to help Canteloupe with shrewd unofficial advice (advice on one occasion at least not far short of murderous) and had continued to do so right up to the fall of the Conservatives in 1964. At this stage Canteloupe, seeing boundless scope for their iniquitous alliance during their forthcoming period in Opposition, suggested that Somerset should now assist him in a full-time capacity. What, Somerset enquired, was in it for Somerset? What reward did Canteloupe propose for the dedicated dirty work which he was doubtless going to require? Office under Canteloupe when the Conservatives came back. And if Canteloupe was in no position to give such patronage when the time came? That was the gamble, Canteloupe had answered, which Somerset must take. In the end, the gamble had paid off handsomely in 1970, when Canteloupe had gone to the Ministry of Commerce and taken Somerset with him. But who, Detterling now reflected once more, could ever deduce even the possibility of such murky trading from the simple, almost idealistic words 'to devote his full time to politics' that covered the affair in Who's Who.

There was little more to read. No publications listed (too busy with the dagger, thought Detterling, to spare time for the pen); address given as care of his bank (Coutts & Co., Piccadilly); no telephone number. 'Clubs: Whites' – membership of which he had only attained, so Detterling recalled, through blackmailing two committee-men.

Detterling was just trying to reconstruct in detail what

he knew of the last little matter when the telephone rang.

'Mackeson here, sir,' said the voice of the Head Porter of Albany. 'There's a shower of journalists down here at the entrance. They want to know where your chambers are.'

Bloody hell, thought Dettering: someone's told 'em I got a look at the body. Carton Weir? The police? Never mind; they always nosed these things out somehow, and they would probably have come after him in any case, knowing him to be a friend of the deceased.

'Keep 'em waiting another three minutes,' he said to the Head Porter, 'and I'll slip out through the coal hole.'

'Very good, sir ...'

Lord's, thought Detterling, as he closed his front door behind him and headed fast for the boiler-room and the back entrance through which coal was delivered: always a good refuge at a time like this. The M.C.C. was playing Surrey, so his fixture list told him, and with luck the Australian touring side would be practising at the nets. He would have a nice peaceful afternoon of cricket, and while it went by he would work out possible (and flexible) methods of tackling Canteloupe at dinner that evening ... and also the best way of putting down that damned rabble of reporters in case they caught up with him later on.

Lord Canteloupe, prompt to the second in his arrival at the Ritz, stalked up to the table carrying an enormous glass of something red.

'Bloody Mary,' he announced to Detterling as he sat down.

'Ought you to have carried it in yourself?'

'Only way, dear boy. Servants drag their feet so these days. But I made sure that they knew it was to go on your bill.'

'How thoughtful of you ... You look very well, Canteloupe.'

This was true. Canteloupe's multi-coloured face, shining slightly from the effort of transporting his Bloody Mary,

gave an impression of sappy vigour; the smashed veins in
the cheeks somehow coalesced to simulate a pleasing tan,
suggesting years spent in mountaineering or exploring
rather than in the copious demolition of rich food and
liquor. The Minister's hair, short, crisp and curly, might
have belonged to a subaltern fresh off the polo ground. His
eyes, despite the little pink worms in them, were bright
and cheerful. He's in good nick, thought Detterling; but
there's something ... wary ... about his mouth. He's in
good nick but he's got problems.

If so, the Minister was in no hurry to share them with
his cousin.

'Fresh Foie Gras,' he boomed, looking down at the menu
in front of him. 'Sole Florentine,' he commanded, and emp-
tied half his Bloody Mary down his throat. 'Entrecôte Chas-
seur,' he concluded, like a colonel bringing his battalion to
the 'Present Arms'.

'When the waiter comes I'll pass the order on,' said
Detterling mildly.

Canteloupe looked at him as if he expected him to
double away and fetch the food himself, and then partly
relented.

'We'll need some decent wine,' said Canteloupe, 'to
drink to Somerset Lloyd-James.' His voice faltered slightly.
'To give the poor bugger a send-off. A magnum of something, to show proper respect.'

Detterling turned and beckoned. An elderly waiter hob-
bled over. Detterling repeated Canteloupe's order for food
and added his own, which was only marginally more
modest. He then tried to attract the wine-waiter, who,
however, was busy snarling at a colleague. Canteloupe at
once observed this failure and—

'—Sommelier,' he bawled and then whistled like a practised doorman.

'No magnums,' said Detterling, feeling it was time he
asserted himself. 'They're no good unless they're specially
ordered first and there's plenty of time to prepare them.'

'Magnums of champagne are all right whenever you

order them,' grouched Canteloupe.

'I don't much care for champagne these days. Those bubbles are so annoying, and I can't be bothered to use a swizzle-stick any more. A bottle of Montrachet '66,' said Detterling to the wine-waiter, 'and one of La Tâche '64.'

'Hmm,' said Canteloupe, mollified. 'Not cheap, the La Tâche.'

'As you say, Canteloupe, we must show proper respect to Somerset.' Then, after an appropriate silence: 'What do you suppose went wrong?'

'Ask me another.'

'Anything to do with his work at the Ministry? Any trouble about that?'

'The only trouble about that is, who the hell's to do it now he's gone?'

'So he was on top of it all right?'

'Right on top.'

'And what about Strasbourg? Was he happy about the arrangements for that?'

'Why do you ask about Strasbourg?'

Canteloupe's lips tightened, emphasizing the look of wariness which Detterling had already noticed about his mouth. I mustn't go too fast, Detterling thought, let's get some food and drink into us first.

'I ask about Strasbourg,' he said reassuringly, 'because it's obviously going to be an important show, and I supposed that Somerset would have had a lot to do with it.'

'He certainly would. He couldn't have chosen a worse time to drop off his hooks.'

But no suggestion at all, Detterling thought, that anything to do with Strasbourg had been the cause of his doing so. Nevertheless, it would be very interesting, to say the least, to know what Somerset and Canteloupe had been up to. Presumably they had been going to discuss it that very evening at that very table. What were the chances that Canteloupe might confide in him, Detterling, instead? Well, here was the Foie Gras and the Montrachet: let them do their work.

When Canteloupe had wolfed his Foie Gras with silent and reverential greed, and when he had drunk two large glasses of wine, Detterling said:

'So Somerset was quite happy about what he had to do at Strasbourg?'

'Quite happy. Right up the cunning sod's street. Just the sort of thing he loved.'

'Might one know what it was?'

Once again, Canteloupe's lips tightened. But then he took a gulp of wine and relaxed. 'In general terms, yes. He was to push one of our products and depreciate everything in the same line that came from ... from elsewhere.'

What product, Detterling longed to ask, and how was he to push it? And who were these rivals from 'elsewhere'? But for the time being he felt it prudent to go along with Canteloupe 'in general terms'.

'Just push our product for what it was?' he said. 'Or crack it up for what it wasn't?'

'It's always hard to know where the first ends and the second begins. Better *not* to know if you want to make a good job of it.'

'Somerset would have known. He always knew things like that.'

'I suppose so. Well, let's say he was getting ready to make a few plausible exaggerations.'

'To tell a few downright lies?'

'Don't be offensive, Detterling. You know the sort of thing which goes on in the world of commerce. If you don't shout your own wares, no one else is going to do it for you ... Ah, that sole looks scrumptious. We need another bottle of Montrachet to go with it, my boy.'

Detterling sent for a second bottle of Montrachet and once again left Canteloupe to eat in silence. Then, pouring his cousin his sixth glass of wine:

'So Somerset,' he said, 'was in charge of the ... propaganda ... for Strasbourg. An important job but not all *that* special. Why are you going to find it so hard to replace him?'

Canteloupe took a toothpick from his pocket and applied it messily.

'It isn't so much a question of boosting our own stuff,' Canteloupe said at last and rather carefully; 'I can get a lot of people who'd do that well enough. The really tricky bit ... is blackening the competition effectively. Somerset had thought of a very smart plan for that ... the sort of plan that needs Somerset to apply it.'

'Sabotage?' said Detterling.

'Not quite that, dear boy. We're not vandals. Let's call it ... industrial satire.'

'Expand, please.'

'Well,' said Canteloupe, 'suppose, just for the sake of example, that you're competing in the sale of motor cars. Now, if a rival car is blown to pieces while it's being exhibited, everyone bloody well knows that there's been a bomb put inside it, and the incident is simply discounted. But if a door falls out for no reason, or if a tyre goes flat while it's just standing there, your rival is made to look ridiculous. You follow the idea?'

'I do,' said Detterling, 'and I quite see that Somerset would have been enjoying himself enormously. Nothing here to make him commit suicide.'

'Nothing.'

'Unless someone had rumbled what he was up to and had found some way of applying pressure.'

'Not a chance,' said Canteloupe: 'he couldn't have been rumbled because he hadn't even *begun* to do anything. It was simply a promising plan which we were still discussing. No one knew of it except him and me.'

'I see ... Here comes the La Tâche. Would you care for a sorbet before you taste it?'

'No, I'll taste it when I've started on the beef. And meanwhile, I *think* I see another drop of Montrachet in the bottle.'

So Canteloupe had the last of the Montrachet, then weighed into his entrecôte, with lip-smacking intervals for bumpers of La Tâche. God, thought Detterling, he's going to want a second bottle of that too. What did Carton Weir mean by saying he's not drinking more than usual? He must have been referring only to *spirits*, I suppose – the consumption he sees of the supplies in the office. And of course it's the spirits that kill in the end, a few bottles of wine more or less can't make any odds to a man like Canteloupe. But all the same, he's a little old to be lapping up La Tâche as if it were water.

A second bottle of La Tâche was now ordered by Canteloupe himself, without reference to his host. After it had arrived and been approved, Canteloupe munched happily on to the end of his entrecôte, wiped up the last of the sauce with his bread, drained his glass yet again, and held it out for more while Detterling filled it. This time it was Canteloupe who broke the silence.

'You're inquisitive, aren't you?' he said.

'Yes.'

'You must be *very* inquisitive – with this La Tâche at sixteen pounds a bottle.'

'Very inquisitive.'

'Well, there's a way you can find out more. Chapter and verse.'

'What way?'

'Take on the job yourself.'

'You're offering me the job of Under-Secretary at your Ministry?'

'Why not? It's about time I did something for the family. And I reckon you could handle this Strasbourg business ... if once you were told the details.'

Detterling took a long steady drink (about thirty shillings' worth) of the La Tâche. He would indeed like to know the details he thought; but he scented danger here, or at least very considerable inconvenience. Clearly the plan which Canteloupe and Somerset had been getting up to 'blacken the opposition' at Strasbourg, though it might stop short of positive outrage, was not the sort of thing to be blithely undertaken. If the price of fuller knowledge of this plan was to be the responsibility of executing it, the price was too high. During Captain Detterling's career as a soldier, his first principle had always been at any cost to eschew the firing line; this principle he had carried with him into politics, and he did not see adequate reason to abandon it now.

'I am not an ambitious man,' he said at length. 'I don't think office would suit me – in your Ministry or any other.'

'Cold feet, eh?'

'Yes. Have a savoury.'

'Thank you : devils on horseback ... I can't say I really blame you,' said Canteloupe, when Detterling had given the order; 'it's not a job to everyone's taste.'

'Precisely so. And don't forget – a lot of my time is taken up with Gregory Stern and the publishing business. I can't go off to Strasbourg for weeks on end and do cloak and dagger stunts.'

'It's much more sophisticated than cloak and dagger these days.'

'Well, that finally rules me out,' Detterling said. 'I'm an old-fashioned man, and cloak and dagger are about my limit. I am not prepared to learn a new technology at my age.'

Canteloupe's devils on horseback arrived, and Canteloupe took a furtive look at the nearly empty bottle of La Tâche.

'No,' said Detterling firmly; 'no more of that.'

'Just as well,' said Canteloupe. 'I'm seeing Maisie later, so I oughtn't to drink too much ... Now look here, young Detterling : I may not have told you any details, but I have given you a pretty fair notion of the kind of thing that's been going on. Now you owe me something in return.'

'You're getting your dinner, aren't you?'

'That's of course. You owe me something more. I'm in a jam, young Detterling; I *must* have someone to do this job at Strasbourg. Somerset can't and you won't : who else is there?'

'Is it really as important as all that? Just a product to be advertised ...'

'*And* the rival product to be done down, remember.'

'All right. But does it really matter if you fail? One more of our products will flop – hardly the end of the world.'

'No. But it could be the end of this Government. One concrete fact I will tell you: the product in question is a new light metal alloy, capable of standing up to higher stress than anything else on the market—'

'—So *you* say—'

'—And so I must bloody well get people to believe. Because if they believe me,' said Canteloupe, ramming in the last devil and mashing it with one side of his mouth while still talking through the other, 'then there will be tens of millions of pounds' worth of export orders, and that will be fucking lovely. But if they *don't* believe me, then a major corporation, whose last fling this is, will go bankrupt, thousands of men and women will be thrown out of work, the shares will be a pig's breakfast, and it will be the Rolls-Royce affair all over again, with sodding great knobs on. Which would likely enough mean the end of our beloved Prime Minister, and would certainly mean the end of yours truly.'

Detterling ordered coffee.

'Port or brandy?' he asked Canteloupe.

'Both.'

'How *much* of both?'

'Just tell him to bring the decanter and the bottle.'

Detterling did so, and at the same time rather pointedly ordered a small Marc de Champagne for himself.

'You were saying...?' he said to Canteloupe.

'In effect,' said Canteloupe, 'I was saying how urgent it is for me to find a capable chap to take over where Somerset left off; and I was asking you to suggest someone.'

'Tell me,' said Detterling thoughtfully, 'how does one apply this ... industrial satire of yours ... to rival light metal alloys? The example you gave just now was motor cars, and I quite see how it might be made to work with them. But with light metal alloy – sheets of it, or strips of it, or whatever – how does one set about making *those* look ridiculous.'

'That was Somerset's secret and mine. But you can surely imagine the sort of man I need.'

'I suppose so. A sort of Somerset. They don't grow on bushes, you know.'

'But for God's sake, dear boy, you must be able to think of *somebody*.'

'All right,' said Detterling: 'Peter Morrison.'

'Morrison?'

'He's been back in the House since '68, and it's time the party did something for him. He's had rotten luck lately – his elder son's been wrecked for good by meningitis – and he'll be glad of interesting work to take his mind off it.'

'I always thought Morrison was ... rather mealy.'

'That's what a lot of people think. You just try him.'

'But he's supposed to be a pattern of integrity and all the rest of it.'

'He is supposed to be, and he likes being supposed to be. But he has a remarkable knack of reconciling his supposed integrity with the more awkward demands of practical necessity. He is good at touching pitch and *not* being defiled. Let me tell you a tale, Canteloupe. While Morrison was a subaltern in India in 1946, he won the Viceroy's Commendation—'

'—That's just what I mean. The kind of chap that's won a Viceroy's Commendation won't take kindly to shifting the shit in Strasbourg.'

'Just listen, Canteloupe. Peter won his scroll of Commendation because during some riots he apprehended a key Indian – the rioters' leader, no less. What wasn't mentioned quite so emphatically was that this Indian was subsequently killed while trying to escape.'

'Killed by Morrison?'

'Oh no. Morrison was too wily to be the man that puts the boot in. But Morrison was behind it. He rigged the whole thing up, Canteloupe, acting under secret orders from some *very* important people who wanted that riot-leader dead.'

*'Why did they want him dead?'

'For one thing, he was an ex-officer of the Indian Army and so was making a troublesome precedent. But there's no need to go into details. Just take my word for it—'

'—Why should I?'

'Because at that time, as you may remember, I was on H.E. the Viceroy's Military Staff. I was in on all of this from the beginning, Canteloupe, and *you can take my word for it* that we wanted this Indian dead. This we had told Morrison, who knew the man by sight, and when Morrison got the chance, he fixed it for us. Even then it was no easy thing to kill a rioter without all hell being let loose by the politicians both in England and India; but so neatly did Morrison arrange it that although quite a few people were suspicious there was nothing they could do about it – except scowl at the Gazette which announced his Viceregal Commendation. Now, does it not occur to you that a chap who managed *that* little piece of business might be fully capable of shifting your shit for you in Strasbourg?'

'I don't quite like the sound of it. You say that the Indian who was killed had been an officer, and that Morrison had known him?'

'More or less.'

'They'd met while the dead man was still serving?'

'Something of the kind.'

'So Morrison killed ... or engineered the killing of ... a man who had been his comrade?'

'But was now an enemy of the Crown. You're not getting fastidious, Canteloupe?'

'I can't afford to be. But I still don't like the smell of this story.'

'To me it smells about the same as Strasbourg.'

'Point taken,' said Canteloupe. He had finished a second glass of port and poured some cognac. 'Do you think Morrison will take it on?'

'I think he'll take on Strasbourg if offered the Under-Secretaryship,' said Detterling, 'provided he's carefully pre-

* See *Sound the Retreat*, passim.

pared. There's a certain idiom you have to use when proposing villainy to Peter: phrases like "concealed moral duty", or "beneficent violence", that kind of thing, to help him keep his ethical self-respect.'

'Are you well versed in the idiom?'

'Tolerably.'

'Then you can sound him out and send him on to me if he agrees?'

'I'd be glad to. He's a very old chum of mine and, as I say, he should have work.'

'So that's settled.' Canteloupe looked at his watch. 'Thank you for a very passable dinner,' he said, 'but now you must excuse me. Maisie's expecting me.'

'So you said earlier. You still find it worth going there?'

'I may have one leg in the grave, Detterling, but it's not the middle one.'

'I'm glad to hear it. I hope you'll be worthy of the La Tâche.'

'I hope I shall be worthy of Canteloupe,' said Canteloupe. He drained his brandy glass and rose. 'See Morrison as soon as possible,' he said, 'and pass him on to me at once. No time to lose.'

'I'll get hold of him tomorrow, if I can,' said Detterling, and himself rose and then waved as the old man marched from the dining-room, as straight as a halberd.

Well, thought Detterling, as he settled down again to finish his Marc de Champagne, he's still a strong old man and no mistake. Putting down his dinner like that and then hacking off to his whore. I wonder how ... effective ... he will be when he gets there ... From what Canteloupe had let slip at one time or another Detterling knew that Canteloupe had more or less retired from the field of love years ago – until, in 1962, he had been introduced to Maisie by Somerset. (*Memorandum*: perhaps Maisie, whom Somerset had been visiting since the middle 1950s, might just happen to know something or other that was pertinent

to his death.) According to Canteloupe, his first encounter
with Maisie had been almost miraculously rejuvenating,
and he had been going to see her two or three times a
week, without a single disappointment, ever since. Maisie,
it appeared, was exceedingly versatile and full of inven-
tion; so that it was quite reasonable to suppose, as Canteloupe himself clearly supposed, that his evening's tryst
would be a success. All the same, Detterling thought, his
cousin couldn't go on like this much longer. Maisie, and
the gargantuan eating and drinking, and all his worries at
the Ministry – between the lot of them any old man, however tough for his age, must surely begin to buckle.

But he hadn't buckled yet. In so far, Detterling reflected,
as the object of that evening's dinner had been to determine Canteloupe's state of health, the occasion had been
highly reassuring. As to the question of Canteloupe's Minis-
terial competence, once again the verdict was in his favour:
he was concerned about the difficult situation in which he
was landed by Somerset's death, but he showed no signs
of panicking, he had been modest enough to seek advice,
and although surprised and perhaps offended by the form
which it had taken, he had been sensible enough to sift and
then approve it, at least on a provisional basis. If Peter
Morrison was his man, and if Morrison was willing, then
Canteloupe was not going to pass him up on the grounds
of his own personal distaste.

For the rest, by the time Detterling had called for and
then paid his formidable bill, he had come to two con-
clusions. First, that he was as far as ever from finding the
motive for Somerset's suicide. On the available evidence
(Canteloupe's) Somerset's death had no connexion whatever with his activities at the Ministry or with the plans
that he had been making with Canteloupe for Strasbourg.
These latter he had positively been relishing; and since no
one except Canteloupe and Somerset knew anything about
them, there was no possibility that he had been in any way
'got at' on their account, let alone compelled to take his
life, by malevolent industrial competitors.

As for Detterling's second conclusion, he reached it somewhat as follows:

He, Detterling, was now charged by Canteloupe to recruit Peter Morrison in Somerset's place. It was quite possible that Peter would subsequently show his gratitude to Detterling by informing him, far more fully than Canteloupe had done, of what was afoot in Strasbourg, and this would be very amusing. But any such revelation must lie in the future. The *immediate* point about Peter Morrison was that he had known Somerset Lloyd-James even longer than Detterling had and might well be familiar with aspects of Somerset's life and character of which Detterling was ignorant. Morrison, therefore, might be able to see into the suicide more clearly than Detterling and suggest an entirely new range of possible motives. So Detterling's next step was quite plain to him: he would go to Morrison, as he had promised Canteloupe; he would use his best endeavours to persuade Morrison to take up the post on offer and the task that went with it; and then he would pick at Morrison's memories of Somerset and see whether anything in them could help to explain why, some time very early that May morning, Somerset should have decided to leave the world, and all that he had in it, in exchange for his coffin.

PART TWO

Knights Errant

The priest flapped a kind of fly-whisk and drops of water pattered on to the coffin. A few stray drops fell, to Detterling's annoyance, on his shining black shoes. Automatically he took out a handkerchief and started to bend down to wipe them off, but then he remembered where he was, and that the water was presumably holy. He straightened up again, and tempered his irritation with the priest and his clumsiness by counting the other people present. Not very many, he thought. But then Somerset's friends had not been the sort that were given to going to funerals. They would all have more pressing engagements. They would come, of course, to the memorial service later in the summer, for the occasion would be fashionable and the attendance recorded; but meanwhile – let the dead bury their dead. Apart from the undertaker's men, the priest and his acolytes, there were only fifteen persons assembled by the grave to bury Somerset, none of them known to Detterling, though he was almost certain that a plump old lady, who was wearing a very long black bonnet reminiscent of the 'Waterloo' style and was accompanied by a tall, scraggy female of upper servant's demeanour (probably her housekeeper), must be Peregrina Lennox Lloyd-James, Somerset's mother.

The bereaved woman appeared to regard the affair neutrally. Her face was composed rather than grave, her eyes tired rather than sorrowful. In so far as she displayed anything other than indifference to the proceedings, it was spasmodic disapproval, indicated, every thirty seconds or so, by a cross twitch of the mouth. Perhaps, thought Detterling, as a Roman Catholic she deprecates Somerset's suicide; but then again the inquest (at which the old lady had not been present but the findings of which must by now have been conveyed to her notice) must surely have dispelled any cause which she might have thought she had for censure.

For the inquest had gone off in accordance with the highest hopes of Detective Superintendent Stupples. Somerset had emerged from it with credit that at times seemed to approach beatification. Dolly, on whom Sergeant Pulcher had evidently done a very good job indeed, had stated with absolute conviction that her employer had been working himself, quite literally, to death and that he had confided this to her in so many words. Detterling and Carton Weir had supported Dolly's evidence, though in more sophisticated terms; Carton, for example, had referred most impressively to Somerset's increasing '*accidie*' or despair of spirit. Canteloupe had spoken of Somerset's 'inhuman task, at once massive and labyrinthine', and when asked by the coroner to say what it was had pleaded national security. Had there been, then, any particular *incident* which might have triggered off Somerset's suicide? Not so far as the Minister knew. Then thank you most kindly, Lord Canteloupe, and the coroner was very much obliged to him ...

Potentially awkward enquiries about Somerset's day out in the country, which had immediately preceded his death, were firmly blocked by Stupples himself, who insisted that the police were satisfied that nothing relevant to Somerset's death had occurred during the outing. The jury had seemed anxious to know why, 'in this day and age', Somerset should have chosen such a cumbrous method of killing himself; but they had been content with Detterling's volunteered statement that his friend had been much obsessed with the customs of antiquity and might well have reverted to them at this moment of stress. In the end the coroner had spoken in lapidary commendation of Somerset's devotion to his duty and his country, and had concluded that he killed himself after his mind had been broken by his labours.

(The undertaker's men now began to lower the coffin. It tilted slightly, causing the sun to flash off the brass plate at its head and into Peregrina's face. The housekeeper (or whatever she was) made a protective gesture, but Peregrina poked her hard in the midriff with one elbow.)

Only after the inquest was over had Detterling realized that the coroner had been a party to the charade. While the Court was in session, he had appeared to find every smallest opportunity to ask awkward questions and knock on embarrassing doors. In truth, however, while making a great banging and clattering, he had never really tried to get through any of them; he had merely poked his head round them, nodded, and then withdrawn with a knowing expression, as though thoroughly satisfied that all was well on the other side. In short, the coroner had been fixed by someone as surely as had the witnesses; it would have been interesting to see what he would have done if any of the latter had departed from the official line.

(Peregrina threw a trowelful of earth on to the coffin, and twitched emphatically. The housekeeper followed. Others formed a queue for the privilege.)

But if everything had gone according to plan at the inquest, this was not the case in other areas. When Detterling had telephoned Peter Morrison's London house, the morning after his dinner with Canteloupe, a rather rattled Mrs Morrison had said that her husband was away. She clearly did not wish to say any more, but when Detterling, using his right as an old friend of the family, had gone on to press the matter, Helen Morrison had admitted that Peter was in Switzerland, at a clinic where a last-ditch cure was being tried out on Nickie, their meningitic elder son. Helen herself had not had the heart to go because she knew the whole thing was useless. But Peter still had hopes, she said, and was prepared to back them with absurdly large sums of money; she only wished he would stop listening to these crooked mid-European quacks. When would he be back? In three or four days. Any chance of getting him back earlier, for something of importance? To Peter, Helen had said, Nickie, poor imbecilic Nickie, was the only thing of importance just then, and futile though his mission was, she did not think it would be either right or kind to try to interrupt it.

With this Detterling was compelled to agree, though privately he thought that the sooner Peter had some sense shaken into him the better; Peter needed distraction from Nickie's plight before he became totally obsessed with it and beggared himself in desperate pilgrimages from sanatorium to sanatorium. But however that might be, the immediate point was that there must be substantial delay before he could talk to Peter. He could not fly out to Switzerland to see him, even had he felt so inclined, because Helen, quite simply, refused to give the address of Nickie's clinic. This meant frustration and annoyance for Detterling, and perhaps rather more serious consequences for Canteloupe, who would be very short of time in which to make final arrangements for Peter to take over the work in Strasbourg, even if Peter, as was by no means certain, immediately consented to do so.

But Canteloupe had put a good face on it ('We can worry till our balls drop off, it won't help anything') and what with the inquest and now the funeral the interval was passing quick enough. According to Helen, Peter would now be back that very evening, together with Nickie, upon whom, as she had predicted, the cure had had no effect. Just how much easier or harder this would make it to persuade Peter to accept Canteloupe's offer remained to be seen.

Detterling, at the end of the queue, finally came to his turn with the trowel. Try as he might, he could think of no other valediction for Somerset than a Greek epigram which went:

> The nettles which flourish on Mopsus his grave
> Are more poisonous far than a hornet:
> I pissed on them once, and the sting that they gave
> Shot right up my stream to the cornet.

Ah well, he thought, Somerset would have enjoyed both the sentiment and the obscenity. Here's luck, old fellow ... Having finished with the trowel he was just about to give it back to the priest, when there was a tap on his right shoulder-blade. He turned, and saw that someone else had come up behind him. Someone who had not been present before; but someone, at last, that he knew or at least recognized: a man who had a face like Mr Punch's, with a chin that curved up almost far enough to meet the nose that jabbed fiercely down at it.

'Leonard Percival,' said the man softly; 'my turn to pay my respects.'

Leonard Percival. The name Detterling had forgotten, though the face was unforgettable. Where had he met him?

Percival threw earth with the trowel, handed it to the priest and followed Detterling, who returned to his former position at the other end of the grave. They stood there together as the last words were said. Then the little congregation, led by the priest, moved away towards the gate of the churchyard. Since they were all strangers, Detterling decided to stay where he was for a little, and Percival stayed with him. Both of them watched as the woman in the long black bonnet (Peregrina it now must be, Detterling thought) took up her station by the gate and started to shake hands with the people that filed past her.

'We mustn't keep the old lady waiting,' said Percival, at last breaking the silence between them.

The pair of them left the grave-side and walked towards the diminishing file at the gate.

'No,' said Percival, as if reading Detterling's thoughts, 'we don't tackle her today. We shan't have a proper chance anyhow. I gather she's not giving a lunch or anything?'

'No.'

'So much the better. We can just disappear and come back to her later ... after the lawyers have sorted out the will and the money and everything. By that time she might have something interesting to say. Though I very much doubt if we're going to need her. She wasn't in his life at all – the part of it that mattered to him. So what would she know of his death?'

By the time they came to the gate, there were only two people in front of them, a soft, balding, middle-aged man and a frumpish woman.

'I'm afraid this must have been a shock, Peregrina,' said the man.

But Peregrina merely twitched, as she had by the grave, and said nothing. The man and the woman both shook her hand and passed through the gate without speaking further.

'Captain Detterling,' said Detterling, offering his hand; 'an old friend of Somerset's.'

'He spoke of you once. It was kind of you to come, Captain Detterling.'

She twitched dismissively, and Percival took Detterling's place.

'Leonard Percival,' said Percival, without explanation.

'Mr Percival . . .'

Peregrina nodded her long bonnet, then turned. A car started up a little way down the street and moved forward to the gate, a small Morris shooting brake, driven by the housekeeper. Peregrina, taking no further notice of Detterling or Percival, or of the priest who was hovering some yards away, climbed neatly into the front seat and twitched at the housekeeper, who drove off, in the direction that led out of London, rather fast.

Detterling and Percival surveyed the empty suburban street. The mourners and the undertaker's men had all disappeared. Two little boys in jeans and jerseys (the disrobed acolytes) ran silently but violently past the priest and through the gate, and fled in the direction opposite to that which Peregrina's car had taken.

'They shouldn't have children at funerals,' said Percival.

'They shouldn't have funerals at all.'

'Disposal service, eh? I agree. Just ring up for the man to come and collect. Less depressing that way. None of this hanging about.'

'My car should be here in a minute,' Detterling said. 'You are from Jermyn Street, aren't you?'

'That's one way of putting it. Rather a tactful one.'

'Then you'd like a lift?'

'Please. I came by train. They're very mean about minor expenses.'

'I wondered when someone would be coming. It was promised, you see.'

'Here am I,' said Percival; 'take me.'

'We've met before,' Detterling said.

'I hoped you'd remember. Hydra 1962. I was staying with your old chum, Max de Freville.'

'He's in Corfu now.'

'So I hear. Very much on my beat at one time, all that part of the world.'

'What brought you back home?'

'Ulcers,' said Percival: 'too much of a risk in the field.'

'Not very handy anywhere.'

'Oh, I'm fit enough for standard domestic jobs, like this one. But I wish that car of yours would come. I don't like standing for too long.'

'Then you shouldn't have come to this funeral.'

'I had to make contact with you, according to my instructions.'

'You didn't need to come here in order to make contact.'

'No, but I like to get the feel of the thing. If you see the body being put away with your own eyes, it gives you a personal interest. And shaking hands with his old mother – that was a help too. It makes you feel part of the family, in a way.'

'I don't think Mrs Lloyd-James quite thought of you as that.'

'No. But now I've got a face to keep in mind. I can look at that face, mentally, and I can ask myself "Could this woman's son have done so-and-so or such-and-such?"'

'Very well. Ask yourself "Could this woman's son have killed himself?"'

'From what I hear, he must have done.'

'Then try asking yourself "Why?"'

'Let's not rush things, Captain Detterling. This your car?'

'Yes.'

A large, deep red Mercedes, driven by a uniformed chauffeur, drew up by the churchyard gate.

'And your chauffeur?'

'My manservant.'

The manservant got out of the car, revealing grey breeches and leather gaiters, and saluted in military fashion. Detterling raised his bowler in acknowledgement.

'You're late, Corporal.'

'Sir.'

'Why? It's not far from here to Mr Morrison's house in Putney.'

'No, sir. But just as I was delivering that note of yours – I was giving it to Mrs Morrison at the door – Mr Morrison turned up in a taxi ... with that son of his, Mr Nicholas. It seemed they'd driven from the airport, and Mr Morrison was disappointed because Mrs Morrison hadn't met them with a proper car and the nurse. *She* said she wasn't expecting him till the evening plane at 5.30, and *he* said he'd sent a telegram changing that, and *she* said she hadn't had it, and in the middle of this Mr Nicholas – well, sir, he forgot himself in the taxi. You know how they are when they're like that. So the taxi-driver took on something fierce about the puddle on the seat, and there was words all round, and I had to help get Mr Nicholas inside and find the nurse, and then Mrs Morrison had to get a bucket of water and a floor-cloth for the puddle in the taxi, and I had to help her, and the taxi-driver just stood there griping, the rotten sod, and—'

'—Oh God,' said Detterling. 'That'll do, Corporal. I understand.'

'But one good thing, sir. In the middle of all this Mr Morrison somehow found time to read your note – he must have known it was urgent, me being there to deliver it – and he says he'll be able to come and talk to you this evening, as you suggest.'

'Does anyone mind,' said Percival, 'if I get in and sit down?'

'Sorry,' said Detterling. 'Corporal ...'

'Sir . . .'

The manservant opened the near-side back door and helped Percival in.

'Rug, sir?'

'Rug?'

'For your knees.'

'No, thanks. It's my belly bothers me.'

Percival moved along the seat and Detterling (having waved politely to the priest, who was still hovering) joined him in the back of the car. When Detterling too had been offered and declined a rug, they set off towards Barnes Common, for Hammersmith Bridge.

'Why was he buried round here?' said Percival. 'You'd have thought it would have been somewhere grand in London or else down in Devon.'

'Expensive, either way. Mrs Lloyd-James doesn't look the sort to spend money on inessentials.'

'Or even on her own kit. That bonnet must have come out of the Ark . . . Who's this Mr Morrison your man was talking about?'

'Corporal,' Detterling said.

The manservant pressed a button on the dashboard; and a glass screen rose from the back of the bench-seat on which he sat and slotted itself into the roof. Detterling then told Percival at some length exactly who Peter Morrison was and what business he, and by extension Percival, now had with him.

'You'd better handle him alone,' said Percival when he had heard Detterling out; 'at any rate when he comes to-night. I'd be *de trop*. You reckon he'll take this job of Lord Canteloupe's?'

'He's wanted a post for a long while now.'

'Well, as to this affair in Strasbourg,' said Percival, 'I hope he'll have proper professional assistance. We don't like amateurs playing games in that kind of area.'

'*Your* area, I suppose.'

'Not any more. We in Jermyn Street are separate from the crowd which goes in for *that* kind of thing – though as it happens I myself used to belong to it, before my stomach started to play up. We in Jermyn Street,' said Percival, 'handle affairs here at home: internal security. Our particular concern is to keep our eye on politicians and important public servants.'

'To protect them? Or to catch them out when they're naughty?'

'To protect them, and to catch them out *before* they can be naughty. Much more decorous that: no mess on the carpet, so to speak.'

'And if the mess is made before you can stop it?'

'We clean up quickly without banging the mop about.'

'Which is what you aim to do here?'

'That depends,' said Percival, 'on whether there really is anything to clean up. One politician who's committed suicide is nothing. The vital thing, as of course you know, is *why*. The *why* could lead us to lots of nasty messes hidden behind the curtains, in which case we mop up *pronto*. Or it could lead us to people who are just about to make other nasty messes, in which case we hold their heads over a basin. Or it could turn out not to interest us at all. But the all-important thing, the thing that has to be found out before we can take – or even contemplate – any action whatever is why Lloyd-James went and did it.'

'Agreed. But just now, when I asked you that very question, you told me not to rush matters.'

'Yes. You were premature, you see, like all amateurs. The "why" behind this suicide is absolutely crucial and we must never for a moment forget it, but there are many other questions to be asked and answered first.'

'Such as?'

'For a start, why do you suppose that I have been sent to make myself known to you?'

'Because Superintendent Stupples promised that I should be brought in on this enquiry, and he has told your chief that I might be helpful.'

'Correct. But why have they chosen *me* to contact you?'

'Because we know each other – or at least we've met before.'

'Correct again. But far more important is where we met before – in Max de Freville's house on Hydra.'

'What's Hydra got to do with it?'

'Nothing. But Max might have a great deal. He knew Lloyd-James quite well, and he knows both of us. Which means that Max, you and I – three men who know and trust each other – might come on something very useful when we combine our efforts.'

'I've never really trusted Max,' Detterling said, 'and I've no particular reason to trust you.'

'Then let's say, three men who know and understand each other...'

'We could certainly have an interesting talk about Somerset,' Detterling conceded. 'Max has always been a collector of information.'

'I know. I used to provide a lot of it – in order to augment my official stipend. In this case, perhaps Max can inform me for a change.'

'The only trouble is, Max may not be very up-to-date. He's been a long time on Corfu, and he hasn't seen Somerset since he had him out there for Christmas in 1970.'

'It's what Max may know of Lloyd-James's past that interests me. I look to you for the up-to-date stuff.'

Percival adjusted his wire spectacles and gazed placidly at Detterling, as if waiting for him to issue 'up-to-date stuff' as a ticker-tape machine beats out racing results.

'I've been trying to sort it all out these last few days,' said Detterling.

'And what have you got?'

'All that about Canteloupe and the Ministry which I told you.'

'Leading nowhere.'

'Leading to Peter Morrison, who may help.'

'*May*. What other lines have you thought of?'

'This whole business of the day Somerset spent out of London just before he died. What I call his "Last Day Out in the Country". That could explain a lot.'

'Only no one knows where he went.'

'You can surely find out.'

'How?'

'He may have been noticed. He may have had an appointment.'

'Noticed by whom? Appointment with whom?'

'Well ... anybody.'

'Exactly. Anybody at all. So we'd have to make a song and dance in order to find out who, thus advertising far and wide our continuing interest in the affair just when it's meant to be finished with for good. I wholly agree with you,' granted Percival, 'that the details of Lloyd-James's "Last Day Out in the Country" could be very enlightening, but we'll have to trust to time and chance to bring us information about that. Meanwhile, what else had you thought of?'

'His mother. But her you want to leave till later, you say.'

'Right. What else?'

'There's a tart he's been visiting for God knows how long. Maisie, she's called.'

'Maisie what?'

'Search me. But Canteloupe will know where to find her.'

'I see. And what else?' said Percival, persistent and almost aggressive.

'His friends. Max, as you suggest – though it'll probably mean going to Corfu. Then the rest of them if we're still getting nowhere.'

'Not bad,' said Percival, his tone turning suddenly to approbation; 'all quite obvious, of course, but at least you haven't made the amateur's mistake of trying to think up brilliant short cuts ... which in this game lead only to short circuits. And here we are at your place, if I'm not mistaken.'

The Mercedes drew up outside Albany. The manservant turned to look through the glass screen, awaiting orders.

'Want to come in?' said Detterling.

'No thanks. You drop me off here – nice and handy for Jermyn Street. So,' said Percival summarizing: 'you'll see Peter Morrison tonight and do your stuff with him. Then we'll get on with the rest of them – his whore, his chums and his old mother if we need her. And that's the only way of it.'

Percival started to leave the car. The manservant had anticipated him and was there to open the door. Detterling too climbed out on to the pavement.

'That's all, Corporal,' he said. 'Garage and maintenance.'

'Sir.'

The manservant saluted, turned to the right, dismissed himself back into the car, and drove away.

'Useful fellow, that,' said Percival.

'He was in my regiment.'

'And hasn't forgotten it, I can see.' Percival tilted his face and caught the sun with his wired spectacles, flashing them in Detterling's face. 'I'll come tomorrow,' he said, 'to hear about Morrison.'

'What time?'

'Expect me when you see me. No need to sit at home though. I'll find you all right.'

Percival bent almost double, gave a quick, sly imitation of a sleuth tracking footprints with a magnifying glass, and darted away through the traffic.

Peter Morrison arrived at Detterling's chambers at ten in the evening in time to be offered coffee and brandy.

'Sorry I couldn't ask you to dinner,' said Detterling; 'my man's evening off.'

'I had to dine at home anyway,' said Morrison. 'My first evening back from Switzerland.'

'Could they do anything for Nickie there?'

Morrison's mouth trembled.

'No,' he said at last. 'No one can. I know that now.'

'What are you going to do with him?'

'He can live down on the farm at Whereham. He might be able to learn to do something in the fields. Either Helen or I will be there most of the time. We can't make much difference, but I think he still knows us ... in a way.'

Morrison closed his mouth very tightly. Then:

'But you haven't asked me here to talk about Nickie,' he said. 'That note your man brought – it implied something pressing. Otherwise I shouldn't have come. My first evening back; Helen wasn't pleased.'

Why, wondered Detterling, does he talk as if he'd been away a year instead of just a few days? Perhaps it seemed like a year to him, while he waited in some ante-room at the clinic, waited for the nurse to summon him into the office, where the doctor rose behind the desk, smiling an antiseptic smile and already beginning to shake his head ...

Aloud he said to Morrison: 'It is pressing, Peter. There's a job for you. To replace Somerset as Under-Secretary in Canteloupe's Ministry.'

'Job,' said Morrison, pursing his lips to make the short word linger. 'That would make a change, certainly. But why are *you* telling me about it?'

'Because there are two conditions, and Canteloupe thought you might like to discuss them with me first.'

'Again, why with you, Detterling?'

'Canteloupe is too shy to mention such matters to you until I have prepared the way. He is overawed by your moral reputation.'

'Whereas you are not?' said Morrison, and smiled bland forgiveness.

'I've known you a very long time, Peter, and I understand – I have done ever since that business in India – that your moral code has a lot of notes in small print written underneath it.'

'Well, talking of notes in small print, let's hear these conditions.'

'The first is that you've got to say "yes" or "no" tonight. If "yes", Canteloupe will want you to start tomorrow.'

'Straightforward, if rather flustering. And the second?'

'You've got to be prepared to undertake ... a very special role ... at this Trade Convention in Strasbourg.'

Morrison sighed. 'I might have known it,' he said. 'Some unfinished affair of Somerset's?'

'Yes.' Detterling started to explain, emphasizing the benefits which it was hoped the new light metal alloy would confer on the country's economy. 'So you see,' he concluded, 'how important it is to the Government, and to Canteloupe within the Government.'

'So important,' said Morrison, 'that he is prepared to use almost any means to do down our rivals.'

'Not "any means", Peter. He merely wants to make fools of 'em. No doubt they're playing the same kind of game against us. It's just like an old-fashioned Horse Fair. A certain amount of ... minor foul play ... is part of the custom.'

'Minor foul play?'

'Just tampering. Nothing crude or violent. Sabotage is out, Canteloupe said.'

'I'm delighted to hear it. But does one ... just tamper ... with rival light metal alloys?'

'Canteloupe wouldn't tell me, but he said Somerset had thought of a way. You'll be told quick enough if you take this on.'

'No doubt.' Morrison passed his right index finger along his upper lip and rested it against the side of his nose. 'Why did Somerset kill himself?' he said.

'That's what I was going to ask you?'

'How should I know?'

'I thought you might have some sort of a clue. Something out of the past ...'

'Nothing out of the past,' Morrison said. 'When I first read about it, in a day-old *Times* in a waiting-room at Nickie's clinic, I just could not believe it, I had plenty of time to kill, so I thought right back, as far as I could, to see if there had ever been anything, however slight, which could have indicated that one day Somerset might do this. There was nothing, Detterling. I thought of the years at school during the war – we were in different houses but I knew him well even then – and I could remember him only as totally equable and competent, never in doubt what he wanted and seldom failing to get it.'

'A bit sickly, wasn't he?'

'Yes, but it never seemed to depress him. He used it very cleverly. He was the average sort of age when he came, getting on for fourteen, but because his build was very slight he looked much younger, hardly twelve. So from his first day there he managed to get it generally accepted, by masters and matrons and anyone who counted, that Somerset Lloyd-James was rather delicate and special and must be allowed time off to rest when he felt like it. In fact he always felt like it when anything dull or difficult was going to happen, a Field Day or a compulsory run, but no one ever resented him for it. In those days we all had to spend one afternoon a week cutting down trees or doing something to help the war effort; never once, that I heard of, did Somerset spend five minutes helping the war effort, far less a whole afternoon, and yet it was never commented on, it was never even noticed. It was just assumed by everyone that such things were not for Somerset. "Lloyd-James not here?" some beak would say at an early morning lesson. "Oh no, sir, it's raining and he's got a cold coming on, so he decided to stay in bed." "Oh, I see," the beak would say. And then later the same day, when the sun had come out and some sort of pleasure was in train, there was Somerset in the middle of it, chatting away to the very same beak whose class he'd cut that morning – and never a single cross word. No, Detterling; there's no clue to be found in Somerset's ill health ... which, incidentally, disappeared fast enough when it was no longer necessary to ensure his comfort. He last used it in 1946 in order to evade National Service; he flannelled the Medical Board just as he flannelled his House matron. From that day on not a word has been heard of it. For the last twenty-five years and more Somerset has had far too many interests to allow time for illness.'

'But there must have been other troubles. Couldn't you

think of *anything* in his past that might have contained the seed of his suicide?'

'Nothing. Oh, he's had his disappointments from time to time. I remember, when he was Editor of *Strix* and I was on the Board with him for a while, he came badly unstuck over several little schemes he had going. But something always came along to make up. In Somerset's life, things have always, on the whole, got steadily better and better. Better money, better positions, better arrangements about sex; first repute, then influence, then real power. Everything improving for him all the time – right up to the day he killed himself. So the only conclusion I could come to – sitting there thinking in Switzerland – was that his suicide must have been connected with something very recent, perhaps his most recent job ... the one which I am being offered now. Not that I knew – then – what was going on behind the scenes. Now that you've told me how – er –questionable some of it was, I'm even more inclined to think that I could have been right.'

'Well you weren't, Peter. The same idea occurred to me. So I went into it, and I've satisfied myself that Somerset's suicide had nothing to do with the plans for Strasbourg or any other aspect of his job.'

'How did you satisfy yourself?'

'I questioned Canteloupe.'

'He could be hiding something.'

'No. I know when Canteloupe's hiding things.'

'So whatever motive Somerset had, it was quite unconnected with the Ministry?'

'I'd swear to it. You don't want to be put off by what happened to Somerset.'

'I'm still not sure I want to step into a dead man's shoes.'

'They're the best pair you'll get, Peter. If you refuse this, you may wait a very long time before you're offered anything else even half as good.'

'The Under-Secretaryship, that's all right, very much all right. But this business in Strasbourg ...'

'What about it?'

'Well, it may not have caused Somerset's suicide—'

'—It didn't—'

'—But it still doesn't seem very wholesome.'

'By which you mean it's not safe,' said Detterling, remembering his own thoughts on the matter.

'I mean it's not straight.'

'That's why Canteloupe wants you. You, my dear Peter, have a way of dealing with what's crooked and somehow making it look straight ... to yourself as well as others.'

'Maybe. It's not an exercise I care for. It's very demanding of one's mental resources.'

'But if the service of your country requires it?'

'Does it?'

'Yes. The country's going broke, you know that. We've little enough dignity left, and if we go broke we lose even that. And when we lose our dignity, we lose our influence, which is still just reckonable and operates, by and large, on the side of decency in an indecent world.'

'Something in that, I suppose. The sale of this metal alloy – will it stop us going broke?'

'No. But it will delay the process.'

'And keep Canteloupe in his Ministry. Canteloupe: is he an influence on the side of decency, Detterling?'

'There are worse men than Canteloupe. You might do a lot with him – and for him – if you become his lieutenant.'

'You're telling me it's my duty to take the job.'

'So it is. You're a talented man, and it's time you were using your talents.'

'You're very tempting. I'd like to take this offer, but I wish I could be clear about my own motive. Do I want it for the public good or for my own aggrandizement?'

'Who the hell cares about that?' snapped Detterling. 'You're simply indulging yourself in moral doubt as other people indulge themselves in fake grief or fake indignation. Will you take the bloody job or won't you?'

'I'll take it,' said Morrison, looking slightly surprised, though whether at his own decision, at Detterling's outburst of ill temper, or at the accuracy of Detterling's diagnosis, Detterling was unable to determine.

'Then ring up Canteloupe straight away,' said Detterling. 'You can use my telephone. He may even want to see you tonight before you go back to Putney.'

'So that was all settled as my cousin Canteloupe would have it,' said Captain Detterling to Leonard Percival, 'but there wasn't much said to help us.'

They were walking in St James's Park at 11.30 on the morning after Detterling had had his discussion with Peter Morrison. Detterling had gone out for a breath of air, and Percival, true to his promise, had encountered him without warning or ceremony.

'Tell me,' said Percival now, 'is Lord Canteloupe certain that the Prime Minister will ratify the appointment? He seems to be going it pretty much alone.'

'That's Canteloupe's affair,' Detterling said. 'I've done my bit. And much good I've got of it. Not a thing did Peter tell me that could even begin to explain Somerset's suicide.'

'No. But some of it was interesting for all that. What he said about Lloyd-James malingering at school – how he managed them all so cleverly. And that remark of Morrison's about how everything got better and better for Lloyd-James all the time – including his "arrangements for sex". That was the phrase, I think?'

'It was. And now I come to think of it, it was rather a surprising remark – coming from Peter, I mean. He seldom refers to that side of life unless he's forced into it. And again, the offhand attitude towards sex which the phrase implies – that's not Peter's usual style at all.'

'But from what you've said to me, the phrase is very appropriate. There's a tart called Maisie, you said, whom Lloyd-James has been visiting for God knows how long. There's an "arrangement" if ever there was.'

'Yes ... Maisie next stop, I suppose?'

'I think so,' said Percival: 'she must have got to know *something* about him by now.'

'Well, I'll ring up Canteloupe. He knows her address.'

'No need. I've got it here.'

Percival gave the number of a flat in Artillery Mansions.

'How did you find out?' said Detterling crossly. 'You don't even know her surname.'

'*You* don't know her surname,' emended Percival. 'We've had her on the books for a donkey's age. She has a distinguished clientele, you see ... with one of whom I was very much involved about ten years ago.'

'I thought you operated abroad then. Before your ulcers.'

'I operated wherever the trail led me. This trail came back to London, at one stage, and right through Maisie's bedroom.'

'You're sure *your* Maisie is the same as Somerset's?'

'Certain. The name rang a bell as soon as you mentioned it yesterday. So I looked *my* Maisie up in the files – her surname is Malcolm, by the way – and it all checked. She used to live in Shepherd Market, where she regularly entertained, among others, two Oxbridge dons, three novelists, a nuclear physicist, and a selection of politicians, which included Lord Canteloupe, as one of course you know, and our dead friend, Lloyd-James.'

'Quite an Aspasia.'

'I can't answer for her intellect, but it seems she's good-natured and honest – *and* an expert impresario of male fantasies. All of which explains why she has retained her appeal despite being rather long in the tooth by now. In fact during the last five or six years she's been more in demand than ever, which is presumably why she left Shepherd Market for Artillery Mansions. A less embarrassing address for her silver-haired gentlemen to give to taxi-drivers and a more commodious arena for romping in.'

'You talk as if she ran a gymnasium,' grumbled Detterling.

'Some people's fantasies take up quite a lot of space and effort. Why are you so huffy this morning?'

'Because *I* was the one who was going to find Maisie for us, and now you've gone and spoilt it for me. And I don't like unnecessary surprises. Why can't yóu meet a man at an agreed time and place instead of popping out from behind bushes in the Park?'

'Because you want waking up.' Percival took Detterling's arm, steered him through a left wheel and set them both on course for Birdcage Walk. 'You're altogether too comfortable, Captain Detterling. You need a little early morning P.T., so to speak. You need to change a few car wheels in the rain, instead of having an ex-corporal to do it for you.'

'I know of nothing in our connexion which entitles you to moralize at me.'

'I dare say not. But you won't resent a little practical instruction? I'm sure you want to be a credit to our partnership.'

'What kind of practical instruction?'

'A simple training exercise, for a start. Here we are in Birdcage Walk. I've told you Maisie Malcolm's address. I'll bet you a fiver that ulcers and all I'm the first of us to ring on her doorbell in Artillery Mansions.'

Percival sauntered away towards the Buckingham Palace end of Birdcage Walk, and thus had his back turned on an empty taxi which had now appeared from the Whitehall end and was at once hailed by Detterling.

'Have a nice walk,' Detterling called through the taxi window as he sailed past Percival. 'I hope you can get that fiver on expenses.'

Percival grinned and sketched a military salute with his left hand. Detterling sighed happily and sat back in his seat. Although he was a very rich man, he always enjoyed winning a wager ...

... So that he was rather put out, having rung Maisie's bell and been admitted, to find Percival already sitting on Maisie's leather sofa.

'You see?' said Percival. 'You need livening up. You

didn't remember that it was just on twelve o'clock and that your taxi would be badly held up by the Changing of the Guard at the Palace.'

'It was only for a minute or two.'

'Long enough for me to slip down Petty France and take a short cut through that new hotel – in at the front and out through the kitchens – while you were driving round in a ruddy great circle at a cost of twenty-seven new pence. Or to be more precise, at a cost of five pounds and twenty-seven new pence.'

Detterling handed over a fiver.

'Would one of you mind telling me,' said the plump and jolly-looking woman who had let Detterling in, 'what all this is about?'

'This gentleman,' said Percival, 'is Captain Detterling. He is an old friend of the late Somerset Lloyd-James, and he is helping me with my confidential enquiries into Mr Lloyd-James's suicide.' He turned to Detterling. 'Meet Miss Maisie Malcolm,' he said.

'How d'ye do?' said Detterling, shaking hands.

'Not too badly, dear,' said Maisie. 'So you've come about poor old Somerset? You don't want a nice dirty, either of you?'

'A nice dirty?'

'You know – a nice old, dirty old time. We can all three do it together if that's what you fancy.'

'Madam,' said Percival, 'it is not yet one o'clock.'

'Lots of my people come and do it in the morning. Gives 'em an appetite for their lunch.'

'Tell me,' said Detterling, who could not resist the question, 'does Lord Canteloupe ever come and do it in the morning?'

'Loopy Canteloupe? Friend of yours?'

'Distant cousin.'

'He comes any old time, Loopy does.'

'More to our immediate purpose,' said Percival, 'did Mr Lloyd-James ever come and do it in the morning?'

'Not as a rule. He was an afternoon man – lately at any

rate. But there was one bit of kinkiness he used to like in the morning. He sometimes had this bit about being a little boy who can't do his motions, see, and I have to be his nanny and stand in the lav. and scold him while he sits there straining. Then when he still can't go I have to bend him over the bowl and smack his bare bottom. He always prefers *that* in the morning,' said Maisie, 'because he says it's the natural time for it. Half-past eight he comes round, right after his breakfast – and a bloody bore it is, 'specially as I have to get myself up in striped gingham with white cross-belts and starched cuffs and cap. A very particular gentleman is Mr Lloyd-James, as well as being inventive. But I can't think why I'm telling you all this.'

'Because I asked you,' said Percival.

'So you did. But I shouldn't be telling about my clients.'

'Mr Lloyd-James won't mind,' Percival said.

'I suppose not. I was forgetting he was dead. Why did he do it?'

'That's what we want to know,' said Detterling. 'We thought you might be able to help us.'

'Haven't a clue, duckie. He's been coming to me for ever so long – 1955, I think it was first – and he's always enjoyed himself, in one way or another, and then just gone off till the next time.'

'When was the *last* time?'

'About a week ago.'

'He seemed his usual self?'

'Very much so. We had the oils out, I remember.'

'Had the oils out?'

'For massage, dear. I had to pretend I was a lady doctor giving him osteopathic therapy. And then suddenly I had to start shaking all over, and lifting my skirt and dropping my knickers, and doing it to myself with the neck of the oil bottle and begging him to let me climb on top. "Oh, you've got a lovely one," I had to say, "it's lovely I can't wait to sit on it".'

'I see,' said Percival. 'And was all this a success?'

'Oh yes. He went off with a bang like a bathroom geezer. And when he left he gave me three quid extra instead of asking for ten per cent off, which is what he usually does because he's such an old customer.'

'Nothing suicidal about all that,' Detterling said. 'Did he tell you when he'd be coming again?'

'No. But that wasn't surprising. He usually rang up a few hours before. "I can feel it beginning to bubble, Maisie," he used to say on the telephone, "and I'll be with you this afternoon at four o'clock" or whatever.'

'How often has he been coming lately?' asked Percival.

'Not as often as when he was younger?'

'Not quite, but often enough. Three times a fortnight, let's say.'

'And his performance when he does come?'

'Well, I told you about the last time. It isn't always as good as that, mind, but he's never dried up on me, and he sometimes stays for a second helping.'

'We should stick firmly to the past tense,' Detterling said. 'Let us conclude that when Somerset died he was sexually in excellent trim.'

'But was he?' said Percival. 'Perhaps he felt guilty or inferior because he was compelled – forgive me, Miss Malcolm – to hire someone. Perhaps he was ashamed of being ugly and repulsive.'

'Ugly he certainly was,' said Maisie, 'but not repulsive. He had a kind of attraction, you know, just because he *was* so odd to look at.'

'Did he realize this?' asked Percival.

'He'd made quite a few girls in his day,' said Detterling; 'smart ones at that. He must have known there was something about him. It's always been my belief that he came to Miss Malcolm only for the convenience of it – to save time and trouble.'

'I wouldn't wonder if you were right,' said Maisie. 'He didn't need to pay for his onions, not unless it suited. Lots of women would have liked old Somerset, because he had a way of surprising you. Not only with all the things he made up – nannies and doctors and the rest of it – but with the sheer strength and vigour of him. He was all so white and weedy that you never expected him to show himself so horny. And when he did, it was exciting. Not that I can afford to get excited about my clients or it'd be the death of me, but when I saw those pale, scraggy thighs, and then saw what power he was pumping up between them ... well, it was very sexy. It was as though all the strength which should have been in the rest of his body had come together in his cock.'

'Priapic,' said Detterling, 'like a satyr. Satyrs were often ugly too. Half men, half goats.'

'So that when you had to say "Oh, you've got a lovely one",' said Percival to Maisie, 'you really meant it?'

'No,' said Maisie. 'It wasn't lovely, it was too bloated, too demanding, you might say, for that. But it was certainly nothing for any man to be ashamed of, and it more than made up for the rest of him.'

'... Which is all very interesting to know,' remarked Detterling as he walked back with Percival across St James's Park, 'but takes us no further at all. No clues in Artillery Mansions.'

'You said something in there,' said Percival, 'about the girls whom Lloyd-James had made in his day. *Smart* girls, you said. What did you mean by that?'

'I'll give you a good example: Lady Susan Grange as was, now married to Lord Philby. She'd been mine for a bit, then Somerset took her on. Or rather, she took him on.'

'Why did she swop over – if it's not an embarrassing question?'

'Not after sixteen years. She was bored with me. The way she put it was that she wanted to try some really bad wine for a change. And then, to her surprise, it turned out to be rather stimulating.'

'Meaning more or less what Maisie said – that Lloyd-James had some unexpected shots in his locker?'

'I suppose so.'

'How long did it last?'

'Nobody lasted very long with Susan in those days. But Somerset went a fair distance – and was only dropped when she got engaged to Philby. Somewhat to his relief, he always said: she was a damned difficult girl and very expensive to feed.'

'So that Maisie came cheaper as well as much more handy.'

'Yes. All of which only confirms what both Maisie and I were saying: Somerset preferred whores because they were in every sense more economical and didn't interfere with the rest of his life. The preference did nothing to make him feel inadequate – far less suicidal.'

They paused by the bank of the lake. It was a blue day but sharp, without much hint of summer. Detterling watched the ducks as they went briskly about their aquatic affairs, and waited for Percival to tell him what they must do next.

'Max de Freville,' mused Percival, 'is in Corfu.'

'Indeed.'

'Fancy a day or two there?'

'Certainly.'

'What about the House of Commons.'

'It won't collapse without me,' said Detterling. 'But what about your boss in Jermyn Street? You say he's mean about expenses.'

'Mean about taxis, because he has to open the petty cash box. Aeroplanes are all right, because he can get tickets on an invoice. It's not the cost he minds, it's dishing out ready money. Civil Service mentality, you see.'

'What about a hotel when we get there?'

'Why don't we stay with Max?'

'Why don't we?' said Detterling. 'It's a very comfortable house. Let's go and telephone him. I've got the Corfu number.'

'No,' said Percival, 'let's give him a surprise.'

'Bad manners.'

'Good tactics. If you warn someone you're coming, he

has time to think of reasons for not telling you things ... or for telling you the wrong things.'

'Why should Max want to do that to us?'

'Because knowledge is power. When you share it with others, you depreciate it. Max of all people knows that.'

'I still think this mania of yours for surprising people is both childish and tiresome. Suppose Max isn't there? Or suppose the house is full?'

'He's there,' said Percival, 'and apart from him and his servants the house is empty.'

'More checking up behind my back?'

'Why not? You wouldn't know how to go about it yourself. And if you did no one would tell you anything.'

'Let's get on, if you don't mind.' Detterling moved along the bank towards the iron bridge. 'I'm sick of these bloody quacking ducks.'

'Not one quack,' said Percival, 'but has a definite purpose to summon, alert, encourage or command.'

'Who told you that?'

'I read it in the *Reader's Digest*. Not your kind of thing, I know, but full of tidily compressed information for those of us who haven't much leisure. Did you know why penguins can't fly? Or the true meaning of the expression a "swan-song"?'

'No, I didn't.'

'There you are, you see. You shouldn't despise the *Reader's Digest*.'

'All right. Why *can't* a penguin fly?'

'Because its wings are too short,' said Percival triumphantly, 'and incidentally, there is no such thing as a "swan-song". It's a poetic fiction.'

When they reached the Mall, cars were whizzing along both ways. Percival dodged neatly in and out of them, and waited patiently on the other side for Detterling, who took nearly three minutes to get himself across.

'You must learn not to waste time,' said Percival, 'in ordinary everyday procedures, like crossing roads. It is

simply a matter of having a sound method and using one's
will-power to apply it.'

'We're not pressed for a few minutes.'

> 'If you can fill the unforgiving minute,
>   With sixty seconds' worth of distance run,
>   Yours is the Earth and everything that's in it . . .'

said Percival as though he really believed it. 'For example,
and here is another practical test, how would *you* propose
to reach Corfu as quickly as possible?'

'Plane to Athens,' said Detterling, 'and an internal flight
on to the island. That's how I did it last time I went to see
Max – the only way, they said.'

Percival clicked his tongue. 'It hasn't occurred to you,' he
said as they walked towards St James's Palace, 'that things
might have changed since then. These days, Detterling, and
at this time of the year, there are direct flights to Corfu.'

'If you say so. Let's get one tomorrow.'

'There are also night flights. We shall go tonight, joining
Olympic Airways Flight 807 at 2130 hours at the Cromwell Road Terminal or 2200 hours at London Airport. And
arriving in Corfu at 0300 hours, local time.'

'And knocking on Max's door at four in the morning, I
suppose, to give him a bigger and better surprise. Thank
you very much, but I'll fly tomorrow.'

'You'd better fly with me,' said Percival lightly; 'tonight.'

Although both the tone and the phrasing were civil,
Detterling was too old a hand not to recognize the discip-
linary menace behind this remark. 'You'll do as I say,' Percival was telling him, 'or I'm finished with you.' Detterling did not wish to be finished with, and now tendered his
compliance, though he made it as cool as he could.

'So be it then,' he said. 'Since you're arranging it all, you
can get the tickets.'

'Bureaucratic difficulties there,' Percival giggled. 'My
ticket will be procured through Jermyn Street. They won't
pay for yours.'

'Why not? I'm helping them.'

'At your own pressing request.'

'All right. You ask 'em to get two tickets, and I'll write them a cheque for mine.'

'That,' said Percival, 'would lead to complications in the accounts. We have to be very discreet, you see. I must ask you to get your ticket yourself.'

'Very well,' said Detterling, who now saw his chance to take a mild revenge on Percival for so stubbornly subjecting him to inconvenience. 'I'll go to my travel agent this afternoon.'

'Yes,' said Percival, 'that's what I should do.'

He stopped at the newspaper stand near Prunier and bought a midday edition of the *Evening Standard*. After a quick look at the front page, 'You could learn something from your cousin Canteloupe,' Percival said. 'He doesn't waste any time.'

He pointed to a paragraph at the bottom of one column. 'Mr Peter Morrison to be Under-Secretary,' Detterling read.

'That means,' said Percival, 'that he's already got the Prime Minister's official agreement. No grass growing under Canteloupe's feet.'

'I dare say not. If you'll excuse me,' said Detterling, pointing to Prunier's door, 'I'll just turn in here for a spot of lunch. I rather fancy some fish.'

'Won't your ex-corporal be expecting you at home?'

'There isn't any fish there.'

'He doesn't know you suddenly want fish. He'll be cooking for you by now.'

'He's very flexible. We taught them to be in our regiment.'

'All the same, rather bad manners to let him down.'

'I'll get a waiter to ring him up,' said Detterling in a brittle voice, wondering why he was bothering to justify his arrangements to Leonard Percival.

'You do as you please,' said Percival, flashing his spectacles in the sun. 'It's no skin off my snout. But remember: 2130 at the Terminal or 2200 at Heathrow.'

'I'll be there ... ticket and all.'

Detterling walked into Prunier's Restaurant, meditating the little surprise he had in store for Percival that evening. Percival needed putting in his place, and Detterling, thought Detterling gleefully, was just the man to see to that.

Captain Detterling had himself driven to London Airport by his manservant and arrived there at 2155 hours. When he had checked himself in on Olympic Airways Flight 807, he went through the passport barrier and found Leonard Percival, who was blinking up through his glasses at a television screen which announced imminent departures. In their case, it appeared, not so imminent.

'Flight's delayed by half an hour,' Percival said.

'Oh dear. That makes thirty unforgiving minutes in which we shall *not* get sixty seconds' worth of distance run. Let us have a drink instead.'

'Just a moment,' said Percival. 'What's that?'

He pointed to Detterling's boarding card, which was sticking out of his breast pocket.

'It's pink,' said Percival in evident dismay: 'first-class.'

'What else?' said Detterling smugly. 'Drink?'

'I won't be long,' said Percival. 'Please order me a light ale.'

He swallowed slightly, then scurried away towards the passport barrier, spoke quietly to one of the officials, and passed back into the outer world. Detterling ordered a light ale and a double whisky at the bar, and sat down at a table with satisfaction. Percival, as he had hoped, was clearly discomfited by the assertion of independence implicit in the purchase of a first-class ticket. He had been reminded that Detterling had his own style of doing things, and that this style was, and always would be, superior to anything which Percival could deploy. Percival, in short, had been put down. But where had he gone? If he wanted to report to Jermyn Street, about Detterling's behaviour or anything else, there was a telephone inside the passport barrier.

And then suddenly Percival was back again, with a pink

first-class boarding card sticking out of his breast pocket.

'Well, well,' said Detterling, 'so you've had yourself upgraded. Jermyn Street won't like that. It will lead to complications in the accounts.'

'No, it won't,' said Percival. 'They'd never allow it. I've had to pay the difference myself.'

'Oh,' said Detterling. 'Why did you trouble to do that?'

'Because we're travelling together. Or that's what I thought.' Percival raised his light ale. 'Cheers,' he said. 'Just as well our flight has been delayed, or I'd never have had time to get my ticket changed.' He took a sip of beer and set down his glass. 'Why did you want to go first-class, Detterling?' he said.

'Better supper, better service, more room.'

Percival nodded pleasantly, as though entirely satisfied by this.

'No,' said Detterling, who in the last two minutes had begun to hate himself. 'I did it to surprise you. To *spite* you. To show off. I'm very sorry.'

'It's good of you to say so. We're not used to apologies in our line of work. But don't worry. I shall be interested to see what it's like going first-class, for once, and I dare say I shall be getting my own back before very long.'

Although supper on the flight to Corfu was indifferent, Detterling rendered it passable by washing it down with four quarter bottles of Olympic Airways claret and topping off the lot with two double brandies. Percival, by his side, muttered something about his ulcers, ate only cheese and salad, and drank water, there being no milk. However, he watched Detterling's progress with interest and talked in a friendly way of the refreshments, some nice but most of them nasty, which he had consumed on various kinds of public transport during his former journeys round Europe. Dining-cars on German trains seemed for some reason to have pleased and even to have obsessed him; and it was while he was giving the details of a luncheon which he and an acquaintance had once eaten between Munich and the Austrian border that Detterling, having finished his second brandy, fell asleep.

'Detterling, Detterling, Detterling,' said a small, persistent voice, whether hours or seconds after he'd dropped off Detterling could not tell. But he was still flying, that he knew, because the cabin of the plane was tilted back at an angle of almost forty-five degrees. Detterling did not care for the implications of this and closed his eyes again to return to the refuge of sleep.

'Wake up, wake up,' said Percival, ramming his elbow into Detterling's side. 'It's bloody bad manners to go to sleep when somebody's talking to you.'

'Sorry,' said Detterling. His mouth felt like pumice stone and the aeroplane started to buck about like a toy.

'No self-control, that's your trouble,' Percival said. 'No concentration. You can't carry anything through.'

The aeroplane lifted like a kite and shuddered all over.

'I should have thought it was jolly sensible to sleep through this.'

'Not when you're travelling with someone who's talking to you. Particularly when he's paid extra for the privilege. No stamina, Detterling.'

'If you don't mind, I shall try to go to sleep again.'

'No stamina,' said Percival, shoving his face close to Detterling's. 'You couldn't even carry through that mean little trick of getting a first-class ticket to annoy me. You thought I was hurt, so you just buckled up and apologized. No endurance, no guts. In *my* regiment we set a lot of value on guts.'

'What was your regiment?' asked Detterling faintly.

'The Wessex Fusiliers. No, don't nod off. I'm telling you you've got to be tougher. In this game you don't apologize just because you've hurt somebody's feelings – not that you *had* hurt my feelings, because of course I'm much too tough. I was just pretending to be hurt to see what you'd do. If you want to be sick, there's a paper bag in there with those maps.'

'I don't want to be sick. I want to go to the lavatory.'

'Number one or number two?'

'Number two.'

'Well, you can't go in any case because the sign up there says you've got to keep your seat belt fastened.'

'Who's stopping me?'

'I am,' said Percival, who occupied the outside seat. 'I'm not going to let you endanger all our lives by walking about when you're meant to stay in your seat. If you only wanted to do number one, I dare say you could use that bag in an emergency. But not for number two. The air-hostesses wouldn't like it.'

The plane dropped a long way like a very fast lift and made a noise as if all the engines had exploded.

'I can't wait much longer,' said Detterling. 'How long before we arrive?'

'At least forty minutes.'

'Oh dear *God*...'

The plane dropped again, tilted left then right then left, dropped farther and faster, hit something, bounced violently, gave a great roar of rage, and then proceeded smoothly up the runway.

'You must have known we were landing. Why did you tell me there was another forty minutes?'

'To teach you not to play silly jokes on me,' said Percival, looking at his watch. '0345 hours, local time. Not bad, since we started half an hour late.'

'Well, I'll just go back to the lavatory. Let me past, there's a good chap.'

'You're not allowed to move until the plane stops taxi-ing,' said Percival, sitting firm, 'and then you won't be able to get back because all the people at the back will be rushing forward to the exit. There may be a loo this side of the customs barrier, but I rather think you'll have to wait till we've been cleared ...'

By the time they had cleared their bags and Detterling had cleared his bowels, it was 0430 hours.

'What now?' said Detterling.

'A walk in the light of dawn. There's something I want to show you. We can leave our luggage here.'

They walked 200 yards from the front of the airport up to the main road, turned left along it, and then, very soon afterwards, wheeled about 130 degrees right on to a subsidiary road which (Detterling thought) must be one of several possible routes into the town of Corfu. For ten minutes they walked past new houses, the roofs of which were flat, the designs distressing, and the colours still mercifully invisible except as light or dark. The wind was high but warm, the clouds low.

'I fear we shan't see the sunrise in this weather,' Percival said, 'but I promise you the walk will be worth it.'

Once more they turned well over ninety degrees to the right, and walked down a lane, on the left of which stood an oddly handsome wedge-shaped house adjoined by a six-foot wall. A few yards along the wall was an iron gate; beyond the gate a grass walk, lined by cypress trees and high-arching shrubs.

'The British Cemetery,' Percival said.

'I can't see any gravestones.'

'You will.'

Percival tried the gate. Locked. He then rang a bell, fiercely. After a few minutes someone shuffled up and grumbled obstructively out of the half-dark. Percival jabbed back a couple of sentences in demotic Greek. The gate opened very quickly, whereupon Percival led Detterling past a gaping man in vest and braces, and then up the grass walk between the shrubs and the cypress trees.

'What did you say to him?' Detterling asked.

'I said that we've come to see the grave of our cousin, whose name-day it is. Since we suspect this cousin of being a vampire, I said, it would be as well for anyone who lives in this neighbourhood to keep in with the family.'

'I didn't know they had vampires in Greece.'

'Not the blood-sucking Transylvanian kind. Greek vampires just get out of their graves and smash people up.'

Percival took a turn to the right, down a narrower walk
with well-spaced tombs, separated by rough grass and
casual flowers, on either side of it. 'They're very strong,
Greek vampires,' Percival was saying, 'and not wholly mal-
ignant. They often cart sacks and things round for members
of their families. In fact they're very family-minded, which
is what made my threat such a potent one. If we had got
a cousin here who was a vampire, then he'd certainly have
it in for anyone who kept us out.'

Although there was still no sign of the sun, the light was
improving with every second. The larger inscriptions on
the graves were quite clear now.

'Nicest cemetery in the Ionian Islands, this,' Percival said.
'There's an amusing one for the British on Zante, but it's
too crowded. And though some of the Jewish ones are good,
they're apt to be used as hen-runs. *This* place is a model of
proportion and propriety – except, I'm afraid, for what
we've come to see. *There*.'

Percival pulled up, and there, at the end of the walk, in
an alcove set into a thick hedge of yew, was a real horror.
Under a cupola, which was supported by four pillars but
nevertheless contrived to look like a beach umbrella, reclined a lightly draped Rubenesque lady whose grinning
face was propped on one elbow, in ghastly parody of the
Etruscan manner. With her free hand she was reaching out
to grasp a wine cup, which was being proffered on a platter
by a group of four lanky and long-haired adolescents (after
Beardsley) each of whom had one hand under the platter
and the other three inches in front of his crutch. Inspection
from any of several angles would indeed have given sight
of their genitalia, but since these were supposedly concealed
they had not been carved. Their absence lent the final touch
of obscenity which turned the ensemble from a curiosity
into an abomination.

'Recognize anybody?' said Percival.

'I can't say I do.'

'Then look here.'

Percival pointed to a small carven scroll, which lay on

the platter by the wine cup, rather as though it was a bill for the refreshment. After some craning, *ANGELA TUCK*, read Detterling on the scroll, *1924 to 1970*.

'Angela Tuck,' announced Percival superfluously. 'Who was Max de Freville's mistress,' he added with a mixture of malice and unction.

'You don't need to remind me of that. I suppose there is a certain grotesque resemblance. That mouth ... Had you seen this frightfulness before?'

'No. But I'd heard it was here. Since early this year.'

'Let's see,' said Detterling, trying to keep a grip on himself. 'Angela died not long before I last saw Max, which was at the end of 1970. When I saw him, he obviously missed her, but he showed no sign of breaking out like this. I mean, I suppose Max *is* responsible for it?'

'Oh yes. Who else?'

'Then what got into him? Angela would have laughed herself sick.'

'Perhaps that's the idea,' said Percival. 'Perhaps it's a joke to entertain her ghost. Anyway, he went to great trouble to get it set up. The authorities said it was unsuitable, but Max insisted, and since he's very important on this island, with his investment in tourism and the rest of it, they let him have his way ... in return for a large contribution to the upkeep of the cemetery.'

There was a spluttering noise behind them. The caretaker, now wearing a cardigan over his braces, was spitting out Greek.

'Oh dear,' said Percival. 'I'm afraid there's been a misunderstanding. He now thinks Angela Tuck is the cousin I spoke of and he's asking if she's really a vampire.'

'Tell him "yes",' said Detterling: 'in some ways she was.'

'*Nai, nai*,' said Percival, pointing at the reclining Angela; '*afti.*'

The caretaker backed off, looking solemn, then turned and retreated rather fast.

'I'm afraid that was naughty,' Percival said. 'If Max hears he'll be very cross.'

'If he put this up for a joke, as you suggested, then he won't mind another one. Nor would Angela. Why did you bring me here, Percival?'

'Joke or no joke, I thought it would interest you. For in either case,' said Percival, 'having seen this thing, we may expect to find that Max has turned rather odd since you and I last met him. *Flighty* is perhaps the word.'

'Then can we trust him to make some sense about Somerset?'

'I think we must be prepared for his approach to be somewhat eccentric.' Percival leant forward and smacked Angela's huge uppermost flank. 'No one who has done this ... in fun or otherwise ... is likely to be entirely straightforward on any topic. Back to the airport for some kind of brekker, I think, and then we'll trundle out to see Max ...'

'Not what one would have expected,' Max de Freville said. He wrinkled his nose, thereby deepening the two purple clefts which ran from his nostrils to either end of his mouth. 'I could hardly believe it when I saw it in the paper. In his bath ...'

Max had received Detterling and Percival, when they arrived at his villa at eight in the morning, without surprise, annoyance or pleasure. He had offered them breakfast, which they declined (having just eaten it at the airport), and the use of two bedrooms, which they accepted. At his suggestion they had spent the morning resting, while Max himself went into the town 'on business', and at his summons they had roused themselves for lunch, which the three of them were now eating in a furnished arbour on one side of Max's lawn.

'Mind you,' said Max, in a tone that showed (Detterling thought) a lack of interest, 'this sort of thing does have precedent. It is by no means unheard of for people to commit suicide even when everything's going well for them, as it was for Somerset. I once knew a chap – Darblay, he was called – a distinguished poet with a rich wife and a beautiful son, his own publishing business to play about with, smart friends and a gorgeous mistress thrown in – he had the lot, you'd have said. But one morning he woke up and just couldn't bear it. He was bored with it all, on the one hand, because it had come so easy, and terrified, on the other, lest it should all disappear like fairy gold. He didn't actually commit suicide, this one, but it came to much the same; he just lay in bed staring at the ceiling and wouldn't move. In the end they carted him off to a bin, and only got him going again with electric shocks.'

'Somerset,' observed Detterling, 'is now beyond being revived by electric shocks.'

'But you see what I mean? There could be a parallel here.'

'No,' said Detterling. 'Unlike your man Darblay, Somerset was neither bored nor terrified. He'd worked hard to get as far as he had and he was still working hard to get further. He was fascinated by what he was doing, and though there were certainly risks in it, he regarded them not with fear but with relish – as a professional challenge.'

'If you say so ...'

'Canteloupe says so, and he was pretty close to him.'

'Well,' said Max, 'I'll believe it. I remember when Somerset used to play in those chemmy games I ran in the '50s. He never got scared, though in those days he hadn't much money to lose, because he was always in control of his play. He used to bet just a little more than he could conveniently afford, to give the thing an edge of excitement, but never more than he could pay. I suppose that's how he played at politics; he'd balance his book so that he stood to make a very pretty win if things went smooth but not get skinned if the cards showed up with the wrong number?'

'That's about it, I'd say.'

'Well then ...'

Max paused and looked rather blankly down his lawn towards the sea. He's not really with us, thought Detterling; he's got something else on his mind, and it's only through politeness he's making himself discuss our subject.

'Have you considered the possibility,' said Max with a

visible effort, 'that someone might have been putting the screws on him?'

'We have,' said Percival. 'No dice so far. I'd hoped that you might be helpful in that area.'

'I live too far away to hear about these things now,' said Max with tired dismissal, 'and I've seen very little of Somerset in these last years.'

'We were hoping you might remember something from the more distant past. I have a hunch,' said Percival, 'that whatever caused this suicide goes back a long way. Can you remember any kind of quarrel or disagreement, anything of that sort, which happened a long time ago but might just have kept a strong enough spark going to cause a blaze later.'

'Somerset,' said Max, 'was always very careful to extinguish sparks. He always tidied up, Leonard, because he was particularly aware of the kind of danger you refer to. Somerset never scotched his snakes, he killed them. And he did the same to the worms, just in case.'

'Even so,' said Detterling, 'there could have been something that escaped. Some little maggot which crawled away and hid itself ... and then grew, over the years, until it was strong enough to come out again, with poison in its fangs.'

'It's always possible, of course. But I don't think you quite realize how incredibly careful Somerset could be.'

Max shook his head and licked his lips. He looked intently at Percival and Detterling, as though making an important decision which had to do with their welfare. His gaze then shifted to a statue on the other side of the lawn : a long-eared faun with flute. The faun returned Max's gaze with a leer, his mouth curving softly over the flute. All at once Max brightened; for the first time he was willing, even eager, to talk.

'I'll give you an example,' he said, 'of Somerset at work. You both remember Angela, my Angela?'

'Of course.'

'Well, years ago, in the summer of 1945 it was, Angela was living with her husband on the Norfolk coast. And there she met Somerset, who was seventeen at the time and staying with a school-friend. Came a night when her husband was away, and Angela asked Somerset and his friend over to her house, meaning to weigh up the form and take her pick of them.' Max chortled at the notion, like an elderly clubman preparing his listeners for the climax of a smoking-room joke. 'She often used to tell me the story, it was one of my favourites, and apparently what happened was this . . .

' ". . . I got us all drunk and playing strip poker," Angela used to tell Max before she died, "and in no time at all, as luck would have it, Somerset was bare except for his shoes and socks, and I had my bra off. But the other boy, Somerset's friend, was still fully dressed, and there was my problem, because he was a pretty boy and I badly wanted to look at him – in fact it was quite definitely him I'd meant to have when I started the whole thing going. And of course poor old Somerset was a real fright in those days, all shag-spots and yellow teeth, so you may wonder why I asked him to come along in the first place. The answer is that he had a way of looking at you, disapproving yet somehow collusive, accusing and excusing at the same time, rather like my father, who used to spank me with one hand and tickle me with the other – very exciting, I can tell you. So all in all, I felt Somerset was worth his seat in the house, and it might be fun to watch him pulling himself while I had it off with the pretty one.

' "But it didn't work out like that. There I was with my tits wagging about – and bloody lovely they were then – and Somerset sitting there nude, as pale and damp as a dishcloth, and the pretty one as randy as a monkey under his trousers, and all I had to do, really, was chuck away the cards, undress him and get off the mark. But somehow I was too pissed to see it clear, I kept thinking I'd got to stick to the rules of the game; so I dealt another hand, hoping like hell I'd win a forfeit from prettikins and have the pants off him – and lo and behold, I won forfeits from both of them, my Ace over their Kings, so in any case I could now line 'em up any way I wanted. So I looked at 'em both, and worked out just what I was going to order – pretty boy under me on the sofa, with Somerset standing over us – and I opened my mouth to say the word . . .

' " . . . And then I saw something I'd missed. Somehow I'd cut myself earlier on, and some of my blood had got on to Somerset, smeared over his leg, it was, a lovely red stain on his skinny white calf; and there was Somerset looking at me as if to say, 'I know you, you dirty bitch, you're longing to lick it off'. So what with that blood on Somerset's leg and that look on Somerset's face, I suddenly found that prettikins didn't matter any more; he was just one more pink little boy, who'd come running along with a stiff tool any time I whistled, and probably shoot his load in five seconds flat. But Somerset, scrofulous, scrawny, *unwholesome* Somerset . . . who understood what went on in one's mind and one's cunt . . . he was something *rare*.

' "So I turned prettikins out of the house, poor lamb, and I leant Somerset back in a chair, and I started to lick that blood. Now, for all that look in Somerset's eye, I thought I'd have to do it all myself, that here was a virgin who'd have to be taught step by step. Boy oh boy, oh Somerset, was I wrong about that. I wasn't licking up blood for long, I was banging my arse on the floor and screaming for more and more of him and more and more of him I got, more and more, but never quite enough, he saw to that. I kept on sort of going off at half-cock, time after time after time, and when I did come at last it seemed to go on for ever, so that long after he'd taken his prick out I was still jerking about on the floor, shivering and shaking and blubbering and squealing, and then begging him – it's a thing I've asked of nobody else – to piss on me as hard as he could . . ." '

' . . . In which particular,' said Max de Freville, 'he obliged most manfully and put Angela clean out for a count of twenty – or so she estimated later.'

'All very entertaining,' said Captain Detterling, 'but I thought this story was intended to exemplify the wariness in Somerset's nature, not the wantonness in Angela's.'

'And so it does if you'll listen to what happened next. It appears that Somerset and his chum went away somewhere very soon after, as had been previously arranged. A few days later Angela had a letter from him, in which Somerset thanked her politely for a pleasant evening and said he hoped they might meet again some time. As things fell out, they weren't to meet again for ten years or more, but that's by the way. What fascinated Angela was this: there wasn't the slightest overt mention, anywhere in the letter, of what had occurred between them; yet if you were in the know, as of course she was, the whole page was heaving with suggestion and invitation. To Angela, as she read it, it was one of the sexiest letters she'd ever had, making her want another steaming session on the spot; but it was so phrased that anyone else who saw it would have imagined he was thanking her for a couple of sedate drinks and expressing a vague hope that he would be able to return her hospitality. For a boy of seventeen, it was a masterly piece of prevarication: he had managed to put his message across hot and strong and yet to write down *nothing* that could possibly be held or used against him, by her or her husband or anyone else in the world who might just get hold of that letter.'

'If he'd been really careful, he wouldn't have written at all.'

'He had to. He wanted her to know where he could be found. He wanted the thing to go on.'

'You said, just now, that it didn't go on.'

'Only through bad luck. He had some engagements he couldn't break, and she had a doting husband to cope with – and before there was any opportunity of a repeat performance, the husband took her off to India. But the real point is this: here was Somerset doing his level best to have things the exact way he wanted them but also making absolutely certain that he took the barest conceivable minimum of chances consistent with his object. Of course he had to take *some* degree of risk, or his life would have been a total blank: what I'm saying is that both here and hereafter he used enormous labour and ingenuity to reduce that degree to near infinitesimal.'

'Hardly as low as that,' said Detterling. 'What about this friend he was staying with? He might easily have opened his mouth and done a bit of damage.'

'Somerset had the whip hand of him.' Max hesitated. His face went suddenly sombre. The gaiety induced in him by his memoir of Angela had somehow been spoilt. 'You know who he was,' said Max in tones at once portentous and peevish, 'that friend?'

'No. How should we?'

'Fielding Gray. Angela always kept a soft spot for him, because he looked so disappointed when she turned him out that night. Pity, a sad pity,' said Max heavily. 'It would have been far better if she'd never seen him again.'

'Why?' said Percival. 'What harm did he ever do her?'

'He helped to kill her. It happened when he was here with a film company back in 1970. Writing the script, he was. So Angela saw quite a bit of him, and one day ... well, he got her over-excited, and then she collapsed.'

Max looked away towards the faun with the flute. This time he found no comfort there. He's looking old, thought Detterling; his clothes are hanging off him and he's scraggy round the neck; and yet he must be younger than I am, fifty to my fifty-five. Perhaps I look like that to others. They say you never see it in yourself.

'In what way ... did Gray over-excite her?' Percival asked Max.

'We needn't go into it. It wasn't even his fault really, I see that now. She'd been ill for some time, and she'd have gone soon in any case. But it was ... what he did ... that killed her, so I can't forgive him. I'm so lonely without her, you see. I told you both, this morning, that I had business in the town. But that wasn't true; my partner, Lykiadopoulos, takes care of all that now. The reason I went out this morning was to go to her grave. I've had a statue put up, and I spend a lot of time there. Most days, I go. It's peaceful there, and I can look at the statue and think of her

... as she was when we first met, not when she got so ill towards the end. She was so vital, always laughing and drinking, full of stories like the one I've just told you, warm, unashamed ... I never slept with her, you know, or rather, we often shared a bed but nothing ever happened. I just wanted her to be there, and now all that's there is that statue. I must take you to see it, it's rather beautiful. At first they didn't want to put it up, it's a bit *risqué* for a cemetery, and even now they resent it. When I was there this morning the caretaker kept buzzing about and pointing at it and jabbering away in Greek. He seemed angry or frightened or something ... as if a statue could do any harm. Well, all I can say is they'd better not try to move my Angela.' He raised his head and his eyes blazed. 'By God, they'd better not try, by God, if I find—'

'—No one's going to move her,' said Detterling, and touched Max's arm.

'No, of course not. I'm imagining things. I get upset very easily these days – that Greek fellow upset me, yittering on and on like that, but of course it didn't mean anything, just some silly fuss about nothing. Anyway, I've given them a lot of money, so they won't want to annoy me. Angela would have been pleased about the money, she always wanted it to be used like that – to make things more beautiful. She hated what Lyki and I were doing to this island, all these hotels and camping sites, so now I'm doing what I can to make up. I'm trying to stop any more horrors being built, but it isn't easy and Lyki's no help at all. He's my front man, you see, I had to have a Greek, so what he says goes, and what he says is more and more hotels, because he thinks they bring foreigners here and make his people richer. He can't understand that it's making them rich in the wrong way, that in a few years they'll be just like everyone else in Spain and Italy and so on, all motor cars and television sets and not a tree or a blade of grass in sight. That's what Angela always said, but I didn't heed her then, when she was alive, only now, but I know she's glad I've understood even if it is so late, I hear her voice telling me when I look at her statue ... But I don't know,' said Max, heaving his whole body in order to collect himself, 'why I'm boring you with this. I'm sorry.'

'No need to be,' said Detterling.

'You came here to ask about Somerset, and all I've done is talk about Angela. I wonder ... is there anything else I can tell you about Somerset?'

'I think not,' said Percival quietly. 'I think we must go back to London and get on with our search there.'

Max did not seem anxious to detain them.

'You can take the evening plane,' he said. 'I'll come and wave you off – and we can all look in to see Angela on the way.'

PART THREE

Knights Vagrant

'It's clear that poor old Max is going quietly barmy,' said Percival on the day after Detterling and he had returned from Corfu, 'but he did make one very important point with that tale of Lloyd-James and Angela Tuck.'

'For God's sake, run up,' called Detterling, on whose insistence they were watching cricket at Lord's. '*What* point did Max make?'

'That Lloyd-James was a master at covering up ... at eliminating or suppressing anything which might have led to trouble later – *or, by the same token, might have been helpful to our enquiries now*.'

'Perhaps,' said Detterling. 'But you must remember this : a man can only eliminate something which may lead to trouble if he knows that it is there. He can only prevent the future results of his misdeeds if he knows what misdeeds he has committed.'

'We all know when we've done something which may lead to trouble.'

'Cross-bat stroke,' said Detterling, looking sorrowfully down from the pavilion balcony in which they sat. 'Very ugly. I don't know what these young pros are coming to. But the point is, Percival, that he doesn't know any better. He's been badly taught and he doesn't know what he's doing wrong. He doesn't even know that he *is* doing wrong.'

'What's that got to do with it?'

'He's a perfect instance of someone who, unknowingly, is doing something that may get him into trouble at any second. He cannot prevent that trouble because he does not know that he's inviting it.'

'If I'd known you were going to be so portentous about this idiotic game, I'd never have agreed to come here.'

'For someone who's been doing what you have all your life,' said Detterling, 'you are in some ways remarkably unsubtle. We all of us resemble that young cricketer. We are all of us apt to do things, every day of our lives, which come so natural to us that we hardly notice we're doing them, but which, if we only knew it, could lead to horrible trouble later on. So now consider Somerset. He knew very well that what he was up to with Angela could certainly lead to trouble, and so he took careful and ingenious steps to prevent this. But suppose that he had done something dangerous – like that batsman down there – without any notion that it *was* dangerous, indeed hardly knowing that he'd done it?'

'What sort of thing?' said Percival, in a more tolerant but still sceptical voice. 'Give me a concrete example.'

'Very well. From my own experience.'

There were only three other spectators up in the balcony, and these were at the other end of it. Nevertheless, Detterling now lowered his voice as if he were about to pronounce something positively treasonous.

'It was early in the war,' he said, 'summer of '41 and I'd just been made a temporary captain and second-in-command of a sabre squadron.'

'By which you mean a fighting squadron of cavalry. But I suppose that by this time they'd taken your horses away?'

'Alas, yes. We'd changed over to beastly tanks in 1939. And they were the start of my trouble, as you'll see in a few minutes ... But as I was saying, there I was, second-in-command of this squadron, which was guarding part of the Suez Canal. Regimental Headquarters were in Port Said, which wasn't too bad in a filthy sort of way, but all four sabre squadrons were out on detachment, each looking after its own section of the canal – and that, my dear Percival, was absolutely bloody. It meant camping in the desert, in acute discomfort, with nothing, but nothing, to look at, except this dreary canal, along which we had to patrol night and day in case somebody tried to fuck it up.'

'Who was going to do that?'

'Dissident Gypos. Enemy agents. Desert tribes on the Axis pay-roll. German patrols in depth, trying a thousand to one long shot ... Not that *we* bothered about the theory of it.

As far as we were concerned, we were there because we were there, and wishing to God that we weren't. If only there'd been a few more ships to watch it might have been a bit jollier; but even those were in short supply, because by that time the Mediterranean was so damn dangerous that everything which could was going round by the Cape. The only thing most of us had to look forward to was being called back to R.H.Q. for some reason or other and having a binge in Port Said.

'But I was one of the lucky ones. (There you are, you see, that cross-bat artist has been bowled neck and crop, and doesn't begin to know what's hit him.) Yes, I was quite lucky, because as squadron second-in-command I was responsible for all rations and supplies and this meant that I had to take a small convoy, once a week, to rendezvous with the regimental supply column which brought up all our stuff from Port Said. All the other squadron second-in-commands would gather at the same rendezvous, which was usually a town called Qantara, and after a time we got a small hotel there to put up quite a decent meal on the days we came in, so that we could have a bit of a party. Later on the owner even produced some girls, and we sometimes fixed it so that we could spend the night and go back to our respective squadrons the next morning. So although I seldom got to Port Said itself, I did have these weekly outings to Qantara, getting pissed and hearing all the gossip from R.H.Q. and the other squadrons, which made me a damned sight better off than most people.'

'Trust you to be,' said Percival.

'No need to be offensive, old man. I just took what I could get, as we all did in those days. Of course, we were riding for bad trouble. The hotel in Qantara was out of bounds to all British troops, the girls might well have been poxed, and officers oughtn't to be drunk when responsible for securing and transporting their squadron's weekly rations. However, it is just the point of this little tale that trouble, when it came, did not come from any of the obvious sources. They were so obvious, you see, that we took precautions. We hired a local doctor to examine the girls just before we had them. We persuaded the local Provost Marshal, whom we found a good-natured chap considering his office, to put the hotel in bounds for "personnel in transit". We let the N.C.O.s and men who came with us have a bit of a fling to keep *them* happy. And in the end I worked out a system with my Corporal-Major (our equivalent of Colour-Sergeant) whereby one of us was always sober enough to see we drew the right kit and got back to the squadron without losing it. So all the obvious dangers were dealt with and everything went as merry as a marriage – until one day I made a tiny but absolutely fatal slip without even noticing, at the time, what I was doing.'

Detterling paused and gave a melancholy smile.

'And even if I had noticed,' he said, 'I wouldn't have worried. What I did was – well – routine. *Anyone* in my situation would have done it. I couldn't *not* do it. Let me explain.'

Below them the cricketers moved into the pavilion for tea. The three other spectators on the balcony departed. It was so quiet where Detterling and Percival sat that they might have been the last two people left in the world.

'As I've told you,' said Detterling, almost in a whisper now, 'it was tanks, bloody tanks, that started it all off. At least indirectly. You see, one of our Troop Leaders needed a particularly rare and difficult spare for an immobilized tank of his. We sent an indent through to the farrier at R.H.Q. . . .'

'The *farrier*?'

'Yes. That's what we used to call the chap who took care of the horses, so we used the same title for the chap in charge of servicing the tanks. Why bother to change? Anyway, we sent in this indent, and as usual in such cases nothing happened. After a bit we sent in a second one marked "urgent", and the next time I got to Qantara a note was handed to me from the farrier, who said that the spare part needed was not available in Port Said, and would I go, in person, to an Armoured Corps depot at a place called

Zagazig (yes, Zagazig) and ask there. When I looked at the map, I saw that this was quite a sensible suggestion. Zagazig was about fifty miles west by south of Qantara, and though it wouldn't be much fun getting there along the desert road, it would clearly be much quicker and easier for me to go myself than for our farrier in Port Said to make a formal application through the correct channels, et cetera, et cetera.

'Well, there didn't seem to be any problems about it. This was one of the occasions when I'd fixed it for us to spend the night in Qantara; so the ration trucks could stay there with the Corporal-Major while I drove on to Zagazig in my armoured scout car. If my journey took too long for me to get back to Qantara that evening, or if there was trouble negotiating for this precious spare part, then I could spend the night at Zagazig and pick up the rest of my convoy the next day for the return to our squadron camp.

'And so it all worked out ... and even better than I'd hoped. The journey to Zagazig was a sod, so I did have to spend the night there; but they made no fuss about letting me have this spare part, in fact they gave me five of it for luck, which I knew would please the Squadron Leader; and I was up and away early in the morning and back to Qantara well before lunch, with the whole afternoon to roll back to the squadron camp, where we were due at any time before sundown.

'But in Qantara I found snags. The Corporal-Major, whose turn it was to get drunk, had seen no reason to forgo the privilege. I'd forgotten to warn him that he'd best not overdo it in my absence, so he'd got himself absolutely *arseholed* in our "transit" hotel, and had then proceeded to beat up his girl, who was threatening to complain to the police. I had to pay through the nose to persuade her to hold her tongue – or it'd have been all up forever with our cosy little arrangements, to say nothing of the Corporal-Major, who by this time was rather a chum.

'The next snag was fuel. My driver, a pleasant old sweat called Tom Chead, said we'd used so much getting to Zagazig and back that we needed a fill to take the scout car on to the squadron. So I applied to the Provost Marshal for help ... only to find him turn up sticky. This was all Armoured Corps business, he said, I should have got more fuel from the depot at Zagazig; he had his own show to run, and he couldn't serve up juice for scout cars to swan all over Egypt. But he was a good-natured fellow, as I've told you, and eventually he relented. He dug out some regulation which made it okay for him to supply vehicles in cases of genuine emergency. There was the usual sort of business with some form I had to sign, and then he sent Tom Chead off to the pump while he gave me a last little lecture on what he called logistic anticipation. He quoted Wellington, I remember: "a prudent officer empties his bowels and fills his belly whenever he has the opportunity". Well, amen to that, I said, and I'd try not to bother him again. Not to worry, he said: "to err is human, to forgive divine". Full of tags he was; I dare say he got them from the *Reader's Digest*.

'And after that all was well. The Corporal-Major was still shaking a bit, but he'd got the wagons loaded up all right; and so off we all went, after a sustaining lunch at the hotel. Home in good time; the Squadron Leader all over me for having had the sense to follow up the farrier's lead and go out to Zagazig; a good mark for Detterling, that promising young temporary Captain; in a word, journey's end – or so it seemed.'

Percival sat looking puzzled and slightly peeved. 'But somewhere you'd made a slip – a fatal slip, you said.'

'Yes. You're pretty sharp; you tell me where.'

'Bribing that whore to keep quiet about the Corporal-Major?'

'No, Leonard. I've told you. It was none of the obvious things.'

'Those spare parts – you drew them without proper forms of requisition?'

'I'd certainly cut a lot of red tape, but the suggestion had come from my Regimental H.Q., so I could hardly be blamed. Anyway there was never any more heard about that.'

'No official authorization for the extra journey to Zagazig?'

'As a captain and second-in-command of a squadron I was fully entitled to authorize it myself.'

Percival licked his lips. 'That Provost Marshal reported you for negligence? For failing to refuel at the depot in Zagazig?'

'He didn't report me. Anyway, I'd already told my Squadron Leader what had happened, and he'd just laughed it off.'

'Food poisoning from the hotel?'

'Leonard, you're just guessing.'

'All right; you tell me.'

'Very well,' said Captain Detterling.

Somewhere below them a bell tinkled.

'The umpires will be out again in a minute. Good.'

'Please get on with your story and never mind this absurd game.'

'As it happens,' said Detterling, 'it is a cricket match at which the next scene takes place. Three, four months have passed. My regiment has been moved to commodious pre-war barracks in the environs of Alexandria, to recuperate and dust itself down. The desert by the canal is only a memory, disagreeable but fading fast; and although more active service is certainly coming, it will not come just yet. And so here we are, amusing ourselves with this cricket match, between Hamilton's Horse and the Second Battalion of the Prince Consort's Own Regiment of Foot. Matting wicket, of course, but reasonable turf for an outfield, and an elegant marquee, full of brave men, fair women and expensive refreshments. Into the marquee steps Captain Detterling (a substantive captain by now) having just made seventy-six runs for Hamilton's Horse and being about to consume a huge beaker of champagne.

'Among Detterling's circle of admirers is his own Commanding Officer – who, when the excitement has subsided, moves Detterling quietly on to one side and tells him to take himself back to barracks a bit smartish, as there are two gentlemen from the Special Investigation Branch waiting to talk to him there. Never mind the rest of the cricket match; the Colonel will explain Detterling's defection. Just let Detterling get his pads off quietly and slink out through the back, where a car is waiting with one of Detterling's brother officers inside it to hold his hand on the way home. But what the devil is all this about? The Colonel knows no details; only that it is something to do with Detterling's conduct in a place called Qantara.'

Detterling paused and gravely applauded a late cut to the boundary.

'And of course,' he said to Percival, 'I instantly imagined that it had all come out about those women at the hotel and so on, and I fully expected to find all the other chaps concerned queuing up to be interviewed too. Not a bit of it. I was taken to my own quarters, and left alone there with a smooth-faced lieutenant in General Service uniform and a bulky Sergeant-Major of the Military Police. The subaltern asked a series of polite questions to confirm that I'd made those regular trips to Qantara, and then got out a large sheet of notes and examined them in silence for several minutes. Here we go, I thought: that's a list of the girls and now he's coming in with the knife. I was as taut as a tent rope by now, and I can still remember the conversation which followed, almost word for word ...

'"... Now, Captain Detterling. You've already told me" – at last looking up from the sheet of notes – "that it was your practice, from time to time, to stay overnight at Qantara."

'"Yes. With my Squadron Leader's approval."

'"Of course, sir. Now, please tell me about one such night – Wednesday, March 15."'

Long pause.

'"March the *fifteenth*?"

'"Yes, sir."

'"Well ... that was the time I went to Zagazig to collect some spare parts from the Armoured Corps depot there."

' "So we understand. You spent the night at Zagazig instead of Qantara, and returned to Qantara the next morning."

' "Yes. What about it?"

' 'Nothing, sir. But what happened when you got back to Qantara?"

' "I had some lunch and took my convoy back to the squadron camp in the desert." '

And bribed a whore on behalf of the Corporal-Major. Going, going, gone.

' "Indeed? You still had enough fuel in your scout car to get to your squadron camp?"' '

Fuel?

' "Sorry, I forgot. I *was* short of fuel by then, so I asked the town Provost Marshal to give me some."

' "How much did he give you?"

' "I've no idea. My driver took the scout car to the pump."

' "But *you* countersigned the AF(ME)2224X."

' "The what?"' '

' "The Army Form (Middle East) which has to be completed in such emergencies. The issuing officer states to whom the fuel was issued and why, and the recipient, in this case yourself, signs for the amount received."

' "All right. I signed for the amount received."

' "How much was it?"

' "I can't remember. Whatever we needed, I suppose."

' "And how much *did* you need?"

' "How should I know? The drivers and the Corporal-Major always take care of that kind of thing."

' "Very well, sir. Your driver, Trooper Chead, states that, allowing for the fuel still in his engine he needed ten gallons to get back to your squadron camp over desert country, and that he actually drew fifteen from the pump 'in order to be on the safe side'."

' "You're not blaming him for that?"

' "No. He behaved very prudently. Unlike yourself, sir, who signed for twenty-five gallons ..."

'... And so there it was,' said Detterling to Percival. 'Exactly how it was worked, I don't know. I imagine the amount was still blank when I signed the form. Perhaps I noticed and perhaps I didn't. If I did, I probably assumed that the Provost Marshal would check up with whoever had actually pumped the stuff out and fill in the correct amount later. But the point is that I wasn't really thinking along those lines at all. Here was a man doing me a good turn, and it never occurred to me to start haggling about pieces of paper.

'But you see what it meant? It meant that the Provost Marshal had issued fifteen gallons and accounted for twenty-five; so he had ten left over to flog on the black market. And of course this was his little vice. Very hard to spot; indeed he might never have been spotted, only he offered some juice to a Gypo who, by a thousand to one chance, was one of our agents and loyal at that. So then the S.I.B. went into the Provost Marshal's affairs, starting with his tickets – and here was one signed by yours truly, name, rank and unit. If they'd come to me first, I might have been able to fob them off; but I was playing cricket, so they asked to see my driver, and Chead loused everything up by being too bloody accurate. Fifteen gallons he'd had, and fifteen gallons he said. "You're sure it wasn't more, Trooper Chead? Twenty-five, perhaps?" "Quite sure, sir. It was an emergency issue, see, and they were that tight they tried to make me only take ten." That kind of thing. And by that time he'd landed me slap in the shit without knowing it, and there was nothing he could do to pull me out.

'And I mean *shit*, Leonard. You see, these policemen thought, or purported to think, that I'd connived at the fraud or even that I'd taken a cut on the profit. For Christ's sake, I told them: I had a private income which amounted to three times my pay; what the hell did I want with half the profit on ten gallons of fuel? Very well, they said, or rather, the smooth-faced lieutenant said: even if he believed me about that, and he wasn't saying he did, at the very best I'd been negligent, criminally negligent. Did I realize that the war was at crisis-point, that the allies were hard-pressed on every front, that oil derivatives were like so much liquid gold? And here was I, so casual, so incompetent – if not positively fraudulent – that I'd signed away ten gallons of our life's blood.

'And they were right. There'd been a great deal of that sort of thing going on. Wastage caused by rackets or mere carelessness had been enormous; and they were minded to make a stern example, as many stern examples as they could. They were busy rounding up all those with whom this Provost Marshal had had similar dealings, and they intended to stage a series of courts martial and cashierings the fame of which would ring round Egypt. And although I, with my ten gallons, wasn't exactly the star name on the list. I would do very well to swell out the scene. So there I was, placed under open arrest pending further enquiries, threatened with possible charges that ranged from gross negligence up to conspiracy against the realm and all because I'd signed an army form when asked to by my superior officer.'

'Come, come,' said Percival. 'Surely a substantive captain of Lord Hamilton's Horse wasn't going to take this lying down?'

'I can't say I did very much about it myself. I was winded, you see. But the regiment came to my assistance. Chead, the driver, now tried to say that I'd told him to draw twenty-five gallons and he'd forgotten to tell me he'd only been given fifteen; but in the light of what I'd told the S.I.B. myself, that didn't help very much – and nearly got Chead into a nasty spot of bother. At a higher level, the Adjutant saw to it that I was not made to suffer the usual humiliations of being under arrest; in return for my parole, I was allowed to dress and go about the place like anybody else. As for the Colonel, he was a common-sense fellow who set about fixing the whole thing in a common-sense fashion. It was absolutely clear to him that this was just a piece of bad luck or at worst of venial slackness, and so he said to the divisional general, who was an old chum of his. But the

S.I.B. wasn't easy to fob off; they wanted a full pound of flesh, and it was only with great difficulty that they were got to settle for a few ounces: the charge was adjusted so that I need not, indeed, submit myself to court-martial – but I had to go in front of the General to receive a severe reprimand.'

'So that was all right. A severe reprimand never broke a man's bones.'

'It can break a man's career though. From that time on there was a big black mark against my name in the book. I was, quite simply, a man not to be trusted. Not to be trusted by the Army Council – "the fellow who fiddled the fuel" – and so never allowed promotion. Not even to be trusted by my own regiment: because although they'd been decent and helped me what they could, they now saw me as a squalid little nuisance. I'd drawn attention to them, you see. My regiment liked to keep itself to itself; and now here were detectives prying all over the bloody place, and rumours all over Alex, and it was all my fault. As the Adjutant remarked one day, it was rather as though I'd farted on parade: by my miserable petty ineptitude I'd turned my regimentals to motley and made the rest of them look like a parcel of clowns as well. They didn't much care what I'd done, or whether or not I'd really done it, but what they couldn't forgive me, and didn't forgive me for years, was being found out.'

'But surely ... you were given some quite respectable appointments later on?'

'*Much* later on. And even then, although the jobs seemed respectable, if you examined them you found they were jokes. I was made, after the war, recruiting officer for the cavalry, which sounds important until you remember that recruiting officers are figures out of low comedy who seduce sluts and can't pay their battels. And in any case I didn't last long at that; someone in the War Office opined that a spiv (you remember the word?) wasn't much of an advertisement. After that I was sent to teach at the Officers' Training School at Bangalore: a very responsible assignment – except that the School, as they very well knew, was about to be turned into a cut-price crammer for low-grade native Cadets. Thence to the Viceroy's staff in Delhi—'

'—Now there at least was distinction—'

'—As a kind of doorman and cloakroom-attendant for social occasions – and chucker-out if one was needed. Luckily I had an old friend there, one of the few who *did* trust me, and he found me some interesting work in Intelligence. I was the chap who chose and briefed the thugs for any dirty work we had in hand. Even my friend, you see, thought I'd be best employed on something shady.'

'But all this was much later, as you say. What did you do immediately after the trouble in Egypt?'

'I was sent on courses. As soon as I came back from one, they sent me on another. P.T., catering, fire precautions, education, religion, welfare. On and on and on. Detterling, the man we can't trust; get him out of the way; send him off on another course where he can't do any damage.'

'A very comfortable existence.'

'And safe. I was delighted to be sitting quietly in Cairo or Alexandra, learning how to interest the men of my regiment in hobbies like raffia-work or kite-flying, while the men themselves were in the Western Desert being shot at. Oh yes, I was very relieved. But in another way I was very angry. Angry because I had become a man of no account, because I had been so shabbily exposed when I had done nothing to be ashamed of. It was the unfairness of it all, Leonard. I had committed a tiny misdemeanour which wasn't really even that. All I'd done was to trust another officer and sign a paper without looking at it – something which everyone in the army did fifty times a day; but as a result the earth had suddenly turned to quicksand underneath me, long after I'd forgotten the whole trivial little affair. It made me feel that the world was made of water; all things in flux, as Heraclitus said. It made me feel foully injured and quite desperate ... that some kind of Fury must have been pursuing me. It made me feel, at one time, nearly suicidal.'

'But you're here to tell the tale thirty years later.'

'To tell it and now to ponder it. If something like this could happen to me, something like it could have happened to poor Somerset. Some small mistake which he neither noticed nor remembered ... something which anyone might have done in total innocence ... and then, years later perhaps, this tiny piece of loose detritus, which he left lying because he never even saw it, is shifted by a chance wind and starts an avalanche which overwhelms him.'

'An ingenious theory, my dear. But there's been no sign of the avalanche.'

'A private avalanche, Leonard. Something in his mind. We never saw it, but we could picture what it might have been like for him, if only we could discover where and how it began.'

'Which means finding this ... "tiny piece of loose detritus" ... which on your theory began it. Not easy. The area of search is large. And surely, it is the essence of the kind of mistake, which you are positing, to be unnoticeable.'

'To the person who makes it. Not necessarily to others. I spotted what was wrong with that cross-bat player although he himself never could.'

'Spare me him again ... though the point is taken. And that's enough of theory,' said Leonard Percival: 'time for more action.'

'What next?'

'Devonshire,' said Percival, 'and Somerset's old mother, Peregrina.'

Chantry Marquess, near Bampton in the County of Devon, the seat of the family of Lloyd-James, proved to be neat and pretty if in no way imposing. It stood about a hundred yards back from a minor road, being separated from the road by a pleasant and well-kept lawn, on the right-hand side of which a drive ran between two rows of elm trees up to a small stone courtyard. This lay off what should have been the west wing of the house but was in fact its front, since the wall that faced over the lawn and towards the road turned out, on inspection, to be only a side wall, blank except for a few first-storey windows. The mild eccentricity of this arrangement had an undoubted charm, thought Detterling as his manservant drove the Mercedes carefully through an arch into the courtyard; for the white Georgian west front, under which the car stopped, had a shy and almost shifty look about it, as if it knew it should be facing another way and was not sure whether it was shunning the road out of modesty or out of cowardice.

'Very lonely,' remarked Percival as Detterling pulled the bell chain; 'not another house in miles. I suppose their kind likes that.'

'Wouldn't you, Leonard?'

'If you have stomach ulcers, it's as well to have neighbours.'

The door was opened by the housekeeper-type woman whom they had seen with Mrs Lloyd-James at the funeral. Since Percival had agreed, contrary to his general principle, that an unexpected arrival would be discourteous to an old lady, Detterling had rung up on the evening after their conversation at Lord's and applied for an interview. They had been invited to afternoon tea on the following day and now, precisely at 4.30 as bidden, they announced their names to the housekeeper, who looked them up and down as if to make sure they were fit to appear on parade and then, without a word, led them across a wide stone-flagged hall and through an open doorway into a study.

Peregrina Lloyd-James, who was sitting with her legs straddled in front of a generous wood fire, did not get up to greet them. She smiled civilly at Detterling, nodded at Percival, and pointed to a table on which stood, not tea, but a decanter of what looked like Marsala. A moment later the housekeeper reappeared carrying a seed cake, which she placed on the table. She looked at the fire and then at her mistress, who shook her head. The housekeeper bowed hers very slightly, took two steps backwards, turned about and left them, closing the door. Detterling and Percival cut themselves slices of cake and poured themselves glasses of wine, in Percival's case a very small one. At last,

'May we sit down, ma'am?' said Detterling, speaking the first words that anyone had uttered since they entered the house.

'If you please, gentlemen.'

Detterling and Percival sat. Peregrina Lloyd-James spread her hands in front of the fire. Something rustled (rats, thought Detterling, surely not?) behind a row of shiny leather-backed books, a ten-volume economic history of Europe by an author of whom Detterling had never heard. A clock on the mantel tinkled primly, prematurely announcing a quarter to five.

'What can I tell you?' asked the old woman, rubbing her left hand on the cheek just below the right ear.

'First,' said Percival bluntly, 'did your son come here on the day before he died? All that day he was away somewhere before going home and killing himself very late at night. We would very much like to know where he went.'

'He didn't come here, Mr Percival. He hasn't been near here for three months.'

'You've no idea where he did go?'

'How should I have? But surely ... you have special methods you can use to find out?'

'Yes, but that would entail drawing some attention to the matter. The whole object of our enquiries is to ensure that from now on it shall receive none at all.'

'I see. You are investigating my son's death in order to suppress any scandal that might lie behind it. In the interest of the Government to which he belonged.'

'Very shrewdly summed up,' said Detterling.

'Shrewdly? The whole thing is perfectly obvious. You, Captain Detterling, his old friend and yourself a Conservative Member. And this other gentleman with the – forgive me, sir – very shady air about him.'

'Shady?' said Percival reproachfully.

'Not exactly that. Surreptitious. I once went, years ago, to a dog race meeting. When they paraded the animals before each race, there was a man who crept along behind them with a brush and pan, ready to clear up their stools. You remind me of that man, Mr Percival. You have the demeanour of someone whose working life is spent sweeping up dog-stools and who very much hopes (like that wretched fellow at the races) that he will not be noticed.'

'Well, let's just say,' said Detterling, 'that Percival's aim is to prevent trouble.'

'Yours too, Captain Detterling?'

'It's a bit more personal with me. Having known Somerset for a quarter of a century and more, I am naturally ... concerned ... to find out why he should have done such a terrible thing to himself.'

'Concerned? Or curious?'

'Both, to be honest. So now you know what we're here for, Mrs Lloyd-James, will you help us?'

Peregrina Lloyd-James leant forward and kicked a log hard with her heel.

'I,' she said, 'have been a lifelong Socialist. Why should I help the Conservative Party bury its scandals?'

'The scandal would also be your family's – if there is a scandal, and if it ever came out.'

'There is no family. Only me now.'

'There is your son's good name,' said Percival.

'My son is dead. He was a poor thing at best, and now he is gone for good. No need to protect him.'

'Look,' said Percival, 'it *could* be a question of national security. Your son, when he died, was working in a very sensitive area. If his death is in any way connected with his work for the Ministry of Commerce, then in the national interest we must know why and how.'

'National Interest. Ministry of Commerce. Why should an old woman ... an old Socialist ... care for either?'

'If you were going to take that attitude, why did you let us come?'

'Idleness. Boredom. To find out what you were going to ask.'

'But not intending to answer?'

'I can't,' said the old lady, and grinned merrily. 'My son never spoke to me about his work for the Government, so I can't tell you anything about that. In any case, as I told you, he hasn't been near me for months. He hardly ever came. Twice a year at most, to make sure that the house and the grounds were in good order. They belonged to him, you see, after his father died. I was his pensioner, and so he regarded me. Important politicians do not tell their secrets – political *or* personal – to their pensioners.'

'Look, Mrs Lloyd-James,' said Detterling gently. 'We have an idea, or at least I have, that Somerset's death may be connected with something which lies a long way back. Would you care to talk about the past?'

'Not much. There's too much of it – and almost all of it boring. Still,' said Peregrina, frowning at Detterling, 'you were his friend, as we all keep saying, and you have come a long way from London. If you have any specific question. I will try to answer it.'

'Very well,' said Detterling, shooting at a venture. 'According to *Who's Who*, Somerset was sent to a preparatory school called St Peter's Court. It's a pretty odd thing, to record one's prep school in *Who's Who*. Why do you think he did it?'

Percival looked at Detterling as if he thought him suddenly deranged. This did not surprise Detterling. What did surprise him was the vicious look of rage with which Peregrina received the question.

'That horrible school,' she said, with a malevolence that brought out goose-pimples on Detterling's skin. 'It destroyed him. Perverted him for life.'

'Oh, come, Mrs Lloyd-James. Somerset was entirely normal. I mean,' said Detterling, recalling Maisie's revelations, 'he was incontestably heterosexual.'

Somerset's mother gave a yapping little laugh.

'I didn't mean *that*,' she said. 'It didn't turn him queer, or not in the sense you took me. But it changed him in a far worse way. You see, until he went there we educated my son here at home. Or rather, I educated him. I was a proficient blue-stocking, and he learned all the usual lessons very thoroughly. Latin, Greek, Mathematics, History, French, and a bit of German and Italian thrown in. He also learned ... how to interpret what he was taught. In the light of Socialist principle. Not Marxism, I was never a Marxist. But with due regard to justice and equality – fair play, as I conceived it and still do. He accepted what I told him; he thrived on it. He also accepted my word that the family religion was so much bunkum. His father was quite a keen Catholic, but not keen enough to insist on Somerset's being indoctrinated, or he wouldn't have married a woman like me. There was a nasty row with the priests, but my husband let me have my way with Somerset – on pain of not having his own way with me in bed. So what with one thing and another, by the age of eleven Somerset had been thoroughly grounded in conventional knowledge and also in correct political and philosophical principle—'

'—*Your* political and philosophical principle,' put in Percival.

'I tell you, he thrived on it. We were close,' she murmured, 'oh, very close in those days, Somerset and I.' She lifted her head high and started to talk loud and fast. 'Then the war came. My husband went off with his Yeomanry – and for the first time in my life I was suddenly very ill. So back came my husband, who'd hardly been gone a week, and packed Somerset off to that loathsome school while I was lying in hospital. Nine months later, when I came home to convalesce, I found I'd lost my son. He'd been taught by them, somehow persuaded, that it wasn't very clever or smart to be a Socialist, or an atheist either. He made a friend, little Lord Somebody or Other, who asked him to stay in the holidays while I was ill. The family was High Church and High Tory, and in no time at all they charmed Somerset back into the fold. Privilege and paternalism, *noblesse oblige*, upper-class responsibility

– he just loved it all when they ladled it out, nicely cooked in a rich, bland sauce and served on the family silver. As for religion, when he realized that the Lloyd-Jameses had been quite famous as recusants, he couldn't go back to Catholicism fast enough. It was the word "Recusant" that did it; it was almost as good as "Cavalier".'

Peregrina paused and positively bared her teeth.

'But of course it all started with his being sent to that school – *St Peter's Court* forsooth. He wanted to go on to Eton. I managed to put a stop to *that*, and soon afterwards little Lord Footleroy went and died on him, but by then the damage was done. In the end he went to a middle-class public school – yours, Captain Detterling, I understand – but they weren't going to cure him there, quite the reverse, and I was still too ill to try. I'd lost him anyway. He'd been taken from me just too early and too long. After that I never had a chance.'

'So now we know,' said Percival lightly, 'why he mentioned St Peter's in *Who's Who*. After all, it had provided him with a very memorable educational experience. It had switched his whole conception of life – and of death, come to that. Tell me, Mrs Lloyd-James: was he *sincere* as a Roman Catholic?'

Peregrina shrugged.

'How should I know? I couldn't understand that kind of sincerity even if I saw it. Anyhow, he never told me anything. He'd been poisoned against me, and for the rest of his life he never spoke to me of anything that mattered to him. Except once, when he spoke of money. After his father was dead he told me what he was going to allow me. He got it almost all, you see. I'd come to the family with very little – it was a love match, believe it or not – and so what was settled on me was tiny. If I'd had to make do with my own when my husband died, I'd have had about 300 a year. But of course Somerset was too good a Catholic to turn me out of the house, and too good a Conservative to let me live in an unbecoming style. So he made me an allowance. "Twenty-five hundred a year, mama," he said; "and I'll pay all household expenses, including Mrs Strange" – that's my companion-housekeeper. "I'll review the arrangement every year," he said, "in respect of current monetary values." Pompous little pig.'

'Nevertheless, he was doing the right thing,' said Detterling, 'and doing it quite generously. I hope he did the same in his will.'

'Didn't I tell you?' said Percival. 'He died intestate.'

'So it's all come to me at the last.' Peregrina snickered. 'I'm the queen of the castle – because there's nobody left of the whole fine recusant family of Lloyd-James of Chantry Marquess, except me. And to whom shall I leave it when I die?'

'Who were all those people at the funeral?'

'A few locals who came to support me. And some of my own blood relations.'

'Ah. You were a Forbes Eden, I think. Why not leave it to them?'

'They hate me. For being an atheist, for marrying a Catholic. Puce Peregrina, they call me.'

'How unkind of them,' said Percival. 'Perhaps some Socialist cause would be a grateful beneficiary.'

Peregrina wrinkled her nose.

'They're a rotten lot now,' she said. 'All greed and envy. They never give a thought to the real poor – those still in England, all those in the rest of the world.'

'Then sell all you have,' said Detterling slyly, 'and give to the real poor yourself.'

'Charity's no answer. It's a proper way of life they need. Anyhow,' said Peregrina, quite unabashed, 'I think I shall leave the house and the estate to Mrs Strange.'

'Your housekeeper?'

'Yes. She's a thoroughly common woman, and it will annoy the landed gentry when she sets up as one of them.'

Detterling rose to his feet. He glanced at Percival, who pursed his lips but then rose also.

'All this talk of wills,' said Detterling, 'reminds me that

Lord Canteloupe is getting up a memorial dinner for your son.'

'A memorial *dinner*?'

'Yes. There was going to be a service, but few of Somerset's friends are of a church-going persuasion and the Catholic thing might have made it tiresome. So Canteloupe's proposed a dinner. If you'd like to come, Mrs Lloyd-James, I know he'll be happy to send you a card.'

'I think it impertinent of Lord Canteloupe to take the office on himself.'

'Why? Were you going to?' asked Percival.

'He should certainly have asked my intentions first. No,' said Peregrina, 'I shall not attend this dinner. I doubt whether the sight of my son's friends assembled would give me much pleasure, and you must be aware by now that I get none from remembering him.'

'We could have given her a little longer, I suppose?' said Detterling in the Mercedes on the way back to London.

'No point. She made it quite plain that they'd steered clear of each other ever since 1939.'

'That's what I thought. But I saw you hesitate when I got up to leave.'

'I was in two minds for just a moment. But then I took a look at her face, Detterling, and I realized, quite finally, that we'd never get anything useful out of Mrs Lloyd-James. You see she wasn't talking about her son at all. She was talking and thinking – and cursing – about someone who'd never existed. Even on the rare occasions she *had* seen him over the years, it wasn't him she saw. It was some ... chimera ... of her own imagining, which moved and acted only in accordance with her conception of it. She wouldn't even have noticed anything about him that you and I might want to know.'

'I don't quite follow you, old chap. Anyway, how did you realize this just by looking at her face?'

'Because it reminded me of my own on a comparable occasion. She was obsessed; totally convinced that she and she alone was right, that she and she alone saw clear and understood. Not to be reasoned with; not caring about any other opinion or interpretation or aspect; frozen as hard as ice in the truth as she saw it. And then I remembered a time, years ago, when I myself had been in the same condition – and had seen the same kind of face looking at me out of the mirror.'

'My dear Leonard ... no doubt you are as opinionated as the next man, but I cannot see you as the bigot you're describing.'

'Well, once I was. Luckily I was taught a very sharp lesson. Unlike that old woman, who will never realize what has happened to her, I was woken up, so to speak, and made to snap out of it. It all occurred on the first assignment I ever had – but I won't bore you with that.'

'You will not be boring me, Leonard. I promise you.'

'All right. You've got yourself to thank.' Percival joined his hands over his breast and rested his long pointed chin on them. 'I was originally got into this game,' he said 'by an uncle of mine, Rupert Percival, who was a country lawyer in a place called Bishop's Cross – not far from here, as it happens, in Somerset. Uncle Rupert had a lot of pull in various quarters, but he didn't find it very easy to fix this for me because I'd had an abominable record at school. I was what these days they'd call a late developer, only just scraping through School Cert. at the age of seventeen – a real muggins. Not the kind of thing they wanted in this profession. But I was dead set on it, always had been, and after one hell of a struggle Uncle Rupert got them to take me on probation. So you see, it was very important that my first job should go off well.'

Percival produced a large wallet from which he took a tattered picture postcard in black and white.

'Recognize that?' he asked, passing it over to Detterling. 'Biarritz?'

'Right. I keep this picture to remind me of the disaster which nearly happened there. Whenever I find myself becoming too dogmatic in my theories, too certain that I must be right about somebody or something, I get out this picture and tell myself, "Leonard, remember Biarritz".'

Percival put away the postcard with reverential care, as if laying up a relic.

'Biarritz, summer of 1950,' he said. 'My first assignment. An easy one, but very lowering, in almost every sense. You remember that in those days the Government was very strict about foreign currency – fifty pounds was all you could take abroad with you. Well, I was one of a number of agents employed to detect people who were cheating. I used to hang about in bars and casinos and whatever, and if I saw an Englishman who was spending suspiciously large amounts I'd try to follow up and discover where and how he came by the money. But of course it wasn't easy actually to pin anything on anyone, so I was instructed, among other things, to act as *agent provocateur*. For example, if I saw a rich-looking type lose a packet at roulette, I'd go up and offer to cash him a cheque, at a heavy discount, drawn on his English bank – I had a special fund of francs for that. If he said yes, then I took his cheque, which had to be made payable to cash or bearer, and sent it off to our H.Q. in London, who made life most unpleasant for him when he got home; because passing a cheque abroad at that time wasn't far off being treason.'

'What a mean trick, Leonard. Like those games the police get up to in public lavatories.'

'I said it was a lowering business. But then, one day, I found a real interest – something which, for a number of reasons, I much enjoyed investigating. There was a girl of about twenty-nine or thirty, attractive, very smartly but plainly dressed, reserved, even haughty, in manner, whom I'd seen come into the "Casino du Palais" – the grandest one – some three or four times the same week and play chemin-de-fer. Now it's not very often you see a *young* woman alone at the chemmy table, and of course the stakes were comparatively high, so this little spectacle would have been interesting whoever the girl was. But very soon I learnt that although she spoke excellent French, she was in fact English – I heard her, one night, dressing down an Englishman who was drunk at the table. And then, of course, I was more intrigued with her than ever. How did she manage it? She always played carefully, but at any one time she'd be winning or losing the equivalent of seventy or eighty pounds, and that's a lot of money for a girl with a travel allowance of fifty. Where did she get it to play with? I'd already tried my old cheque routine on her – one evening when she'd lost – but she hadn't taken the bait. Which meant she had a source of her own.'

'A source which could have been quite legitimate, at least from your point of view. Suppose she was whoring, for example. The Treasury had no rule against *that*.'

'Whoring was what I thought it was – at first. And I even wondered whether I might not use some of my special fund to buy myself a treat with her. But she just didn't fit the part. You can always tell whores in casinos. As soon as they lose, they sit about showing a lot of thigh and start drumming up custom. The second night I saw my girl lose, she just got up, marched out like a queen, and sailed off in a taxi.'

'A rich protector somewhere?'

'Another theory of mine – but only one out of dozens. By this time, you see, she had me really fascinated and determined to find out what kept her propeller running. And quite apart from being exceedingly curious to know what was going on, I also had hopes that it might lead to really important charges, if not for currency offences then perhaps for something even more serious and exciting. *Then* London would know what a good man they'd got – and how proud Uncle Rupert would be.

'So here was my own heaven-sent mystery woman, and I, Leonard Percival, was going to rumble her. Perhaps she was working a con-game of some kind; or involved in some criminal racket like drugs; or perhaps she was a beautiful spy – one of ours, why not? – who was blowing Government funds at the tables; or a double agent who was in French pay as well as British. She might have been almost anything; but the great point was, as I saw it, that she just had to be something shady – something wicked, or immoral, or secret, and with any luck all three. A pretty young woman who came out by herself to play chemmy ... who would sit down in her place as cool as mint with two hundred quids' worth of chips piled under her dainty knockers ... she couldn't but be more or less bent.

'And then Detterling, I got an important clue – or so I thought. I'd taken a day trip to San Sebastian, just over the Spanish border, to do some cheap shopping. Shirts and things like that, which were still more or less rationed in England and very expensive in France, were going two a penny in Spain. And whom should I see, while carting my haul of haberdashery towards the bus-station, but my own gorgeous chemmy girl – stepping into a car the size of a cathedral, with the assistance of a character who had a face like Fu Manchu and was got up like flash Harry. A crook if ever I saw one. Whatever madam was mixed up with, part of it happened in Spain. When I saw her the night after, at chemmy again in Biarritz, she had a much larger stack of chips than usual in front of her. Obviously, when I'd seen her in San Sebastian, she'd been at some stage of a mission – which had paid off very sweetly, thank you.'

'But you were still no nearer to discovering what she was at?'

'No. And the problem was, how to go about it. I thought of several schemes; like following her home, then burgling the place when she went out to see what I could find. But eventually I decided that the safest way would be to button-hole her in the Casino in my role of dubious character (already established by my offer to cash her cheque), to pretend that I knew what she had been up to in San Sebastian, and then ask for a large sum to keep my mouth shut. That should elicit *some* response, should make *something* happen, and if I kept my wits about me I should learn a lot about her, particularly if I could make her lose her temper.'

'A rather ... tenuous scheme?'

'In those days I was still an apprentice – as indeed I was about to be very forcibly reminded. When I appeared at the gaming-rooms that evening, I found the entrance barred to me by a round and doleful Frenchman, whom I had often seen standing gloomily about the place but whom I did not know, so ignorant I still was of the world, to be the casino detective. He took me away to an office, where he said that I had been observed pestering the customers, that I had in general the look of a shabby and undesirable nuisance, and whatever my business was would I kindly take it elsewhere and cease to pollute the air in the "Casino du Palais". I then told him what my business in fact was and satisfactorily identified myself, whereupon we enjoyed a hearty laugh as being, in a sense, colleagues; but I was told that nevertheless the ban against me must stand, as it was no part of the policy of the Société des Bains de Mer de Biarritz to assist the British Government in catching currency offenders, and I had already caused grave offence to clients. To which clients? To the young English lady, who had complained that I had impertinently offered to discount her English cheques at an exorbitant rate – as if totally ignorant of her character and standing, and offensively assuming that she was short of ready money. All right, I said: I knew a lot – if none of it very exact – about *her* character and standing and goings-on, and if they were going to make a fuss on *her* account— *What* did I know of her? the casino detective interrupted. That she was a thoroughly bad lot, I said, who was up to something highly suspicious just across the border. I followed up with a detail or two and told him how I'd planned to unmask her.

'At this my friend (for such he was to prove) gave a long sad sigh, and informed me that the young English lady (*Madame la jeune Anglaise*, as she was locally known) was a hero of the wartime resistance, who had been parachuted into France in 1943, had figured in many brave adventures, and had married, at the end of the war, her comrade in arms, M. le Comte de St Jean de Luz, whose château she now adorned, being all but worshipped for

forty miles around as the friend of France and the pride
of the Province. Her independence of demeanour, which
had doubtless misled me, was due to her military experience; her companion in San Sebastian was a retired bull-
fighter gone to seed but generously maintained at the
château by M. le Comte, a great aficionado; and her fond-
ness for chemin-de-fer was a foible which she could well
afford and indulged but moderately if one considered the
amplitude of M. le Comte's finances. In short, such was the
lady's position that if I had accosted her that evening in
the manner I had intended, I should, said the casino detective, have been languishing in a French prison for many
months to come.

'It was at this moment I caught my face in a mirror on
the office wall. I remember the letters in gilt at the top of
it – *S.B.M. de Biarritz*; and underneath them my face, scowl-
ing, incredulous, absolutely set in its brutal and irrational
insistence, *knowing* that it was right and that this fat fool
had somehow or other been deluded by the young woman
into believing the tale he'd just told me. When I blurted
out something of the kind, he grabbed my shoulders very
tightly, shook me for half a minute like a pup who'd peed
on his chair, and then showed me a photo of Mme la Com-
tesse, with her name underneath it, in the local paper.
"Evidence," he shouted in English: "where is yours?"

'And at these four words my sanity was restored. I saw
that I'd been the victim of a colossal delusion which, out of
loneliness, discontent, sexual fancy and an overheated
imagination, I had manufactured solely by myself and for
myself. So I apologized most humbly. After which the good
fellow patted me on the head (literally) and mumbled something about in youth is folly and in age is death; I must
haunt no more casinos, he told me, but if I promised to be
a "sage garçon", he would give me a letter to a friend of
his who was hotel detective in the "Maurice" at Cap
Breton, just up the coast. This friend would give me a tip or
two about likely currency offenders in exchange for a tip
or two in currency.'

'How did that work out?' Detterling asked.

'Very well, as it happened. I netted one rather big fish whom they were very pleased to put in the pan. With the result that my appointment was made permanent and I have become what you see today, an ulcerous and washed-up nosey parker, who will retire on a pension of peanuts. But you take the point of my tale?'

'I'm not sure that I do.'

'Well, instead of looking at what was under my eyes and simply asking who the girl was – a question that could have been answered by almost anyone in the streets of Biarritz – I wilfully and perversely preconceived and elaborated a ridiculous myth, and then allowed it to enslave me. Now, Peregrina Lloyd-James has done rather the same. *Her* myth is of a promising young Socialist intellectual, who weakly let himself be duped and flattered into betraying the ideals she had taught him, and thereafter spent a worthless and frivolous life in his own worldly advancement. But of course that's not the truth at all. Somerset just found a rig he liked better, changed his mind as all children will, and threw in his lot with the Old Gang, because pound for pound and penny for penny he thought they offered quite as much in value achieved and value forthcoming as Peregrina and her levellers. Somerset may or may not have been right in his decision, but the decision itself is entirely understandable – to everyone except that old fanatic in Chantry Marquess, who was so jealous and angry, so incapable of mental flexibility, that she ceased to see her son as a human being at all.'

'How does that help us?'

'It doesn't,' said Percival: 'the whole point of this conversation is that she never could have helped us and can now be written off entirely. As far as Somerset is concerned, she has not properly *seen* him since he was twelve. Just as I failed to *see* that card-playing countess and saw something I'd dreamed up instead.'

'All of which has made for an interesting philosophic lesson – and for an entirely fruitless day. What now?'

'More of his friends.' Percival took out a notebook. 'Quite a list, with some impressive names. I thought we might start, tomorrow afternoon, with Provost Constable of Lancaster College, Cambridge. There we shall also find another old acquaintance of Somerset's, Tom Llewellyn, the historian.'

'We could go on, quite easily,' suggested Detterling, 'to Broughton Staithe on the Norfolk coast. Fielding Gray still lives there.'

'Yes. Fielding Gray, the novelist ... You're a publisher. Is he well regarded these days?'

'I'm *his* publisher. So-so, I'd say. He's spent most of the last two years or so working on a book about Conrad for us. A lot depends on that.'

'So he's done no novels just lately?'

'No.'

'Good. I do not want him in the fictitious vein when we talk to him ... By and large, an interesting old lot to talk to,' said Percival, considering the list. 'I'm looking forward to the next two or three days. And to spending them with you,' he said.

'Thank you, Leonard,' said Detterling: 'ditto.'

PART FOUR

The Pundits

'No,' said Provost Constable; 'I hardly knew Lloyd-James when he was up. It was later that I became well acquainted with him.'

'We'll be coming to that,' said Detterling. 'But first – did you know *nothing* of him while he was here?'

'Very little. Except ... I do remember clearly that he won the Lauderdale in 1948.'

'The Lauderdale?' said Leonard Percival.

'A University prize for an historical essay ...'

Provost Constable had received Detterling and Percival in his study in the Provost's Lodge of Lancaster College. Detterling, with whom he had some very slight previous acquaintance, he recognized with bleak civility; Percival, who was a stranger to him, he greeted with a suspicion which almost amounted to open distaste. The same old Constable, thought Detterling, as cold as a cod and as close as a crab; but at least he will tell us absolutely nothing which is not the unqualified truth – even if he may wrap it up in layers of donnish allusion.

'... The essay must not be less than 30,000 words in length,' Constable was saying now, 'and the prize is open to all resident members of the University beneath the degree of Doctor. Since Lloyd-James was still an undergraduate when he won it, it was a somewhat notable performance on his part.'

The word 'notable', to Detterling's ears at least, was not kindly uttered.

'So he must have been quite a figure about the place,' said Percival.

'I dare say. He and I did not frequent the same circles. Even so long ago I was already Tutor of this College, and so considerably his senior in every way.'

'But you did know him by sight?'

'Yes. Just.'

'Did you ever hear any gossip about him?' Percival persisted.

'I don't listen to gossip, Mr Percival.'

'Then what did you hear about him in a *serious* way? For praise or blame?'

'For praise, that he was a diligent student who achieved outstanding results. For blame, that he was ... more interested in awards than in studies.'

Here's my cue, thought Detterling.

'You never,' he put in, 'heard any hint that he might have been given to cheating? In his exams, for example?'

Constable looked silently at Detterling and then at Percival.

'What makes you ask that?' he said at last.

'I have heard it mooted – admittedly with no proof at all and only in the thinnest of whispers – that he might have cheated in his Tripos.'

'I told you: I do not listen to gossip.'

'But *we* have to,' said Detterling. 'As you know, we are looking for a clue to the true cause of Somerset's suicide. We cannot afford to overlook anything that might give us this clue. No matter how long ago it happened, no matter how remote from his death it might seem. You see, if Somerset *had* cheated in his exams, and somebody else had proof, then it is just conceivable that this proof was used to blackmail him on threat of humiliating exposure.'

Constable nodded reluctantly. 'Just conceivable,' he said. 'But what is not conceivable is that anyone should cheat in his Tripos examinations. They are far too closely invigilated, and the papers are far too closely guarded beforehand.'

'If you say so ...'

'So much for your whispers. I can, however, offer you in exchange for them ... a piece of informed speculation.' Constable glared at Detterling and Percival with extreme severity, as though they were a pair of delinquent undergraduates whom he was about to expel for ever. 'So long,' he continued, 'as it is firmly understood by both of you that

I am speaking only in order to assist you as servants of the State, and that you will in no case use the information to entertain your acquaintance.'

'*Is* it entertaining then?' Percival asked.

'Some might find it so. As I say,' said Constable, 'there can be no suggestion that Lloyd-James cheated in his examinations. But I once heard it ... convincingly argued ... that the essay with which he won the Lauderdale contained a very culpable element of plagiarism.'

'Surely, the judges would have spotted that straight away?'

'Not if the material which he exploited had not yet been published.'

'You mean,' said Percival, 'that he filched some stuff from someone else's work in progress?'

'Not exactly, no. Let us begin at the beginning. The subject set for the Lauderdale Essay Prize in 1948 was "Eighteenth Century Concepts of Monarchical Function". Lloyd-James's prize essay proposed the theory (a totally original one, or so it seemed to the judges at the time) that after the English Crown passed to the House of Hanover, the outlook and mentality of successive monarchs was that of petty German princes more fit to rule over a province than a great kingdom—'

'—Nothing original in that—'

'—And that this outlook so far qualified their sense of function that they were incapable of acting as independent sovereigns and *became, in effect, the vassals of their own nobility*.'

'But surely, they were very much at odds with their own nobility?'

'*Not* a valid objection, Captain Detterling. Vassals are usually at odds with their overlords. They remain, none the less, vassals.'

Constable raised his square jaw as if deprecating the insolence of Detterling's interruption. For a well-known Socialist, Detterling thought, the man had an outrageously aristocratic manner. But then of course the Constables were indeed aristocrats : hereditary castellans of Reculver Castle from some time way back in the Middle Ages. But he, Detterling, was damned if he was going to be put down so easily.

'Isn't this theory just an elaborate way of saying that the Hanoverians did what they were told – and not only told by the nobility? Walpole and Pitt were very powerful as commoners.'

'You have misunderstood my statement. Lloyd-James was positing a definitely *feudal* relationship, with all the special conditions of service, protection, duty and privilege. But whereas in properly feudal times the nobility gave service and duty to the king in return for tenure of their lands, in this case the king gave service and duty to the nobility in return for tenure of his kingdom.'

'Or in plain words,' said Detterling obstinately, 'he was told to toe the line or get out. The relationship was no more feudal than me and my aunt Fanny.'

Oh God, he thought, I'm beginning to talk like Leonard.

'Of your relationship with the lady you mention,' said Constable, 'I do not presume to speak. But it is quite irrelevant whether or not you or I agree with Lloyd-James's approach; I am simply telling you what it was – or trying to. What you must also understand is that in the opinion of the judges, back in 1948, this was an original thesis urged with style and argued with ingenuity. So they gave Lloyd-James the prize – a cheque for two hundred pounds and a small gold medal – and that, one might have thought, was that.'

'Only it wasn't?' said Percival with relish.

'It would have been,' said Constable, 'but for a very curious accident. A good four years after the prize had been awarded, a close friend of mine, an historian called Carnwath, had the task, as Vice-Master of his College, of writing an obituary for the Annual College Report of a recently deceased Fellow called Pennington. The task was delicate, because Pennington's private affairs had caused substantial and enduring scandal as a result of which he had for many

years resided away from Cambridge – though still retaining
his Fellowship, which was for some technical reason in-
alienable. But however all that might be, appearances had
to be upheld. As a Fellow of the College, Pennington must
have a minimum of two and a half pages in the Annual
Report, and none of this must be less than cordial. My
friend Carnwath therefore eschewed much mention of his
personality and concentrated on his published work. Unfortunately there was very little of this, and that little
mostly indifferent and entirely forgotten. At last, in some
despair, Carnwath visited his College library and extracted
the typescript of the Dissertation on the strength of which
Pennington had first been awarded his Fellowship in 1925.
The College, though small, was not undistinguished, and
there must have been *some* quality about the dissertation –
so my friend told himself – for it to have led to Pennington's election. With any luck the typescript might provide
material for a page or more's discussion in the obituary of
Pennington's "early promise", after which some charitable
reason might be assigned for its sad lack of fulfilment.

'Pennington's dissertation turned out to be an analysis of
the moral and religious ideas which informed the Feudal
System. There was also a long passage about the survival
of such notions and their influence on later politics. Carnwath found it quite enlivening by comparison with Pennington's published work, but he was puzzled because one
chapter had an oddly familiar flavour. He knew he had read
something like it before . . .'

'And of course,' said Detterling in a blasé manner, 'he'd
read it in Somerset's prize essay?''

'Nothing as crude as that, Captain Detterling. Carnwath
had indeed been one of the judges of the Lauderdale in
1948, and it was indeed Lloyd-James's essay of which Pennington's work reminded him. But whereas Lloyd-James
had applied the "inverted feudalism" theory to the relationship between the British nobility and the Hanoverian kings,
Pennington had applied it to the relationship between the

populace and the monarchy in modern Scandinavian coun-
tries.'

'A pretty embracing sort of theory,' observed Detterling.

'And what's more,' said Constable icily, 'Lloyd-James's
supporting arguments were of a totally different kind, and
there was no idiomatic or stylistic resemblance between
the two pieces of work. Only the basic theme did they
apparently have in common.'

'Then it must have been a coincidence,' said Percival,
looking disappointed.

'So my friend thought – and would have gone on thinking had it not been for one more thing. Pennington had
two or three times perpetrated what Carnwath thought
was a solecism but was in fact an archaism: he had used
the word "baronage", not in the accepted modern sense
of "the barons collectively", but in the sense of "barony",
i.e. the dignity, rank, estate or domain of a baron. When
he checked in the dictionary, Carnwath found that the
latter usage was very rare but in theory just permissible –
and then suddenly recalled that he had gone through exactly the same experience while perusing Lloyd-James's
essay four years before. Lloyd-James, discussing the legal
powers and privileges of peers in the eighteenth century,
had at one stage written: "One Scottish peer, the Lord
Kilmarnock, could still preside over his own private court
and could even hand down sentence of death; but the privilege was peculiar to the baronage." Now if "baronage"
there is taken in its usual meaning of "the barons collectively", the passage is slovenly nonsense ... so on that occasion too, Carnwath now recalled, he had gone to the
dictionary, and, after noting the archaic usage, had been
able to construe the clause as meaning that this murderous
privilege was peculiar to the estate and domain of the
Barons Kilmarnock.'

'There are said to have been good reasons for it,' Detterling began.

'Good or bad, they are nothing to our purpose. What
concerns us,' said Constable, 'is that my friend Carnwath

was convinced that their similar and eccentric misuse of the same term established a connexion between Pennington's work and Lloyd-James's. Perhaps Lloyd-James had repeated Pennington's error without noticing it, or perhaps he had simply assumed (being a tyro) that Pennington's use of "baronage" was correct, that a successful Fellowship dissertation could not contain error in such matters. But no matter exactly how it had happened, Carnwath was convinced that in one way or another Lloyd-James had caught the usage from Pennington. In which case he had also caught his basic idea from Pennington, stolen it, in fact, from a thesis that had never been published and survived, as far as was known, only in one typed copy which was locked away in the back room of a small college library.'

'Rather thin – the evidence,' Percival said.

'Ah. There was more to come. "Baronage" began it; more concrete things followed.'

'But surely,' said Detterling, 'Pennington was still alive when Somerset wrote his essay. Wouldn't Somerset have been afraid that Pennington would spot the stolen idea even if no one else did?'

'Pennington, as I have already indicated, was a discredited scholar of dissolute habit, who lived at the other end of the country. He no longer concerned himself with academic affairs – or certainly not to the extent of procuring and reading a prize essay. Lloyd-James need not have been deterred by any fears on the score of Pennington. A far greater objection to Carnwath's hypothesis was this: how could Lloyd-James ever have had access to Pennington's dissertation? When I say it was locked away in a back room, that is the literal truth – and what is more, the College in question wasn't even Lloyd-James's. If it comes to that,' intoned Constable sternly, 'how had Lloyd-James ever known such a work existed and might be of use to him? But my friend Carnwath was a determined man, who trusted his instincts. "Baronage" and the resemblance of ideas had convinced him. He began to enquire further ...'

There was a noise of girlish laughter from outside. Constable went to the open window, looked out of it and down, and brooded like Jupiter.

'All these wretched women here for May Week,' he said, more to himself than his guests. 'These days they even think they're entitled to walk on our lawns. How can you keep a lawn in good order with hundreds of people trampling on it – even if half of those young trollops do go barefoot?' He turned heavily away from the window and now spoke directly to Percival. 'How would *you* have gone about Carnwath's enquiries?' he asked.

'I'd have started with the librarian and his assistants. Although the dissertation was locked up, Lloyd-James might have applied to see it; and since, as you say, it wasn't his College, such an odd request would certainly have been remembered, even four years later.'

'Neither the librarian nor his assistants could recall that anyone had ever asked for Pennington's thesis except Carnwath himself when he was working on the obituary. No one else had had it since they'd been there – and they'd all been there for over ten years.'

'Did they never have vacations?'

'Never all at the same time. At least one of them was in that library, in term and out of term, every day of the year except Christmas Day, when the place was locked up as tight as the Bank of England.'

'In which case,' said Percival, 'I should have asked whether there was not another copy in existence which Lloyd-James might have seen somewhere else.'

'Very good. But *whom* would you have asked?'

'Typing agencies who might have typed the thing originally.'

'Their records did not go back to the mid-twenties.'

'Pennington's colleagues and contemporaries.'

'None of them could recall having seen a second copy. Few of them even knew about the first.'

'Then I should have asked a question of myself – whether the game was still worth the candle.'

'It was to Carnwath. He was morally certain that Lloyd-

James had stolen another man's ideas – a cardinal crime in our circles, Mr Percival – and he wanted proof in order to be able to exact justice. So he asked himself this question: if there *were* other copies of the thesis, where would they be?'

'Among Pennington's own papers?'

'Not according to his executors.'

'He might have presented someone with a copy?'

'Too vague. Presented whom with a copy?'

'You tell me,' said Leonard Percival.

'His old school – or so Carnwath reckoned. In 1925, when Pennington won his Fellowship, he had still been young, hopeful and proud of his achievement ... his *first* achievement. What more natural than that he should have sent a copy of his dissertation to his old school – like a child bringing its prize to show to his mother? So to Pennington's old school Carnwath went; and there in the school library, in a special section for the books of old boys, was what Carnwath was hoping for – another typescript copy of Pennington's thesis, with a rather touching inscription of gratitude to "the friends and tutors of my boyhood at the best school of all". There was a prominent notice saying that no books from this section could be removed in any circumstance; but the shelves were open, and anyone at all could examine any of the books in them. So there it was. A second copy of Pennington's thesis, which had been readily available ever since 1925, at Pennington's old school.'

'Which was also Somerset Lloyd-James's?'

'No,' said Constable. '*Not* Somerset Lloyd-James's. Very different. A grammar school.'

'Well,' said Percival, 'that was a bit of a damper.'

'Not at all. A grammar school but a prominent one – in the West Country. Sir Thomas Martock's School for Boys, founded in Yeovil in 1727 and later removed, in 1789, to one of the Martock properties near a town called Bampton in Devon. It had a Governing Body largely made up of local magnates – one of whom was Seamus Lloyd-James, of

Chantry Marquess in the County of Devon, Esquire. The father of Somerset Lloyd-James. The latter no longer came into the neighbourhood very often, as Carnwath now learned, but had quite often been there, during his school holidays and university vacations, as a boy. A studious and responsible boy, who needed a good library and was granted, at the request of his father on the Governing Body, the freedom of the library at Sir Thomas Martock's. Even when Martock's closed for its holidays, the caretaker had instructions to open up the library for Mr Somerset Lloyd-James. Who was very grateful for the privilege; who, it was rumoured, was on uneasy terms with his mother and therefore particularly glad to slip away from home and work at Martock's ... where he was most appreciative of the fine selection of historical volumes bequeathed by the late Sir George Martock, Baronet ...'

'... And where,' said Detterling, 'he one day examined, in a mood of idle curiosity, the section devoted to the books that had been written by the school's *alumni* ...'

'... And was surprised to see,' put in Percival, 'that one of them was in fact unpublished. The typescript of a Fellowship Dissertation. Rather a rarity ...'

'... So he took it down and read a few pages, was perhaps favourably impressed ...'

'... And some time later, when deciding to enter for the Lauderdale Prize in 1948 ...'

'... Remembered that there was a passage in this unpublished thesis back at Martock's that might be helpful. So on his next visit to Chantry Marquess,' Detterling pursued, 'he went over to Martock's in the depth of the vacation, was admitted to the library by a deferential caretaker, spent some hours reading the Pennington thesis and making notes on it, then returned it to its shelf and went his way, as usual leaving everything just as he found it but taking with him the seminal idea – someone else's – which was to win him, before the year was out, a cheque for two hundred pounds and a small gold medal. *Quod erat demonstrandum.*'

'But it was very far,' said Constable, 'from being demonstrated. To Carnwath it was now clear what had happened: something, by and large, of the sort you've just suggested. But was his case strong enough for him to take action? It was at this stage he first consulted another person, an old friend, myself. He told me the entire story, as I have told it to you, and then asked me to give an opinion ... not as an historian, for I am in fact an economist, but as a man, he was kind enough to say, of balanced and logical judgement. In four words: would the charge stick?'

'And your answer?'

'In one word: no. There were extremely strong grounds for suspicion, but absolute proof was not possible. If Lloyd-James had transcribed whole sentences, or even some important phrases, of Pennington's, that would have been proof. But the echo of an idea and the similar misuse of the word "baronage" were not enough. There was no *proof* that Lloyd-James had read and exploited Pennington's material, even though we knew that this material had been available to him. Mind you, I thought Carnwath was almost certainly right; but Lloyd-James's plagiary had been too cleverly and cautiously carried out for anyone to make an official accusation; and indeed if anyone did make such an accusation, he would be laying himself open to an action for libel or slander. With some reluctance, Carnwath agreed. But did I not think, he asked as a man eager for the academic honour and purity of Cambridge University, that something ought to be done? And indeed I did so think.'

'But what?' said Detterling. 'What could either you or Carnwath possibly do?'

'We could do nothing official. We could make no open accusation, and even in private it would be unwise, the only evidence being what it was, to speak explicitly. But by *unofficial* action, by *implicit* accusation, we could exact a punishment to fit the crime. We could let Lloyd-James know that we knew; and we could so far discredit him by indirect means that he would never again be recognized by his College or his University – except with contempt. All this we could and must do, as we told each other, so delicately that Lloyd-James would never be able to make legal charges of malice against us – just as he had plagiarized so delicately that we would never be able to make official charges of cheating against him. We were determined, in short, to spike him on his own weapons.'

'But I dare say,' said Detterling, 'that you found him, even at that age, quite a formidable opponent.'

Constable gave a low grunt of assent. Once more he looked fiercely out of the window, as though wishing (like the Emperor Nero, Detterling thought) that the May Week mob had one throat only which he might cut. Then he moved nearer his two guests, seated himself on a hard chair, and leant forward to resume his tale.

'First,' he said, 'Carnwath took Pennington's thesis from his college library and had another three copies made, two of which he deposited in his bank. The third copy Carnwath sent to Lloyd-James, who was at that time working for a well-known financial newspaper in London. Carnwath marked the passages from which Lloyd-James had pillaged his key idea, and enclosed a letter saying that he had been much interested by the obvious influence which Pennington's early and unpublished work had had on Mr Lloyd-James's prize essay for the Lauderdale in 1948. Since Pennington was now dead, and since very few people were acquainted with his work at all, let alone his dissertation of 1925, Dr Carnwath would be most grateful if Mr Lloyd-James would prepare a paper for *The Historical Quarterly* (which he, Dr Carnwath, edited) on Pennington's contribution to historical scholarship. This would be of great interest to subscribers to the *Quarterly* and also a graceful gesture towards the neglected scholar to whom Mr Lloyd-James clearly owed so much.

'A week later Carnwath received the reply he expected. Mr Lloyd James thanked Dr Carnwath for his interest in Mr Lloyd-James's work and for his invitation to contribute to *The Historical Quarterly*; but Mr Lloyd-James had never heard of a scholar called Pennington and in any case was far too busy at that time to prepare historical papers. However, he was grateful to Dr Carnwath for letting him see Pennington's thesis, which he had now sent back to Cambridge under separate cover, by the parcel post.'

'Love-fifteen in Somerset's favour,' grinned Detterling. 'Next service, please ...'

'Carnwath then wrote again, expressing his disappointment at Mr Lloyd-James's refusal. However, Mr Lloyd-James might be interested to know that Dr Carnwath himself now proposed to write the paper in question. It would take the form of a comparative study between Pennington's theories on latter-day manifestations of feudal attitudes and Mr Lloyd-James's equally stimulating theories on the same subject as expressed in his prize essay. Such notice of Mr Lloyd-James's essay was clearly called for in the *Quarterly*, since the Administrators of the Lauderdale, recognizing the essay's importance, had now decided to subsidize its publication by The Cambridge University Press under the terms of the Lauderdale benefaction. Normally, wrote Carnwath, this decision would have been made at the time the prize was awarded, in 1948; but at that time paper and printing materials had been very scarce, so a final decision had been deferred. Now, however, publication of the essay could be readily undertaken by the C.U.P., and Mr Lloyd-James might expect to receive the galley-proofs very shortly. Would Mr Lloyd-James accept Dr Carnwath's congratulations ... and rest assured that Dr Carnwath, in his forthcoming paper for *The Historical Quarterly*, would do ample justice to Mr Lloyd-James's essay on the happy occasion of its public appearance.'

'How much of this was bluff?' asked Percival.

'None of it. The Lauderdale Committee were indeed empowered to pay for Lloyd-James's essay to be published, albeit it was now rather late in the day, and Carnwath had persuaded them to do so. As for the paper, Carnwath could certainly have written a piece for the *Quarterly* which purported to be a comparison between the original work of two men but in fact made it plain, without ever saying so straight out, that one had pilfered from the other.'

'And of course Carnwath as editor could easily arrange for his piece in the *Quarterly* to coincide with the C.U.P.'s publication of Somerset's essay.'

'Precisely. Carnwath intended, you see, to award Lloyd-James a minor academic triumph, which would then be subtly transformed, under the very eye of the spectators, into academic disgrace.'

'And although there would not be many spectators,' mused Detterling, 'there would be quite enough to pass the word around – and pass it as far as Somerset's employers in London.'

'As to London, we were more or less indifferent. Our primary object was to discredit Lloyd-James here in Cambridge, where it really mattered.'

'I see, Provost. And how did Somerset get *this one* back over the net?'

'He never had to. He enjoyed what is sometimes known,' said Constable wryly, 'as Bentley's luck.'

'Bentley's luck?' Percival said.

'Richard Bentley was appointed Master of Trinity College in 1699,' said Constable didactically. 'He so scandalized and outraged his Fellows that they summoned the College Visitor to enquire into his conduct. The night before the enquiry the Visitor passed in the best guest-room – where he was found dead the following morning.'

'Of natural causes, I trust?'

'Indisputably. The enquiry was of course postponed *sine die*. Bentley's luck. Something rather similar,' said Constable with a quick twist of malice over his usually marmoreal face, 'occurred quite recently in a senior College at Oxford.'

'What and where?' said Detterling.

Constable's face resumed its state of stern repose.

'It does not concern us,' he said shortly. 'What does concern us is that before Carnwath could bring his plan into action he fell dead of a stroke. Bentley's luck for Lloyd-

James, and sorrow for myself. Carnwath was perhaps my oldest friend. Despite our disagreements over politics – Carnwath was High Tory in his views, while I, as you may know, am a Socialist – we had been very close to each other since we were boys. We had served together in the Gurkhas during the war; in Burma, under Wingate.'

Constable fastened his eyes close on Detterling's and then went on: 'Carnwath's dead was undoubtedly hastened by the appalling physical hardships which he had endured in the jungle.'

There was a cool innuendo conveyed by this statement (when did *you* ever serve in the jungle?) which Detterling did not consider to be justified.

'You at least seem to have survived in very sound health,' he said.

'Yes,' said Constable neutrally. 'I survived. And I decided that I owed it to my friend to continue his work of justice for him. Lloyd-James must still have his lesson. But how to give it to him? I was not an historian; I could not write Carnwath's piece for the *Quarterly*, and I had no influence with the Administrators of the Lauderdale, who, now that Carnwath was dead, quietly cancelled the publication of Lloyd-James's essay on the grounds of expense. Clearly, Carnwath's plan was in the coffin with Carnwath, and I must think of another. But I did not share the Machiavellian talents of my friend, and a whole year and more later I was still thinking, not to much purpose. Then two things happened. I was appointed Professor of Economics at the University of Salop, and some fifteen months afterwards Somerset Lloyd-James was appointed editor of *Strix*. The Professor of Economics at Salop is, *ex officio*, a member of the Board of *Strix*. Thus time and chance had at last brought Lloyd-James and myself face to face.

'It was at this time that my personal acquaintance with Lloyd-James commenced. When he was up here at Cambridge, I had known him, as I told you, very barely by sight and by repute. After he left, while I'd heard a great deal of him from Carnwath in the Lauderdale connexion,

I had still neither met nor corresponded with him myself. But now ... now we were sitting round the same table, discussing the policies and fortunes of *Strix*. Now if ever I must find a way of carrying out my old friend's intentions – or else devise a new set that would serve as well.'

'Your original intention – yours and Carnwath's – had been to expose him in Cambridge,' Percival remarked. 'You didn't mind about London, you said. But by now I suppose the emphasis had shifted a bit?'

'Let's say ... that I felt he must be shown up for what he had done before one or more people who mattered to him and by whom the meanness and fraudulence of his act would be fully appreciated. I no longer cared much whether these people were in London or in Cambridge. But since it was clear to me soon after he came to *Strix* that he now regarded Cambridge as long since behind him, I inclined to think that he should be discomfited before one of his London circle.'

'I never heard that he was discomfited before anybody,' Detterling said.

'I dare say, Captain Detterling, that even you do not hear everything. Now, at that time a regular and prominent contributor to *Strix* was a young man called Tom Llewyllyn. Although I did not know Llewyllyn, indeed never met him until several years afterwards, I had a high regard for the personality revealed by his writing. His articles were honest and accurate, and showed a genuine concern, informed but never sentimental, over social issues. He was known to be less than reputable in his private life, but as far as I could gather he was not a vicious man, only a cheerful and Chaucerian sinner. And however that might be, I knew that Lloyd-James valued him both as a friend and a writer, and that this regard very much increased (as did everyone else's) on the publication, in 1956, of Llewyllyn's book *The Bear's Embrace*, which was, in its kind, a minor classic. I imagine you've both read it?'

'I was abroad in 1956,' said Percival shiftily.

'And I myself can hardly think of it,' said Detterling, 'as

a minor classic. Too many gimmicks. But I can tell you this. It was published by Gregory Stern, whose partner I later became, and even now we find it still goes on selling. Not enough to keep Tom in caviar, but enough to tickle his vanity.'

'Well,' said Constable, who clearly deprecated the terms of Detterling's assessment, 'it certainly brought him substantial and enduring esteem, and of course this was at its height in 1956 – both with the public and with Lloyd-James, who constantly reminded the Board of *Strix* what a privilege it was to have Llewyllyn writing for us and how clever it had been of Lloyd-James to secure his services. So it occurred to me that Llewyllyn was the man before whom Lloyd-James must be exposed. In this way Lloyd-James would be much chagrined and incommoded, and what was more, gentlemen, the information would have gone to a man who knew how to make just and effective use of it. For both just and effective, on the evidence of his writing, I took Llewyllyn to be.'

'So you told Tom Llewyllyn, did you?' said Detterling. 'What on earth did he say?'

'I didn't *tell* him anything. As I've told you, I never met Llewyllyn until some years later. I merely ... put him in the way of finding out what had happened.'

'Ah,' said Percival: 'more tricks?'

'Stratagems, let us say.' Rather unexpectedly, Constable gave Percival a thin, apologetic smile. 'I did not want to involve myself directly,' he went on in a careful and meditative tone. 'After all, this was Carnwath's affair more than mine. I was only so to speak his executor.'

'And of course,' said Percival, 'it was wiser to keep your distance, Mr Provost, in case the thing back-fired?'

'Yes,' said Constable flatly.

'Well then, tricks, stratagems, call 'em what you like,' said Percival with a grin of enjoyment, 'how did you set them going?'

'If you'll both excuse me,' Detterling said. 'Before you tell us that, Provost, I'd like to have one thing clear. Was

it your intention, or any part of your intention, to get
Lloyd-James removed from the editorship of *Strix*?'

'It was my intention,' said Constable, 'to expose the un-
scrupulous piece of plagiarism, of which Lloyd-James had
been guilty in 1948, to a fair-minded man of Lloyd-James's
close acquaintance. What followed would not be in my
hands. All I was concerned with was the revelation which
justice required.'

'But you've admitted that you hoped he would be "discomfited" and "incommoded"?'

'Yes. Justice certainly required that.'

'Yet you had no *specific* result in mind?'

'No. The only *specific* result I had ever desired from all
this was that Lloyd-James should be prevented from returning to Cambridge in an academic capacity. With his ostensible record, you see, he might well have been invited to.
But now that it was plain to me that he would never wish
to return to Academe, my interest had become almost ab-
stract. Justice required that he be shown up and take the
consequences, and that was all. With what those consequences might be, I could not concern myself.'

'So there was no element of personal spite in this?'

'None.'

'And you had no axe to grind with regard to *Strix*?'

'Speaking for myself,' said Constable patiently, 'I despised
Lloyd-James as a cynical self-seeker and I rather admired
him as an efficient and perspicacious editor. But all that was
quite beside my purpose at that present – which was only
that the truth about the Lauderdale should be made known
to someone with whom it would count for what it was.'

'Even though by this time the Lauderdale incident was
nearly ten years in the past.'

'That could not signify. There is no ... statute of limi-
tations ... for fraudulence of the kind which Lloyd-James
had practised. Scholarship must not be mocked.'

'Agreed,' said Percival. 'We cannot allow people to cook
the Books of Truth and get away with it. So now back to

the nitty-gritty, Mr Provost. You wanted to let this man Tom Llewyllyn know what Somerset had done but you were not prepared to commit yourself to a direct assertion: so how did you work it?'

'I asked myself how Carnwath would have set about it, and then proceeded as follows. I sent a copy of Lloyd-James's prize essay to Llewyllyn's publisher, Gregory Stern, and explained in my accompanying letter that I was an executor of the late Dr Carnwath, who had been very interested in this essay and had hoped to achieve its publication. Unfortunately, I went on, the C.U.P. had now dropped the idea of printing it, but I thought it might be worth Mr Stern's attention; for I knew he sometimes took on historical work with a modern application, such, for example, as Mr Tom Llewyllyn's distinguished book *The Bear's Embrace*. Perhaps, indeed, he might ask Mr Llewyllyn to read Lloyd-James's essay and give an opinion?

'A little later I heard from Stern that he had passed the essay to Llewyllyn, as I had hoped he would. I myself then sent a copy of Pennington's dissertation direct to Llewyllyn. Might I presume, I wrote, as a member of the Board of *Strix*, to congratulate him on his articles – and to ask a favour? My late friend, Dr Carnwath, had been very concerned to promote interest in the ideas of the historian Pennington, whose Fellowship dissertation of 1925 I begged leave to enclose. If Mr Llewyllyn could find in it the substance of an article for *Strix* or any other journal for which he wrote, such an article would afford me pleasure and earn my gratitude on behalf of Pennington and Carnwath.'

'I see,' said Detterling. 'So now Tom would be reading Pennington's thesis within only a day or two of reading Somerset's copy-cat essay. Or so you hoped. You didn't suggest he should compare them?'

'Oh no. I didn't nudge him in any way. In accordance with my policy of non-involvement, I was responsible only for contriving that Llewyllyn should have both pieces of work on his desk at the same time. The rest I left to him. It was, you see, in part a test of the evidence: if Llewyllyn, umprompted, drew the same conclusion as Carnwath and myself, then clearly we had been right.'

'And if Llewyllyn did not draw that conclusion?'

'Then we might have been wrong, and Lloyd-James would, quite correctly, receive the benefit of the doubt – for nothing would then be done about it.'

'So in effect,' said Percival, 'you were dumping the entire onus both of judgement and action on Llewyllyn?'

'I believed him to have strong shoulders,' said Constable, with the air of a man well-pleased with his own skills in delegation.

'So you have told us. What happened?'

'Lloyd-James's essay was not published by Stern and Pennington's thesis was not used as material for an article by Llewyllyn. But Llewyllyn wrote me a line or two when he returned the thesis. The exact phrasing is perhaps worth your attention. "Thank you for sending me Pennington's work," he wrote, "but my order book is full and I haven't the time to give it the care it doubtless deserves. As for Lloyd-James's essay, which is also, I gather, under your sponsorship, what sort of care *it* deserves is rather a tricky problem." And that was all.'

'So the penny had dropped in the slot?' said Percival.

'Perhaps. And then again, perhaps not. Perhaps he was simply referring to the problem of whether or not the essay should be published. All I could ever be certain of was that my part was done. I had sent Llewyllyn the evidence, without any prejudicial comment, so that he might make of it what he would and then act as he saw fit. My duty was discharged.'

'But this was the *crunch*, Mr Provost. Did nothing further come of it?'

'Nothing ... that I know of.' Constable smiled blandly at Percival's evident exasperation. 'Some five years later I came to know Llewyllyn quite well. Early in the sixties he was awarded a Research Fellowship at this college, and he was later given a permanent appointment. But in all the time since he's been here, he has never once referred to this affair, and I cannot remember that the name of "Lloyd-James" has ever passed his lips in my presence.'

There was a knock on the door, and a thin white female face snaked into the room on a long, scraggy neck.

'They're here for lunch,' the face said.

'Very well, Elvira.'

'You've got to come and talk to them. They're too clever for me.'

'Two minutes, my dear.'

The face withdrew.

'My wife,' said Constable with well-bred contempt. 'She has rather a nervous disposition. So if you'll excuse me, gentlemen ...'

They all rose. Detterling felt like a schoolboy who had worked through some huge equation, only to find, after five pages of wrangling, that 'x' equals 'x'. But whenever that happened, he told himself, it always turned out that one had made a mistake. There must be some positive value in Constable's story; otherwise he would not have wasted the time to tell it.

'Provost,' he said. 'You've told us all this because you felt it might help us. But how? You say that nothing at all came of it.'

'I said no such thing.' Constable preceded them to the door. 'I said nothing came of it that I myself knew of ... nothing *overt*.' He seized the door-handle and opened the door wide with one long circular sweep of his arm, like a state janitor in a palace. 'Let me wish you, gentlemen, a very good afternoon.'

'He certainly made us work for it,' said Percival, 'but it's pretty plain what he meant.'

'Not to me,' said Detterling.

They were walking together in Lancaster College Chapel, Percival having opined that they might as well take a squint at it while it was handy.

'Ah,' said Percival, 'a tomb. I like a good tomb.'

He led the way through an elaborate screen of stone

tracery and into a little chantry, much of which was occupied by a high box tomb.

'Really grand,' said Percival. 'The sort of thing that Provost Constable ought to be lying in. With his effigy in
armour on top.'

'Funny you should say that. He comes of a fighting
family. A line of knights and captains going back to the
Plantagenets. It's a wonder they've never been ennobled.'

'Too grand to bother with it, I expect. I was impressed
by Provost Constable.'

'You looked pretty annoyed with him once or twice.'

'Because I found him perverse. But later on I began to
understand his technique and respect it.'

'Then for heaven's sake, Leonard, tell me what he was
getting at.'

'He was saying,' said Percival, 'that it was about even
money that Llewyllyn got the message.'

'I gathered that much.'

'He was also saying that he neither knew nor wanted
to know what happened then, but that if anything *did*
happen it might be very much to our purpose to find out
what. Because as he kept reminding us, this Llewyllyn is a
capable man – that's why Constable picked him. Is Llewyllyn capable, Detterling?'

'Yes. And persevering. A Socialist like Constable. Despite
his dissolute youth he takes very tough moral views.'

'Exactly. So the very fact that whatever action he took
was *not overt* – a point which Constable stressed for us –
makes it sound all the more formidable. When persevering
men of tough moral views take covert action, it's time to
fall to one's prayers.'

'We don't know that Llewyllyn took any action at all.'

'It's my bet that it's Constable's bet that he did.'

'And if he did ... it might have led, all these years later,
to Somerset's suicide?'

'It entirely depends,' said Percival, 'on how and when
Llewyllyn used his knowledge. The question is, will he tell
us?' He stooped down to examine a Maltese Cross which

was carved near the base of one end of the tomb. 'That Head Porter chappie said he had rooms in college but would be staying away from the place during the May Week celebrations. Why May Week,' he said crossly, 'when we're well into June?'

'Academic perversity – like Constable's. They're so keen to avoid being obvious that they end up by being obscure.'

'Will Llewyllyn be obscure?'

'I don't think so. He wasn't bred up as a don, you see, and I think he's too rugged to have been infected since he got here. Did the Head Porter say where we could find him?'

'At a house he has in Grantchester.'

'God,' groaned Detterling. 'That wife of his will be there. A real pain in the neck.'

'Then I'll buy you a nice lunch before we go out there,' said Percival, 'to give you strength.'

The front door of Tom's house in Grantchester was opened by a very pretty little girl of about twelve (Detterling guessed) who was wearing white knee-socks and a very short tartan dress.

'Professor Llewyllyn's residence,' she said, rubbing her silky bare thighs together.

'I didn't know he was a Professor.'

'He's not,' said a tired voice. 'How are you, Detterling?'

He looks very much older, Detterling thought as Tom Llewyllyn stepped up behind the girl in the doorway; nearer sixty than his real forty-odd. It must be his wife. Everything else has gone well for him; he's respected at Lancaster, it seems, and that last book of his was a success, in academic circles at least. No great problems about money – or there shouldn't be, not now. Yes; it must be his wife.

'Hullo, Tom,' he said. 'I suppose this is Baby?'

'Yes,' simpered the girl deliciously, 'I'm Baby Llewyllyn, I am.'

Detterling offered his hand to her. She clutched two of his fingers in her left hand and two plus his thumb in her right, stared up into his face with adoration, and went on rubbing her thighs together.

Dear God, thought Detterling, as he introduced Percival to Tom and Baby, wait till she sprouts tits and then watch the balloon fly. Even while being introduced to Percival, Baby continued to hang on to Detterling's hand with both of hers, and indeed she was now kneading his palm against the woollen jersey which she wore above the tartan skirt.

'How's Patricia?' Detterling said to Tom, pretending not to notice Baby's advances.

'Well enough,' said Llewyllyn. 'She's gone to London for the day.'

'To the dentist,' volunteered Baby. 'Mummy was mean. She wouldn't take me with her.' She looked spitefully at her father. 'I think Mummy'th got a *man* in London,' she lisped, 'or why else wouldn't she take me? It wath the thame last week – when she went to have her new coth-tume fitted.'

Tom Llewyllyn heard this speech out calmly, then took firm hold of both of Baby's wrists and detached her hands from Detterling's.

'I shan't be a moment,' he said.

Baby opened her mouth very wide, whether to howl or to perpetrate some further obscene conjecture Detterling never knew, as Tom now clapped a palm across her face and whisked her into the house. For about three minutes, while Detterling and Percival waited by the front door, there was absolute silence within. Then Tom Llewyllyn re-appeared alone.

'Sorry about all that,' he said. 'Let's take a turn by the river.'

'Will Baby be all right by herself?' said Detterling, prompted by curiosity rather than concern.

'She's not by herself.' Llewyllyn hesitated slightly. 'There's a governess,' he said, 'and it's her time to take over. That's why I told you on the phone to come now.'

He led the way round the house, down a long and ill-kept garden, and out through a gate into a meadow which sloped down to the river.

'Baby doesn't go to school,' he said abruptly, 'and Patricia has to be away a lot. Hence the ... the governess.'

'Well, give my regards to Patricia when she gets back this evening,' said Detterling easily.

'I'll do that. When she gets back from London.' To judge from Llewyllyn's tone, she might (or might not) have been coming back from the South Pole. 'Now, what did you want to talk about?'

'Somerset Lloyd-James,' said Percival.

'Poor old Somerset. God alone knows what got into him.'

'We're trying to find out,' said Detterling, and explained why.

Tom Llewyllyn listened carefully. Then,

'I doubt whether I can help you,' he said. 'I haven't seen him in years.'

'But you knew him well once?' said Percival.

'Intimately.'

'In the old days of *Strix*,' said Detterling.

'I did a lot of work for him when he was Editor there.'

'But you *didn't* write an article on an historian called Pennington?'

Llewyllyn's face went quite blank. Either he doesn't remember, thought Detterling, or he doesn't want to.

'Constable wrote to you about him,' Percival prompted, 'some time in 1956 or '57. He sent you a dissertation which Pennington had written.'

'I didn't know Constable. Not then.'

'But Constable was on the Board of *Strix*. He wrote to congratulate you on the standard of your work ...'

'Yes,' said Llewyllyn slowly. 'Ye-es.' He paused. 'He sent me somebody's thesis which I didn't have time to read. I remember now. I was too busy, because Gregory Stern had just sent me something of Somerset's which he wanted an opinion on. So I read this thing of Somerset's, but then, when the *other* thing arrived from Constable – from a man I'd never even spoken to – I got fed up. So I let a decent interval pass, and then I sent it back with a polite note.'

'And that's all.'

'That's all.'

'Well,' said Percival heavily, 'you *did* read Lloyd-James's essay. What did you do about that?'

'In the end I told Gregory not to publish it. You see, there was something wrong about it.'

'You knew that,' said Detterling, puzzled, 'just from reading it ... and that alone?'

'More or less.'

'But surely, you say you didn't read the Pennington thesis, so how did you know there was something wrong with Somerset's essay?'

'What the hell has Pennington got to do with it?' said Llewyllyn.

Detterling opened his mouth to attempt an explanation but Percival held up his hand like a policeman.

'Halt,' he said very firmly. 'Let us not get ourselves confused.' And then to Llewyllyn, '*What* did you find wrong with Somerset's prize essay?'

'It was a long time ago. Let me try to get it straight.'

Llewyllyn stopped walking and started to examine a clump of river-reeds as though they had been rare orchids.

'Somerset's essay,' he said at last, 'was about the function of the monarchy in the eighteenth century. Some of it was quite brilliant; there was one long passage, about the survival and perversion of feudal practices, in which Somerset put forward a striking new theory. But the trouble was that in the rest of the essay a lot of the material was faked.'

'You mean stolen?'

'No; faked. And very ingeniously. For example : Somerset opened his essay with character sketches of the first three Georges. Now, if he'd just lifted these clean out of some well-known work – Thackeray's *The Four Georges*, let's say – and tried to pass them off as his own, it would at once have been spotted. But what he'd done was entirely different and far more subtle. He'd taken passages from Thackeray and elsewhere, and quoted them with full and precise acknowledgment; but every now and then he'd altered the text very slightly, or even inserted a phrase or two of his own, so as to slant everything which he'd quoted in such a way as to make it consistent with the theories (especially the one about feudal survivals) which he was later going to propound. He was manufacturing support for himself, and lending this support prestige by falsely attributing it to prestigious men. And yet his alterations were so neat, his insertions so plausible and brief, that it was a hundred to one against anyone's getting suspicious and going to check with the original.'

'Then how did you come to spot that he was cheating?'

'Ironically enough, through a piece of my own cheating. One of Somerset's quotations was a sentence from Edmund Burke's *Address to the King*. Now, as it happened, I'd just been sent a new edition of Burke's speeches to review for *The Observer*. I was pressed for time, and not very anxious to grind my way through Burke, so I decided I'd fudge up an article just from reading the introduction to the book and a few selected passages. Since I'd been rather impressed by the sentence which Somerset quoted in his essay, I thought I'd look the passage out in the book, in case it might suit me to quote it at greater length (which would help fill out my review) or in case there were any more useful gobbets in the adjacent text. This had to do with the attitudes which Burke thought George III ought to adopt towards the American Colonies and the disastrous nature of the advice which the King had received from his Privy Council – or so I gathered from Somerset's transcription in his essay. But when I turned to Burke himself, I found that in fact he was excoriating, not the Privy Council, but Parliament as a whole. What Somerset had done was to substitute the phrase "Privy Council" for the single word "Parliament", thus giving the impression that the King was in the hands of a small group of aristocrats who determined his every act for him – an impression very much in line with the theory he would later produce about the neo-feudal dominance held *over* the king *by* the aristocracy.'

'It could have been a slip of Somerset's.'

'It could indeed. But I knew my Somerset; so I checked on the rest of his quotations, and found that he'd played very much the same kind of trick with passages from Macaulay, Froude, Thackeray and Trevelyan, to name only a few. The thing was quite clear: Somerset had been fiddling the evidence, but in such a way that he would never have been found out but for the pure chance of my being up to a similar fiddle over my review of Edmund Burke.'

'At least *you* weren't out to falsify.'

'Only to save myself trouble. But it often comes to the same thing.'

'Did you disapprove of what Somerset had done?'

'Very deeply. Just as I disapproved of the way in which I myself had meant to treat Burke. So then I did two things. I set about reading Burke fully and properly, in order to write a pukka review and purge myself, so to speak, of my intended treachery to letters. And secondly, I went to see Somerset and told him I'd rumbled his prize essay.'

'How did he react?'

'He was very put out. He hadn't known Gregory was thinking of publishing it – he thought, as well he might, that it was safely buried in the past. And now here was I, telling him I could prove it was a fraud, and that it was my duty to expose him to Gregory to make sure Gregory didn't publish. When the story got round, and Gregory would see to that if I didn't, Somerset was going to look exceedingly silly to say the least of it. I had him strapped over a barrel, buttocks spread for a whipping.'

'But you never,' said Detterling thoughtfully, 'handed that whipping out. Did you keep it hanging over him? Did you remind him, from time to time over the years, that you could make him a public laughing-stock whenever you wanted? How did you *use* your knowledge, Tom?'

Tom laughed softly, still looking at the river-reeds.

'You're not suggesting,' he said, 'that *I* drove Somerset to suicide? All because of a crooked essay?'

'You had the power,' said Percival, 'up to the day he died *you had the power*, to humiliate him cruelly. And the higher he went, the crueller the humiliation.'

'I dare say,' said Tom; 'but I am not vindictive, and Somerset was an old familiar. Besides, I wanted him at *Strix*, where he could help me, not grovelling about in a crap-heap – then or ever. So what I did was to put up a deal.'

'Money, I imagine,' said Detterling with weary disappointment.

'Money, but not in the way you think. Some time before my book *The Bear's Embrace* was published – indeed before it was even finished – Somerset had lent me five hundred pounds, which I desperately needed, on condition that I paid him half of every cheque I received for rights or royalties after the book was ready.* He'd got it all on paper, all sealed and signed, in case I tried to rat. Fair enough, I suppose, remembering the sort of chap I was then.'

At last Tom turned away from the river-reeds. He smiled at Detterling and Percival and gave a modest shrug.

'Well, in the event,' he said, '*The Bear's Embrace* did much better than anyone had hoped, and by the time we're talking of, what with American rights and all, Somerset had already received well over £3,000 – and jolly good luck to Somerset, because he'd taken a long shot with his five hundred quid and done me a good turn when it counted. But by now I reckoned he'd had enough. So I told him that his secret would be safe with me, and that I would tell Gregory to send the essay back where it came from as being unsuitable, merely on general grounds, for publication; but that all this must be on the strict understanding that Somerset would no longer invoke his piece of paper to demand any share of the money which might still accrue from *The Bear's Embrace*. He could keep the paper as a guarantee that I would keep the secret; but let him

* See *The Rich Pay Late*.

ever again try to enforce that paper, and I would shout the
story of his Lauderdale Prize from the rooftops.'

'He agreed?'

'Of course. So that was how the contract stood between
us and it remained unbroken on either side. Other little
differences we had from time to time, and Somerset at least
did not always observe the Queensberry Rules. But when it
came to our Lauderdale agreement – well, he always
needed my silence and I always needed my royalties. The
bargain was kept as firm as a rock by both of us ... until
today, when poor old Somerset has ceased to care about the
Lauderdale or any other of the earthly prizes for which he
fought so dirtily. So dirtily, and yet' – Tom smiled, almost
with love – 'with so much sheer bloody guts as well, and
bless his rotten heart for it.'

'An interesting old day,' said Detterling, as the Mercedes
carried them through the loitering fenland afternoon towards the Norfolk coast and Broughton Staithe.

'Yes ... What in God's name was the matter with that
child of Llewyllyn's?'

'Perhaps it saw something in the woodshed.'

'That generally frightens them off it,' said Percival. 'This
one couldn't wait to start. And why did she say her father
was a professor?'

'Infantile paranoia.'

'But what brought that on? She's got nothing to complain of – as pretty as paint she is.'

'Something to do with her mother may have upset her.
Patricia Llewyllyn has been behaving very oddly of late.
There's some tale that she got keen on an undergraduate a
few years back, and ever since then she's wanted them
younger and younger.'

'Is she a good looker, this Patricia?'

'Frumpish. But she's got a lot of good firm flesh and a
warm motherly way with it. So if you were a healthy
growing boy with nothing to do on a summer's afternoon,

you might be rather glad of Patricia to teach you a trick or two. Anyway, she finds plenty that are.'

'Where does she get 'em?'

'According to Jonathan Gamp—'

'—Jonathan Gamp?—'

'—An old London friend of Tom's, the original Madame Tattle. According to Jonathan, who's often accurate, Patricia picks up her little friends in public swimming-baths. Not in Cambridge, Tom's put his foot down about that—'

'—But while visiting her dentist in London?'

'That's it, I suppose. Jonathan says she spots out the talent while she's in the pool, then makes her pick and asks him to a flat she's got for tea—'

'—And serves it up with hot buttered crumpet. No harm in that so long as he's over sixteen. Nothing illegal.'

'The trouble is, so Jonathan says, she's getting greedy. It's not just tea for two any longer, it's bring all your friends.'

'Now that,' said Percival, 'could be naughty. It's still just all right provided they form an orderly queue outside the bedroom door. But if she once gets party games going and the word slips out, somebody's mummy might turn up very nasty.'

'God knows what goes on. Even Jonathan Gamp doesn't claim to know the details.'

'But it doesn't sound as if she's giving poetry readings.'

'No. So what with all that, and what with Baby shaping up as a teenage vampire, it's small wonder that Tom looks about a hundred. He probably thinks it's all his fault. He has a comprehensive conscience.'

'Well,' said Percival after a pause, 'at least he hasn't got Somerset Lloyd-James on his conscience. If we believe his story that is. And we do believe it, Detterling, because if he had anything to hide he wouldn't have admitted that he ever knew that essay was faked.'

'I agree. No clue to Somerset's suicide here. But we have learnt,' said Detterling, 'something of great interest about

Somerset. Think of the incredible pains he went to in order
to pass off that fraud on the judges.'

'We always knew he was painstaking.'

'But the point is, Leonard, that it took him almost more
pains to write that essay crookedly than it would have
done, given his knowledge and abilities, to write it
honestly. It's as if he didn't want to win that prize honestly,
which he might well have done if he'd tried, but was determined to win, if at all, by cheating. You see, Leonard ... *it
gave him more pleasure that way*. That must be it. He
enjoyed deceiving people, enjoyed getting away with it. On
the face of it, no one was more concerned to uphold moral
and social systems – but that was because, if the systems
hadn't been there, Somerset would not have had the
pleasure of finessing and defrauding them. I suppose that's
what Tom meant by saying he had a lot of guts: he preferred to do things the dangerous way.'

'It's the same with some people about sex. They do it
better if there's a risk of someone coming in and catching
them at it. The extra excitement caused by anxiety stimu-
lates their performance.'

'But what happens to such people if they *are* actually
caught? What would Somerset have done if he really had
been exposed?'

'He was. He was rumbled both by Carnwath and by
Llewyllyn.'

'But only by them. One of them died, and he did a deal
with the other. Constable knew too, of course; but he was
on the side line; he couldn't take any action by himself
because he just wasn't qualified, which Somerset knew as
well as he did. No, Leonard, what I meant was, suppose
Somerset had been subjected to full public exposure. How
would he have behaved then?'

'Interesting question. But nothing to our purpose now.'

'More to our purpose than you might think, Leonard.
The line I'm following is this. On the one hand, we have
reason to suppose that Somerset enjoyed playing things
dirty more than he enjoyed playing them straight. On the

other hand, as we have often told each other, he took immense care to cover his tracks. But he must have known that there was always a risk, however careful he was, of his being caught out. And therefore, simply because he was indeed so careful, he must have had contingency plans in case he *were* caught out. All right so far?'

'Yes ...'

'Now. Somerset being what he was – full of sheer bloody guts, to quote Tom Llewyllyn – it's my bet that his contingency plans would have been pretty strong ones. They would not have included surrender; they would have been plans for carrying on the fight.'

'I dare say. And so what of it?'

'Well, several times today we have assumed the possibility that the threat of exposure over this Lauderdale business *might* have led to Somerset's suicide. We now know that there was never any real such threat and therefore that this didn't happen. But my point is that even if the threat of exposure had been a thousand times stronger, even if Somerset had actually been exposed – whether over the Lauderdale or anything else – he still would not have committed suicide, because he would have had these contingency plans ready to cope with the situation.'

'But when all this is said, Detterling, we know that he *did* commit suicide.'

'Exactly so. And therefore whatever drove him to it must have been something *for which he had no contingency plan*. Whatever the threat or the danger or the sorrow, it was something which, with all his care and foresight, Somerset had never anticipated. Something totally devastating that came right out of the blue. Which brings me back to the proposition which I formulated that afternoon at Lord's: I'm sure that the train of events which led to Somerset's suicide originated in some action of Somerset's so natural to him and so commonplace that he didn't notice it at the time and never even thought of it again.'

'And hence the lack of contingency plans in that area?'

'Right, Leonard. And it is particularly important that we

should remember that proposition just now.'

'Why just now?'

'Because we are on our way to see Fielding Gray.'

The Mercedes cornered sharply, passed a derelict pub, and mounted a narrow bridge.

'The Ouse,' said Detterling.

The car descended a steep gradient off the bridge and took a left turn of ninety degrees. On the left of the road was a grassy dyke between the road and the river; while on the right an apparently unsown expanse of dark brown earth lay absolutely flat to the horizon, hedgeless, treeless, lifeless, unbroken by anything whatever except a line of telegraph poles which carried a single wire only from nowhere to nowhere else across the mud.

'Hell,' said Percival. 'That's what hell will be like. That mud, with you all alone in the middle of it. Only "middle" won't have any meaning because the mud goes on for ever. Why,' he said, 'is your proposition – which, by the way, I had not for one moment forgotten – so particularly to be remembered now that we're going to see Fielding Gray?'

'Well ... what do you know of Fielding?'

'I knew him twenty years ago when he was still in the army and I was on a job in Germany.* And I had quite a lot to do with him ten years later, when he was doing an enquiry for the B.B.C. in Cyprus.† My department was trying to turn that enquiry to its own ends.'

'I remember.'

'He made a botch of the thing,' said Percival. 'He didn't stick to it. He let himself ... be distracted.'

'It wasn't his kind of work,' said Detterling; 'he should never have taken it on. There's only one thing he does passably well, and that's write books. Have you ever read any of them?'

'No,' said Percival flatly.

'One of the early ones, a novel called *Love's Jest Book*,

* See *The Sabre Squadron*, passim.
† See *The Judas Boy*, passim.

is largely autobiographical. It's about the time when Fielding was a boy at school. One of the characters is based on Somerset Lloyd-James.'

'So where does that get us?'

'It gets us right back to 1945 ... and the earliest known instance of foul play by Somerset. The book is a blow-by-blow account of how – among other things – the boy Somerset did the dirty on the boy Fielding.'

'Who resented it, I suppose?'

'Not overmuch. According to the novel, Fielding seems simply to have observed and accepted it. For one of the points made by the story is that the young Fielding thoroughly deserved everything he got, including Somerset's knife between his shoulders.'

'How did Somerset react when the novel came out?'

'He shrugged it off. Only those few who remembered him as a boy would have recognized his portrait; and nobody holds his schoolboy antics against an adult. It couldn't do Somerset any damage worth talking of.'

'Then if Somerset wasn't injured by the book, and if Fielding had more or less forgiven him the deeds recorded there, surely nothing more ever came of it?'

'Nothing.'

'So for Christ's sake, what help is this bloody book to us?'

'It's of no direct help to us, Leonard, but it shows us how Fielding himself might be. The young Somerset in that book is very subtly observed. Fielding really knew his Somerset. And so Fielding, if anyone, will understand my theory about Somerset's suicide. He will know just what I mean when I postulate some action which came so naturally to Somerset that Somerset would hardly have noticed it. He will know exactly the kind of thing Somerset might have done in this way, and where it might have led without Somerset's being aware of it until too late. Indeed, with any luck, he may have seen what Somerset did, and taken note of it where Somerset had failed to.'

'All right,' said Percival. 'I'll buy that – on appro. But

now another thing. He was living with some widow woman, or so I was told—'

'—Harriet Ongley. She scraped him out of the mess he got himself into in '62, over that Cyprus enquiry; and then they set up together.'

'Is she still with him?'

'Not as far as I know. She was a possessive woman, and after a time – quite a long time, to be fair to both of them – he got fed up. There was some kind of crisis nearly two years back, and to my belief she's not been near him since.'

'So he lives down in Broughton by himself. Lonely for him. Perhaps we should have asked ourselves to stay.'

'We'll be more comfortable at the hotel. I do not see Fielding Gray in the role of housekeeper.'

Nor did Fielding Gray, it appeared. For when, later that evening, Detterling and Percival entered the dining-room of the L'Estrange Arms Hotel in Broughton Staithe, they immediately spotted Gray, who was alone at a small table in one corner. As they crossed the room, Gray raised the one little eye in his shining pink face, rose from his seat, gestured quickly to the Head Waiter, and steered Detterling and Percival to a larger table, at which he sat down with them.

'We didn't expect to see you till tomorrow morning,' said Detterling.

'I should have told you on the phone: I always dine here, so we were almost bound to meet tonight.'

The Head Waiter gave menus to Detterling and Percival and a wine list to Detterling.

'It's absurdly expensive for the rubbish they dish up,' said Gray, in a voice audible to the hovering Head Waiter, 'but they know me, and I get some kind of service. Anyway, I've no patience for cooking my own food at home.'

Detterling and Percival ordered their meal. Gray took the wine list from Detterling and closed it firmly. 'You'd better have what they keep for me,' he said. And to the Head Waiter, 'A bottle of Les Pucelles, Charles, and one of Cent

Vignes. I'll have coffee and brandy here, while these gentlemen eat.'

'Yes, Major Gray,' said the Head Waiter, whose tone and manner (Detterling thought) showed the kind of wary affection that a zoo-keeper might bestow on a man-eating animal which had been many years in his charge and was now, supposedly, tamed. 'The Hine as usual, sir?'

'The Hine,' said Gray: 'my measure.'

'Well, old fellow,' said Detterling as the Head Waiter left them, 'it's nice to see you. And how's the book on Conrad coming along? Gregory's getting very excited.'

'The final draft will be with you by the agreed date,' said Gray: 'please ask Gregory to be equally prompt with his cheque. He was two days late with the last one.' He turned his eye from Detterling to Percival. 'Leonard,' he said; 'long time no see. I trust you've been having happy hunting.'

'My hunting days are over,' Percival said: 'I'm only a scavenger now, sniffing after dead meat.'

'Somerset Lloyd-James's meat. Or so Detterling said on the telephone. I should have thought it would have had a very distinctive smell.'

'On the contrary, there's been no smell at all. That's our trouble.'

The wine arrived.

'I should have told you,' said Percival to Gray; 'I can't take my juice any more. A glass at most.'

'Then I'll drink some of this before my coffee. Another glass, please, Charles – two glasses, one for each bottle. And some Cheddar to go with it.'

'Yes, Major Gray. And still *your* measure of Hine, sir?'

'Of course,' said Gray dully. And to Percival, 'What's the matter, Leonard? Ulcers?'

'That's it. Caused by worry and irregular meals. Occupational hazard.'

'Will they increase your pension?'

'Will they fuck. They'll try to cut it down, because from now till I finish it's home duties only.'

'But so much nicer, Leonard, than mixing with all those

beastly foreigners. You know how you hated them ...
especially the Greeks.'

'Something in that,' said Percival.

'And this time at least you've got someone to help you.
Detterling here.' Gray's face changed from ironic concern
with Percival's affairs to ironic puzzlement. 'But Detterling's strictly an amateur, Leonard. Is this wise, we ask ourselves? I should have thought you'd be leery of amateurs –
after the way I buggered you up over Cyprus.'

'Captain Detterling is a volunteer. You were conscribed
by us. Anyway, this is very different from Cyprus.'

'Is it?' Fielding Gray giggled and drank off a glass of
wine. 'It seems to me very much the same. The only difference is that in Cyprus you were looking for dirt which
you could throw at someone else, whereas here you're
looking for dirt which someone else might throw at you
– or rather, at the Government – if you don't find it first
and have it disposed of. But either way, your problem is
the same: *cherchez la merde.*'

Gray giggled again, then nibbled at a fragment of cheese.
Detterling looked suspiciously at his 'Fresh Caught Local
Plaice'. Percival sipped his wine and smiled gloomily at its
forbidden excellence.

'You were *always* a scavenger,' Gray went on. 'Even in
your hunting days, Leonard, all you hunted was shit.'

'All right,' said Percival calmly; 'and that was why I
tried to use you in '62. Because you had a natural nose for
it.'

'And Detterling? Has he got a natural nose for it?'

'His nose has twitched once or twice. But I told you:
there's been no real scent.'

'And what makes you think I can find it for you?'

'You knew Lloyd-James, at one time, better than anyone.
We think you might show us new places to start sniffing.
Detterling will explain to you.'

Percival looked across at Detterling, who started, very
deliberately, to explain his theory.

'My word,' said Gray when Detterling had finished,

'what's he gone and done to you, Leonard? Do you *believe* all this nonsense?'

'I think there could be a good deal in what Detterling says.'

'You – gritty old grimy old Leonard, charmed by an amateur into believing that load of goolies? You of all people? So there was a teeny-weeny mistake which Somerset didn't even notice, was there? And this was the spark – was it, Leonard? – which set a hidden fuse-train slowly burning down the corridors of time? And then at last the long-delayed and fateful explosion? In a pig's arsehole. Jesus Christ, Leonard, he's talking like a fucking novelist.'

Fielding Gray laughed, painfully stretching his thin little mouth as he did so, and then uneasily inspected the enormous cognac which the Head Waiter had just set before him (at least a quadruple, Detterling estimated) as though fearful lest he might have received short measure.

'Poor old Leonard,' he said: 'no wonder they'll try to cut your pension.'

'I don't ask you to accept my theory,' said Detterling to Gray, part-angered at the unexpected rejection and part-humble in the face of it: 'I do ask you to help us in our efforts to apply it.' He leant forward and almost whispered to Gray: '*Res unius, res omnium.* Remember, Fielding?'

'What's that?' said Percival.

'Our old regimental motto,' said Detterling blandly. 'It recommends us to assist one another.'

They both looked at Fielding Gray, whose face had now ceased to mock and had become, very suddenly, very sad.

'Of course,' he said, lifting his cognac. 'If you're going to put it like that ... But how can I help you?'

'We want you,' said Percival, 'to think over all the time you knew Somerset Lloyd-James, right back to the beginning, and tell us in what areas he might have made errors of conduct or judgement or sentiment, and what such errors, if any, you ever observed him make.'

'You don't want much, do you? Only the wisdom of Socrates and the memory of a bloody computer.'

'Try, Fielding. Try.'

'All right,' said Fielding Gray. '*Res unius, res omnium*. I'll try.' His eye blinked, and he passed a finger under his collar. 'God, it's hot in here.' He took a long, avid drink of his cognac, as though hoping this might cool him. 'Finish your dinner and let's get out. Then I'll try.'

'The trouble is,' said Gray, as they walked along the beach in the dying mid-summer evening, 'that whatever Somerset did, he behaved at the time with such an air of righteousness and authority that it was impossible to think he might be wrong. Either tactically or morally wrong. It was only a confidence trick, but a very effective one. Years after I'd first learnt how crooked he could be, I would still be made to feel, when Somerset came up with some new scheme or suggestion, an overwhelming sense of Somerset's rectitude, though intellectually I knew jolly well that he was almost certainly up to something rotten. He diffused a mixture of self-confidence and sweet reason that anaesthetized one's faculties of judgement.'

'But only for the time being,' said Detterling. 'Sooner or later one always woke up to the reality.'

'Usually later; just as the guillotine was coming down on one's neck. And even then one couldn't exactly blame Somerset. Even then one felt that what was happening was somehow inevitable, that he was the executioner appointed by a superior court against which there was no appeal.'

'Concrete instance, please,' said Percival.

'Very well. Somerset was largely responsible for getting me sacked from school.* He leaked certain information to certain people – and I was out. He wanted me out because he was afraid that they might make me Head of the School later on, and he coveted the post for himself. But although I knew that was his motive, I still found it difficult to feel angry with him. It was all done in such a way that it seemed to be entirely justifiable – as from many points of

* See *Fielding Gray*, passim.

view it was. Somerset had simply seen to it that I got my proper deserts.'

Fielding led the way off the beach and in among the sand dunes. The spiky grasses, which sprouted from the sand in clumps, swayed in the seaward breeze, giving off a low hiss.

'He came to stay with me here in the summer of '45, not long before it all happened. We went for walks, just where we are walking now; and Somerset talked of school. It was obvious then that he was getting ready to do me down. But even so I was ... paralysed into acceptance. I couldn't resist or resent it; I was his creature and must obey his will. Somerset's will be done.

'Now, you're interested in his mistakes – "errors of conduct or judgement," you said. But how could I ever have spotted such errors if, in all my dealings with him, my own powers of judgement were suspended? You see, it wasn't as if he only served me bad turns. I was all the more under his spell because he also did me kindnesses – with the same monumental air of righteousness and with great efficiency. When I came out of the army with this' – Fielding pointed up at his face – 'Somerset found me work as a writer, although I was completely untried, and set me on the road to being quite successful. Or again, less than two years ago he came with you and Canteloupe, Detterling, and rescued me from those brutes at Vassae.'*

Detterling nodded and held up a hand to silence Percival, who was clearly about to investigate this last remark.

'Nothing there for us, Leonard. Let him get on. Yes, Fielding?'

'There's been a pattern. Somerset trampling all over me, going away for years, and then reappearing to help me to my feet. So whenever he turned up, I knew he was going either to harm me or to help me, depending on what fate had in store for me at the time, almost as if Somerset himself *were* fate ... or at any rate the agent or executive – even, as I said just now, the executioner – that fate had

* See *Come Like Shadows*, passim.

appointed. Impartial, carrying out his orders.'

'But of course he was no such thing,' said Detterling firmly. 'Whenever he came across you, Somerset just dealt with you as happened to suit his own plans at the time. It suited him to get you sacked from school; it suited him, or did not unsuit him, to help you when you left the army. He must have known very well that you had potential talents as a writer, and he could use these for *Strix*.'

'Yes; I did a lot of work for *Strix* at one time.'

'And also, of course, other things being strictly equal, he would have been glad to earn your gratitude. Rest assured, Fielding: Somerset was no emissary of God's will, he was simply concerned to check you or to exploit you as might best conform with his own projects.'

'Oh, I always knew that at bottom. Nevertheless ... he always gave this impression of having some absolute or divine warrant. In his presence I became totally unable either to defend myself or to criticize him. Even if I did try to act or fight back, I did it so feebly and ineptly that I would only deliver myself further into his hands.'

They passed a rubble of brick and concrete which was fenced round by rusty barbed wire.

'Whatever's that?' said Percival.

'Gun emplacement. One of six left over from the war. You'd think they would have shifted them by now,' said Fielding, 'but instead they've fenced them off so that people can't go inside to copulate. Somerset used to like them when we came on our walks here. That was a very long time ago, of course, but even then they looked almost as forlorn as they do now – as if they'd died on the day the soldiers left them. "It's remarkable," Somerset said, "what decay can do for a building. However commonplace or functional the design, as soon as a building falls into ruin it attains to romance. These rotting gun-sites have a melancholy appeal quite as powerful as the stones of the Acropolis." "Have you ever been to the Acropolis?" I said – this was in 1945, remember, and no one had travelled for years.

"Yes," he said: "in spirit." That was the sort of thing I was always letting him get away with.'

'Which brings us back to the point,' said Detterling. 'Although you let him get away with things like that, you came to realize, in the end, what he was getting away with. So despite this mental and moral paralysis from which you say you suffered in his presence, you would have realized – if only much later – when he was making mistakes the sort of mistakes we wish to hear of.'

' "Errors of conduct," you said, "or of judgement or sentiment".' Fielding shook his head and raised a hand to his eye, as if some long effort of reading or writing had tired it.

'Let's put it even more simply,' Detterling said: 'you must, at some time or another, have seen Somerset when he was caught on the wrong foot or in some way looking silly.'

For answer Fielding only shook his head once more, still holding his hand over his eye.

'You said you'd try,' prompted Percival.

'I am. Be patient. I know there's something. Something.'

They were now walking along the fairway of a golf course. Though it was very nearly dark, Detterling knew by the smell that they were approaching the salt-marshes.

'My house is just by here,' said Fielding abruptly. 'You'd better come in for a drink.'

As he spoke they came to the end of the golf course. There was a lonely green, slightly raised, the sandy banks being held in place by vertical planks of heavy wood; beyond this stockaded outpost, the no man's land of the salt-marshes. Fielding led them along a path, through a gate in the hedge, across a lawn, and up stone steps to a verandah, from which a glass door led into a living-room. Fielding switched on a light. Detterling saw a large desk at a window which looked towards the sea, two comfortable armchairs, a scruffy but expensive carpet, some Norwich School landscapes on the walls, and a table which bore the remains of a meal.

'My breakfast,' said Fielding, in tones of explanation, not apology. 'I can't go out for every meal, so a woman comes in to tidy up and cook breakfast. She's meant to clear it up before she goes, but she usually forgets.'

He fetched three glasses.

'Whisky?' he said.

'Milk,' said Leonard Percival.

'Poor old Leonard.'

Fielding went out of the room and returned with a pint of milk.

'It's cold and fresh,' he said; 'I drink a lot of it myself. But not at this time of the day.'

He poured very stiff whiskies for himself and Detterling.

'Where were we?'

'You were trying to remember,' said Percival. 'You think there is something that might help us ... some occasion on which Lloyd-James made a fool of himself ...'

'It couldn't,' said Detterling, 'be anything to do with that time you and Somerset played strip-poker with Angela Tuck? We've heard about that.'

'No,' said Fielding. 'He made no mistakes there. Although he was so ugly and weedy, he kept his head and won that game hands down. I was the one who was sent packing.'

'So we heard. But he might have slipped up somewhere?'

'Not from what I saw. She was all over him.'

'Later? Something might have gone wrong later?'

'Not that I ever heard. Anyway, it wasn't that I was thinking of. I'm sure it wasn't.'

'Then what was it?'

'It'll come. I'm sure there was *one* time when Somerset stepped out of line ... did something ill-judged or incongruous. Just talk about anything. It'll come. Go on, talk.'

'All right,' Detterling said. 'You've finished with Harriet Ongley?'

'She's finished with me. She lit out of here just before I got back from scripting that film. She wrote later, saying I could keep the house – she paid for most of it – and anything of hers still inside it.'

'Generous.'

'Yes. Provided she doesn't use it as an excuse for coming back.'

'You think she might?'

'If she's short of someone to mother.'

'Could be a good thing.' Detterling glanced at the greasy remnants of breakfast. 'You need a proper servant.'

'She was an admirable housekeeper, I grant you. The trouble was, she also thought of herself as a wife.'

'You must have got used to that. You lived with her for eight years.'

'Only because she wouldn't bloody well go sooner.'

'But you found her money handy?'

'Yes.'

'And you might again.'

'I can do without it. I've got some money in Switzerland if things get really rough – stashed away from that film. Meanwhile, Gregory's advances on Conrad are enough to keep me in liquor.'

'*Good* advances. Which means that it'll be some time before they're recovered and you start receiving a royalty. Don't rely on Conrad too much, Fielding, or you'll be drinking pretty cheap liquor.'

'That's it.'

'That's what?'

'Cheap liquor. Somerset's one little mistake. The only time I've seen him commit an error.'

'Explain.'

'You'll probably laugh at me. It *can't* have had anything to do with his suicide. But it's the only thing I have for you. The only little thing of the sort you seem to want.'

'*Then explain.*'

'All right.' Fielding took a very long drink and then liberally subsidized his glass. 'Back to summer 1945 again. Back to school. The end of the Summer Quarter – a few weeks before Somerset came to stay with me down here. The very last night of the Quarter, of the whole school year. Party night. Fashionable boys give little parties in their

studies and groups of us roam from House to House joining
in. It is the done thing. The Headmaster distrusts the custom but tolerates it, indeed could not stop it if he tried. And
now observe: one such party going full swing, given by
Somerset.'

'A mistake on his part?' put in Percival. 'After all, Somerset wanted to be Head of the School, or so you said just
now. Silly of him to annoy the Headmaster by giving one of
these parties.'

'Not really, no. Anybody who was anybody either gave
or attended such a party, and Somerset was definitely somebody. The Headmaster knew all that. He would have preferred Somerset not to give a party, but he would not hold
it against him if he did. And then the school was a big place,
Somerset was not in the Headmaster's house, probably
the Headmaster never knew. No mistake there, Leonard;
not yet.'

'Ah,' breathed Percival.

'So. Four or five of us come over from my House to
Somerset's, "to take a glass of wine with him", as he had so
elegantly put it when inviting us. And there is Somerset at
his desk, dispensing Woodbine cigarettes and cocktails from
a bottle. Gimlets, if I remember: a kind of ready-mix gin
and lime. *Not* very elegant, even given the war-time short-
age of decent drink, and not at all the thing for ten o'clock
in the evening. Where was this wine Somerset had promised? Somerset explains: he had asked for a case of fine
hock from home, but it was never sent because his father
said it would be pilfered *en route* by railway workers. A
very common thing at that time. All allow this to be a
plausible excuse, and happily get on with the Gimlets.'

'Who was there?' said Detterling lightly.

'Peter Morrison, for one. I remember walking over with
him. Under the moon. There was a very big bright moon
that night.'

'Who else was there?' asked Detterling.

'No one else you'd know. Does it matter?'

'It might.'

'Several boys from Somerset's House whose names I've forgotten. Ivan Blessington from my own House.'

'I know *him*,' said Detterling. 'He came into the regiment while I was still in the army. Had quite a good career – always being chosen as an attaché, that kind of thing. He's out now, though; with some merchant bank.'

'Shall we get on with the story?' said Percival.

'In a minute,' said Detterling. 'Who *else*?' he said to Fielding.

'Christopher Roland,' said Fielding shiftily.

'Thank you,' said Detterling with the air of someone who has made an interesting private point.

'Who was he?' asked Percival.

'A particular friend of Fielding's. Long since dead, as it happens.'

'He's no real part of this story,' blurted Fielding, and drank savagely at his whisky.

'But he *was* just there at the party,' said Detterling with quiet satisfaction.

'Drinking Gimlets with everyone else,' said Percival. 'What happened then?'

'We had a few toasts,' said Fielding, clearly grateful (Detterling noted with further satisfaction) to be done with Roland and resume his narrative; 'toasts to departing friends and happy holidays and next year and the captain of cricket and the Headmaster ("wish he was with us") and the school tart ("wish *he* was with us"), and by this time, as you can tell from the tone, the Gimlets were doing their work. More people came, and Somerset told them what a pity it was the hock had run out before they arrived, but would they like a Gimlet, but oh dear the Gimlets were all gone, but Somerset thought there was some sherry. Which, to do him justice, there was. So we all poured ourselves some sherry, and then Peter Morrison, who was leaving that quarter, said he wanted to propose a toast: THE SCHOOL.'

'The School,' said Detterling, raising his glass. 'I hope you all did it with dignity.'

'Peter Morrison burst into tears,' said Fielding, 'and while we were comforting him, Somerset Lloyd-James was sick all over his desk.'

Percival laughed and Detterling looked cross.

'Somerset passed out,' said Fielding, 'with his head in his own mess. The sherry, as Ivan Blessington observed, had been a mistake.'

There was a long silence.

'Well, go on,' said Detterling.

'That's the end of it. We all went home to bed, leaving Somerset sleeping it off with his head on his desk. Best not to disturb him, we thought. I didn't see Somerset again until he came down here to stay about four weeks later. He did not say anything about his party, then or ever.'

'I'm rather surprised that you have now,' said Detterling. 'What good can this sordid little anecdote possibly be to me and Leonard?'

'It's the kind of thing you said you wanted to know. Some mistake, you said, some small mistake, something so commonplace that he wouldn't even have noticed it himself.'

'He'd have noticed this one all right,' said Percival, 'when he woke up surrounded by sick.'

'Yes. But it was hardly anything very serious. We were all inexperienced, and on the rare occasions when we were allowed to drink, something of this kind usually happened. When it did, it was good for a coarse laugh, and there an end of it. Peter and I discussed it on the way back to our House that night. I said Somerset had made an exhibition of himself, but Peter just wouldn't have it. "Five bob to a skivvy to clear up the mess," he said, "and tomorrow is a new day".'

'Exactly,' said Detterling. 'So why tell us about it?'

'Because,' persisted Fielding irritably, 'it's the kind of thing you asked me to tell you. Some little mistake, in this case a crapula brought on by inferior sherry, that appeared at the time to be almost a matter of routine, but might conceivably, on your theory, have started a train of events which led to crisis and disaster much later.'

'But what train of events could *this* conceivably have started?'

'That's for you to find out. It's *your theory*. I told you it was balls, but you begged me to help you, to think of any little incident I could from which Somerset came off badly. So now I *have* helped you' – Fielding poured himself whisky – 'I've told you of the only time I remember when Somerset lost control of himself, and it's no good blaming me if you can't make anything of it.'

'It was so very long ago,' said Percival mildly, and sipped his milk. 'Tell me: why was Detterling so interested, just now, in establishing the presence of that friend of yours – what was his name, the one that's dead – Christopher Roland?'

'You ask Detterling,' said Fielding miserably. He looked at his glass, raised it, but then retched slightly and set it down. 'You'd better go now, both of you. I've got to work on Conrad in the morning.'

'Well, thank you for trying,' said Detterling in a disappointed voice.

Fielding shrugged and led the way through a hall to his front door.

'Straight down the lane,' he said; 'don't stray on to the salt-marshes, or you'll be in trouble. And don't forget, Detterling: tell Gregory to be prompt with my next cheque.'

'Well,' said Percival to Detterling the next morning, as the Mercedes headed towards London, 'why *were* you so persistent about Christopher Roland? It obviously made Fielding unhappy.'

'Christopher Roland,' said Detterling, 'was Fielding's favourite. There was a scandal about it some time later. Somerset got the scandal going.'

'I see. And that's what Fielding meant by saying that Somerset leaked information which got him sacked?'

'Yes. Now, when Fielding started to tell us about this party, it occurred to me that Roland might well have been there. I wanted to know, Leonard. You see, if, as turned out, Roland was there, it made the scene so much more entertaining. Woodbines and Gimlets on the last night of the school year. Somerset, shambling, grubby and pustular, telling lies about hock. But also a huge and beautiful moon, looking through Somerset's study window on a pair of pretty schoolboys in love. A delicious mixture of the squalid and the romantic – particularly piquant since the scene was being re-created for us by one of the erstwhile lovers, now a paunchy middle-aged drunk with one eye and a face made of surgical plastic.'

'So ... you tortured Fielding into telling about Roland just for your personal enjoyment. Solely in order that you might indulge your fancy with a few amusing ironies.'

'Yes, Leonard. And serve Fielding right. He behaved very badly to Roland later on, and he deserves to be punished now and then. And if I need any other excuse – well, the Roland thing might have been relevant.'

'Only it wasn't. There's nothing in all that for us. All Somerset did, in that connexion, was shop Fielding for buggery or whatever and get him sacked. As Fielding himself admits, this action of Somerset's can be readily justified, and anyway Fielding has long forgiven Somerset, who did him many kindnesses afterwards, one of them as recently as 1970. Nothing in any of that can help us to explain Somerset's suicide. So I suggest we pass to the real point of Fielding's story – which is that Somerset got pissed at the party, and passed out publicly after being horribly sick.'

'Nothing for us there either. It was a lovely little scene, that party, but there's nothing there for us from beginning to end of it, and that's why I was so sour with Fielding when he'd finished.'

'He did his best, and he was quite right when he said that this was just the sort of incident we were asking for. That's why you were so sour, Detterling. There was nothing the matter with Fielding's story. It was your theory that came unstuck, or at least didn't rise to the occasion.'

'The occasion was *wrong*,' said Detterling crossly. 'It all came to an end too abruptly. If only Somerset had done *anything* rather than be sick and pass out, there might have been a line we could follow. But as it is ... nothing.'

'Ah well,' said Percival kindly, 'better luck next time.'

'What's your plan now?'

'First, you go to that Memorial Dinner which Lord Canteloupe is getting up. See if you can find out anything new there. Someone may come up with something better than Fielding Gray did.'

'Yes ... I'm sorry I can't get you asked to that dinner, Leonard.'

'Why should I be asked. It's for Somerset's old friends. No place there for me ... though I'm beginning to know him quite well.

'And after the dinner? If I find nothing for us there?'

'There are still some more people we could talk to.' Percival produced his list. 'Donald Salinger and Jude Holbrook. They owned some printing firm which tried to buy *Strix* while Somerset was Editor. There could be something there.'

'Jude Holbrook disappeared years ago. He's said to be in Hong Kong ... though no one has an address.'

'Salinger?'

'In a home somewhere.'

'A home?'

'His wife was drowned by accident five years back. He loved her, although she was a slut, and after that he just fell to pieces.'

'Holbrook of no fixed address in Hong Kong, then, and Salinger in a nut house. Not very helpful.' Percival looked at his list. 'Lord Philby,' he said: 'proprietor of *Strix* when Somerset was Editor. Anything there?'

'Could be, I suppose.' Detterling twitched slightly in embarrassment. 'His wife ... Susan. Somerset had a brief affair with her before she married Philby. The trouble is, I was the chap before Somerset. Philby's never said anything, but I really wouldn't relish talking about the old days with *him*. Or her.'

'I see. So all in all,' said Percival, 'we very much hope

that we shan't have to concern ourselves with Messrs Holbrook, Salinger or Philby. But I'm afraid we shall have to, my friend, unless you can find us another lead at that dinner.'

Detterling looked as glum as he felt.

'I'm beginning to think there is no lead,' he said, 'or none that we'll ever find. All this time – and all anyone's really told us is that they can't begin to imagine how Somerset could possibly have done it.'

'He did it,' said Percival. 'There must be a reason somewhere. If we are patient we shall find it. Your theory is as good as any, because in practice it means we just go on talking to everyone we can, which is the only thing we could have done anyway. So fettle yourself up for this dinner, Detterling, and be of good cheer, and when you arrive there just get them all talking and listen. Sooner or later someone will tell us what we want to hear. Listen and wait. Theories come and go, good, bad and indifferent, but in the end there's only one way to do this work, my friend – listen and wait.'

PART FIVE

The Envoys

Captain Detterling was in a taxi on his way to the Memorial Dinner for the late Somerset Lloyd-James, for which occasion Lord Canteloupe had hired Annabel's Club in Berkeley Square. Since this was only a few hundred yards from Albany, Detterling would normally have walked; but Lord Canteloupe had ordained 'Evening Dress with Trousers and Decorations', and Detterling did not fancy parading himself through the streets in a white tie and tails. He was, indeed, very annoyed with Canteloupe for insisting on such formality, not because he objected to formality in itself, but because his medals, which commemorated survival rather than gallantry, always made him feel a fool. 'Here's Detterling in his NAAFI Gongs,' Canteloupe would undoubtedly say, fingering his own *Croix de Guerre*. The fact that this had been awarded to Canteloupe in return for his procuring a much needed issue of British Army Sheaths Rubber for De Gaule's Free French Troops was no help whatever. For if Detterling brought it up, Canteloupe would merely admit it and roar with laughter, whereas Detterling's cheap ribands and tinny discs weren't even good for a giggle.

But never mind that, Detterling now told himself firmly. I have more important things to think of. Leonard and I need a new line, and here, if anywhere, I should be able to find it. The trouble is, shall I know it if I see it? For about one thing I am right, I must be right: whatever caused Somerset's suicide must have been something for which he was totally unprepared; otherwise, being Somerset, he would have had tough plans ready to meet it. But if it was something for which he, of all people, was unprepared, it must have been something the origin of which went unnoticed. Whatever incident or action started it all off was so commonplace that Somerset ignored it. But I might hear of any number of such incidents or actions this evening,

and how shall I possibly know which to follow up? Come
to that, how *could* I follow them up? That is why I have
found no use for this tale of Fielding Gray's; even if the
incident had led on to something else (and why should it
have done?) there is now no way of picking up the trail in
order to follow it. The whole thing just appeared to come
to a dead stop. But something of that kind it must be;
something more open-ended, no doubt, and probably much
more recent, but nevertheless something of that order. How
am I to spot it? How am I to come at the trail that leads
on from it? Only by luck, thought Detterling as he paid
off his taxi: as Leonard says, I can only listen and wait –
and at least Annabel's will put up a damn good dinner
while I do it.

'Here's Detterling in his NAAFI Gongs,' said Lord Canteloupe.

'Don't be so childish, Canteloupe.'

'Hoity-toity. Remember I'm your host.'

'Then where can I get a drink?'

'At the bar, where else?' Canteloupe pointed to it. 'Dinner in twenty minutes,' he said; 'seating plan on the wall.'

He walked away to welcome another arrival. Detterling
went to the bar, where he was given a generous tumbler of
Mimosa, and then turned to study the assembly.

This, he now realized, was much smaller than he had
expected. Tom Llewyllyn, who gave him a smile and a
wave, was talking to Gregory Stern. Canteloupe, attended
by Carton Weir, was now greeting Peter Morrison. And
that, so far, was all ... except for Jonathan Gamp, who
came prancing out of a doorway opposite the bar and
crossed the room to join Detterling. He was wearing a
miniature M.C. and one of his campaign ribands carried an
oak-leaf.

'I've just been inspecting the dinner table,' Jonathan
said: '*very* tasteful arrangements.'

'Where is everybody, Jonathan?'

'This is everybody, sweetie. Except for just one more.'

Jonathan pointed to the seating plan, which was hanging on the wall, framed and glazed like a minor masterpiece. 'Only eight of us. It was to have been ten, Canteloupe told me, only Fielding Gray wouldn't come up from Norfolk, and Max de Freville was tied up in Corfu.'

'No wives?'

'Oh, dear me, no. It's going to cost Canteloupe a small fortune as it is. You wait till you see what's in that dining-room.'

'But isn't it rather pointed? No wives, I mean?'

'Did any of them know Somerset? Not really, when you come down to it.'

'It's going to look jolly odd in *The Times*. "A dinner was given by the Most Honourable the Marquis Canteloupe in memory of the late Mr Somerset Lloyd-James" ... and not a single woman on the list.'

'Correction, duckie. One woman.'

Who was now arriving: Maisie.

'Is this Canteloupe's idea of a joke?' said Detterling. 'Getting us to come here in full rig and clanking with medals, to meet Miss Maisie Malcolm.'

'Don't be such an old snob, dear. Canteloupe's idea was to invite only those who really appreciated Somerset or whom Somerset really appreciated. On that reckoning, from what I hear, Maisie Malcolm has earned her place with the best of us.'

'Just as well the old mother wouldn't come.'

'Ah well, if she'd accepted it might have been different. It was when Canteloupe heard she'd refused that he hit on the idea of doing it like this. Just a few people who understood what Somerset was all about. So much better than having rows of civil servants and their middle-class women. Besides, it wouldn't have been physically possible to lay on what Canteloupe's laid on for more than a very small number.'

'What has he laid on?'

'A little surprise. You'll see. Here comes naughty Tom to talk to us, with poor old Gregory. *Comè va, Gregorio mio?* Detterling's just been saying that he wants you both to publish Maisie Malcolm's memoirs.'

'What nonsense is this, Detterling? I never heard of the lady until she walked in here just now. I forbid you to take on her memoirs.'

'I think Jonathan's pulling your leg, Gregory.'

Gregory Stern tapped his decorations with his fingernails. Less impressive than Gamp's, they were nevertheless more reputable than Detterling's. My only consolation, thought Detterling, is that Tom Llewyllyn has none at all.

'People are always pulling my leg,' said Gregory Stern with huffy amiability. 'Isobel my wife does nothing else. Her latest joke,' he said with pride, 'is to pretend I wish to be knighted like George Weidenfeld. "Poor Gregory," she says, "you will never win your spurs until you publish lots of books with glossy pictures, just like George's. The Queen likes only picture books, and that is why she has made Georgie a knight." "Pictures are expensive," I tell her : "Detterling and I cannot afford them." "Never mind," she says, "to me you are always my own true Yiddisher knight, my shining Hebrew horseman, my Jewish jouster with the peerless lance".'

'Was Isobel cross at not being asked to this?' said Detterling.

'No. "You have your night out with the boys," she said, "and don't mind about me. Englishmen are all queer really, even you, my lovely Levantine, which is why they are always having parties for the boys." She did not know, you see, that this Miss Maisie was coming. I think,' he said, looking at Maisie, who was deep in conversation with Canteloupe, 'that she is a tart.'

'Darling Gregory,' said Jonathan Gamp.

'But we shall not talk of that. We shall talk of Somerset our friend whom we are here to remember. Ai-yai,' he smiled wistfully at Tom, 'it seems only yesterday that we were young, and you were writing *The Bear's Embrace*, and our friend Somerset was in Gower Street, Editor of *Strix*.'

'We are not so very old now,' said Tom.

'And yet already Somerset is gone. We shall not look upon his like again,' said Gregory, 'and just as well, perhaps. But he is a loss, Somerset our friend. Come, Tom, Detterling, Jonathan, a toast to our old friend. To Somerset, sailing over Acheron.'

As they drank they were interrupted by Carton Weir.

'Canteloupe says it's time to go in,' he told them in his fussiest A.D.C. manner; 'please don't hang about.'

He shepherded them all towards the door which led to the dining-room. Peter Morrison was just disappearing through this, while Canteloupe, with Maisie, was standing to the left of it.

'Your hostess, Miss Maisie Malcolm,' said Canteloupe.

Maisie smiled like a princess, and held out her hand to each of them as they filed past her and into a short corridor.

'What's all that about?' whispered Detterling to Weir. 'Our hostess?'

'Don't ask me. It's the way he wants the thing done. He's planned it all very particularly from beginning to end. Now go on in.'

Detterling stepped from the corridor into what he supposed was the dining-room, looked about him, and then shuddered with delight.

For he had not entered a room; he had passed, as it seemed, out into the open air, into a little grove of trees, which must surely be high up in the mountains, because the view from where he stood was of a re-entrant that descended almost sheer from the far end of the grove, and then slowly widened and levelled until, thousands of feet below, it ran into a broad plain which was traversed by noble aqueducts and bounded by the distant sea. On either side of Detterling, he now saw, peaks towered into a gentle early-evening sky; a stream cascaded from rocks just behind his left shoulder, ran across the grove at his feet, and descended with the re-entrant into the plain, where it became a broad river on which barges and caiques rode

slowly between fields and townships, to and from a harbour
at the river's mouth. On the right of the grove was a wall of
rock and in the wall the mouth of a cave; set on the grass
between this and the stream was a table of marble,
crowded with wine-jars and cornucopias and birds of brilliant plumage. In a circle round the table stood young boys
and girls, ready to serve, dressed in dainty white tunics
which ended just above the knee; and in a larger circle, a
few feet outside the ring of pretty little servants, were the
couches on which the guests would recline, each couch
being shaded from the evening sun (which was sinking towards the sea) by a small tree of holm-oak or lady-birch.

The seating plan had shown eight names but nine places;
and on the ninth couch, which was set before the mouth
of the cave, was a skeleton caparisoned in ermine, which
lay open to show the bones beneath.

'Very quaint,' whispered Jonathan Gamp to Detterling.
'It was Canteloupe's idea, but I helped him work it all
out. We got Oliver Messel to do the décor and the *trompe*.'

But Detterling hardly heard him. He and the other guests
stood speechless, now looking on the reclining skeleton
(whose skull was propped by the hand of one splintery
arm), now gazing out over the plain towards the sea. At
last the silence was broken by Maisie:

'Loopy dear, how he'd have loved it,' she said, and kissed
Canteloupe wetly on the lips.

Canteloupe looked gratified.

'Places, please,' he said in a gruff voice.

Canteloupe and Maisie went to their couches, Canteloupe's to the left of the skeleton, Maisie's to its right.
On Maisie's right was Tom Llewyllyn, on his Peter Morrison, and on his again Captain Detterling; Weir, Stern and
Gamp completed the circle to Canteloupe. As they settled,
there was a sound of flutes among the trees, and the cup-
bearers came forward from the table to serve each guest
with a beaker of wine.

'To our Guest of Honour,' called Canteloupe: 'a bumper
to Old Death;' and all the revellers raised their winecups

while the servants stretched out their arms before their faces and bowed to the ground.

It is not easy to recline comfortably in evening dress with medals, and before long all the guests (except Old Death) were in fact sitting on their couches, bending forward to feed themselves from the little tables on which each course was served to them. As the second course (a soup of écrevisses) was being cleared, the diners joined each other, two to a couch, the better to converse. Tom Llewyllyn joined Maisie, and Detterling joined Peter Morrison. In the grove behind them nymphs and satyrs rustled and flitted and tittered; and against the tree which overshadowed the couch just vacated by Detterling a cross-legged faun now leaned, piping a ditty of thin, spiteful tone.

'What do you make of all this?' said Peter Morrison.

'Unexpectedly imaginative – for Canteloupe.'

'He has more imagination than you might think. I've learnt that since I've been working for him. Canteloupe, Detterling, is a romantic.'

'And your work for him ... is that romantic?'

'The conception behind it is. Or at any rate the conception that is behind our activity in Strasbourg – which is the main part of our work at the moment.'

'From what Canteloupe told me some weeks back, it seemed essentially a matter of common sense. Whoever went to this Convention at Strasbourg, he said, must discredit rival products on exhibition at the Trade Fair there. Our great hope, I remember, is some new light metal alloy; so I suppose you spend your days running down other people's light metal alloys. Not very romantic, Peter.'

'Yes, very,' Morrison insisted. 'That's why I'm back in London at the moment and able to come to this dinner. The romance is coming to a crisis, and I have to consult very urgently with Canteloupe.'

'Well, I'd be glad to know how you squeeze romance out of light metal alloys.'

'It all starts with Somerset. You remember that before

he died he'd interested Canteloupe in a special plan for Strasbourg?'

The sun sank close to the sea below them and lights began to appear in the towns along the river. Somerset's plan for Strasbourg, Detterling thought: there could be something here. Although Canteloupe had denied that Somerset's operations for the Ministry had anything to do with his death, that might (just might) have been policy on the part of the Minister.

'Yes, I remember,' he said to Peter Morrison. 'So you've inherited Somerset's plan – and romance along with it?'

'Yes. I'm afraid I can't go into details.'

'But you can tell me the general principle?'

'If you like ...'

The third course was served to them, quails' eggs in aspic. A nymph ran out of the cave and started, reverently but fiercely, to make love to the skeleton. Grinning satyrs capered with delight as she unrobed and embraced it.

'That,' said Morrison, pointing at the spectacle, 'that is the general principle behind the plan which Somerset left to us.'

'Be plainer, my dear.'

'Assume that skeleton is the rival product you wish to discredit. You start by paying someone to show interest in it and evince mounting pleasure, just as that poor girl is doing. The pleasure rises until it approaches climax; the audience looks on breathless; the girl has her orgasm and very nearly faints with delight. But of course everyone really knows that the whole thing has been faked. Cleverly faked, no doubt,' said Peter, as the girl swooned to the ground and was carted off by the satyrs, 'but nevertheless faked. Now, consider: if, as I say, the skeleton equals the product to be done down, and the girl equals the agent you have hired to simulate enthusiasm, what have you achieved?'

'I've achieved nothing. Indeed, I've helped my rivals. I've advertised their product by getting up a public demonstration of how desirable it is.'

'Except,' said Peter, 'that the public realizes the desire was *faked*. So you then start a rumour that the agent was in fact employed by the makers of the product, in a bid to achieve false prestige for it. What a pity for them, you say scornfully, that they couldn't afford a better actor, that the final orgasm over their product clearly wasn't genuine. Are you with me, Detterling?'

'Not entirely, old man.'

'Well then, in real terms. We have set up what appears to be an international consortium (I'm sorry, but I mustn't name it to you) which wishes to buy light metal alloys. This consortium shows interest and then intense pleasure in the product of our rival, whom we shall call "X". The affair culminates in a dramatic deal – so dramatic that there is something suspect about it, we see to that. And then we spread a highly circumstantial rumour, to the effect that the "international consortium" is in fact a phony which "X" himself has rigged up to advertise his product by feigning enthusiasm for it. What a pity for "X" we tell everyone with a sneer, that the enthusiasm was so evidently theatrical; no one will be taken in by *that*. Thus "X" and his product are discredited by the charade; and the audience comes flocking to buy our metal alloys instead.'

'Suppose,' said Detterling, 'that the news gets round that it was really your phony consortium and a charade of your making?'

'We should be in trouble,' said Peter Morrison; 'but at the moment all is well over that. Our problem just now is that although we are approaching the fake climax on schedule, it promises, for various reasons, to look very much too genuine. There has not been enough spurious ecstasy. If we are not careful, we shall wind up with a performance so realistically played that people will actually believe in it and we shall have provided, *gratis*, a valuable advertisement for "X" instead of making him look silly.'

'I see. And hence the necessity to consult with Canteloupe?'

'Yes. You understand what I mean by calling the strata-
gem romantic?'

'I do. It is not the first time that "romantic" has been
used as an euphemism for dishonest.'

'Let's call it ... an exercise in sleight of hand. Other
people over there are being much nastier, Detterling. Our
rivals use violence, blackmail, political pressure. Compared
with theirs, our methods are positively decent ... as well
as being rather witty, as Somerset might have said.'

The old Morrison, thought Detterling: always ready
with the right reason for doing the wrong thing. In telling
Canteloupe to appoint him, I certainly gave good advice.
Aloud he said:

'One thing, Peter. It's important I should know. Is there
the remotest chance that the preparations for producing
this illusion could have laid Somerset open to something –
this blackmail you talk of, perhaps – that might have led
to his suicide?'

'None whatever,' said Morrison flatly. 'At the time Somerset died, the thing was only an idea, and known only to
him and to Canteloupe.'

Another dud trail, Detterling thought. A pity; but then I
never had much hope of it. I must start somebody else off
talking. Will Peter be offended if I move to another couch?

As Detterling wondered how to shift his place without
giving offence, the sun slipped into the sea and the evening
star appeared high over the nearest peak. The table and the
circle of couches were now lit by torches of pine; a little
breeze shivered in the leaves above them; and as the boys
and girls cleared the third course, the music of flutes began
again in the heart of the grove. Then sudden silence. Then
the sound of crying, the flutes once more, thin wails of
anguish both from human throats and from the instru-
ments. A figure in white *cap-à-pie*, pointing up at the evening star. A sweet, pure voice:

> 'Weep no more, woeful shepherds, weep no more,
> For Lycidas, your sorrow, is not dead,

Sunk though he be beneath the wat'ry floor;
So sinks the day-star in the ocean bed,
And yet anon repairs his drooping head ...'

I can't move while this is going on, thought Detterling. A silly poem, I always considered. Yet the old man at school used to say that this passage was the most musical in all English poetry.

'So Lycidas sunk low, but mounted high,
Through the dear might of him that walked the waves,
Where, other groves and other streams along,
With nectar pure his oozy locks he laves,
And hears the unexpressive nuptial song
In the blest kingdom meek of joy and love.'

Ridiculous, thought Detterling. Imagine the old twister risen up to the 'blest kingdom meek' and listening to the 'unexpressive nuptial song'. Clothed all in white, like this fellow who's reciting. Too absurd. And yet ... the lines soared on in irresistible triumph; and now the stars were coming out, one by one, and gathering round the evening star, that was Hesperus ... Lycidas ... Somerset ...

'There entertain him all the saints above,
In solemn troops and sweet societies
That sing, and singing in their glory move,
And wipe the tears for ever from his eyes.
Now, Lycidas, the shepherds weep no more;
Henceforth thou art the Genius of the shore.'

But Detterling was still weeping and so was Peter Morrison, tears and snot dribbling down his face and off his chin. I can't leave him just yet, Detterling thought, I'd better sit here and get control of myself. Say something; we can't sit here blubbering like a pair of schoolgirls; say something to get a normal conversation going again.

'If only we knew,' he said off the top of his head, 'where he went to on his last day.'

'What was that?' snivelled Peter.

'I've been trying to find out,' said Detterling, 'why he did it. There has been absolutely no clue.'

'What was that you said about "his last day"?'

'The last day of his life. Before he came home and killed himself. His servant said he went somewhere; out of London, she said. Nobody knows where.'

The boys and girls were distributing the next course: tiny chickens stuffed with truffles and foie gras.

'Listen,' said Peter to Detterling after they had been served: 'you know Ivan Blessington, don't you? He was in your regiment.'

'Yes,' said Detterling. We might as well talk about him as anyone, he thought, though God knows what made Peter think of him. 'Yes. He's a lot younger than me, of course, but he joined some time before I resigned. I never knew him well, but I kept in touch, for a time at least. I used to hear interesting things from him when he was military attaché in Washington.'

'He's out of the army now.'

'Working for a merchant bank, I believe.'

'Yes. The Corcyran. Off-shoot of the Corinthian. He's been in Strasbourg – at this Convention.'

'Don't tell me he's anything to do with this fake consortium of yours.'

'As a matter of fact he is. But that's not the point.'

'What is the point, Peter?'

'Somerset's last day.'

'What's that got to do with Ivan Blessington?'

'He told me something. It might help you.'

'What could he possibly know about it?'

'Listen. Listen.'

A beat of drums, very low, very slow, was coming from the centre of the grove.

'Drums,' said Detterling.

'No. Listen to *me*, Detterling.' Peter leaned close to his companion and started to talk fast and earnestly. 'A few days ago I met Ivan Blessington in Strasbourg. After we'd discussed our ... our business, I mentioned that I was coming to London, and to this dinner for Somerset. Now, Detterling, listen very carefully ...

' "... Pity about old Somerset," Ivan Blessington had said to Peter Morrison in Strasbourg.

"Yes."

"I saw him only a day or so before he died. I was at the Ministry of Commerce for something, so I popped in on him to say 'Hallo'. He seemed in very good nick. Top of the world. Very pleased with himself about something."

"Pleased with himself?" Peter Morrison had said. "Only a day or so before he died?"

"Yes. So pleased that it rather got on my nerves. Made me fell quite ill-natured, you know how it is. So just to give him a prick, I reminded him of that party he threw years ago – you remember, on the last night of the Summer Quarter in '45. When he was sick all over the place."

"I remember. Fielding Gray was there. And Christopher Roland."

Silence for a moment. Then,

"I didn't make anything of that," Ivan Blessington said; "I just ribbed him about how he was sick. You know, to pull him down a peg or two. But it didn't. He seemed more pleased with himself than ever. 'That party,' he said; 'thereby hangs a tale.' Which he told me there and then. So tickled he was, he couldn't keep it to himself. Not at all the usual canny old Somerset – he was just bubbling at the seams with it."

"What did he tell you?"

"Well, you remember we all left him, clean out, with his head on his desk. It seems he woke up about three hours later, was sick again before he could stop himself, but this time was strong enough to get off to bed. And before he went he pulled himself together and wrote a note of apology for the boys' skivvy, who'd have to clean up the mess in the morning, and with the note he left her half a crown for her trouble." '

'It should have been five bob. Five bob was the going rate for sick.'

' "Ah. When he woke up in the morning he found the boys' skivvy standing over his bed and saying just that. In a loud voice. 'Five bob, Mr Lloyd-James,' she said, waving his note in the air: 'it's five bob for cleaning up filth like you left, and so I've come up here to tell you.' So Somerset blinked and sat up, and then he realized it must be quite late, because the two other senior boys, who shared his dormitory with him, had already gone. 'What time is it?' he said. 'Time for me to get my five bob,' said the boys' skivvy, 'that's what time it is. And time for you to get up and go home like the rest of 'em. The whole place is empty,' she said, 'except for you and the cat.' And then Somerset looked at the boys' skivvy, and saw a well set up young woman with a red round face, an angry face just then but underneath the anger a pleasant one. And the boys' skivvy looked at Somerset, and saw an acne'd adolescent with a hangover, but also saw something else which women, I'm told, often seemed to see in Somerset, a kind of elemental libido pushing up under the shag-spots. And so they both looked at each other, and all around them was the strange, eerie silence which the boys had left behind them, the sort of silence which says you've got no business to be where you are, but since you *are* there you can do anything you want to, because you're in a place which isn't real at a time which doesn't count. 'Empty?' said Somerset. 'Empty,' said the boys' skivvy, not angry any more, standing over the bed ... bending over the bed and slowly pulling back the bedclothes and very pleased with what she saw – there's nothing like a hangover to bring you on in the morning – and starting, there and then, on a nice healthy piece of mid-morning exercise."

"Rather odd," Peter Morrison said to Ivan Blessington, "that Somerset was so pleased with himself just because he'd had the boys' skivvy one morning long ago."

"That wasn't the end of it – though Somerset thought it was at the time. A few weeks later, before the next quar-

ter began, he had a letter from the skivvy (addressed c/o
the school and forwarded by the porter) which said she
was going off to be married and leaving her job at the
school, so ta-ta for good, but hadn't it been jolly? Yes it
had, thought Somerset, but just as well she'd be out of the
way when he got back in September. And out of the
way she remained for twenty-seven years. Until a few
days before Somerset and I were having this conversation.
And then he'd had another letter from her. Did he remember that morning long ago, after the boys had gone? She'd
left the school to get married, as she'd written at the time;
and then she'd had a child. Not her husband's, Somerset's.
But she'd passed the boy off on her husband all right, and
indeed she would never have told Somerset at all, only her
husband was just dead, leaving her and her son, who was
unmarried and still lived with her, really rather poor. Since
Somerset was really rather rich (or so she gathered from
the newspapers) would he care to help? She was aware she
had no legal claim, and she wouldn't dream of making a
fuss – *couldn't*, after all this time, as she very well knew –
but all the same she would be most grateful, et cetera, et
cetera. And if Somerset wanted to be sure the boy was his,
would he care to come and meet him? He'd be certain the
moment he saw him."

"And that's why Somerset was so excited. He'd never
been a father, he said, and he was intrigued by the idea.
There could be no danger of scandal – it was all too long
ago, and the tone of the woman's letter had been very
agreeable. She couldn't and wouldn't make trouble. So he
was going to help her, see what he could do for her and
the boy; it would be great fun, helping him on in the
world, like an eighteenth century grandee and his bastard,
like Chesterfield and Stanhope. He was looking forward
very much to meeting his son – and he was going down to
the country to do so the very next morning ...'"

'...And that,' said Peter to Detterling, as the drum beats
from the centre of the grove began to quicken, 'was what
Ivan Blessington told me in Strasbourg. But you see what

I'm getting at? According to Ivan, he'd heard all this from Somerset "a day or so before he died", and Somerset was going down to the country to see his newly discovered son "on the very next morning" ...'

'So *that* must have been what Somerset was doing on the day before the night he killed himself.'

'Exactly,' said Peter. 'Somerset's last day ... about which you could find out nothing ...'

'... Until now. He went into the country, as Dolly the servant told us ... saw his son and the mother ... came back ... and committed suicide. *Why*, Peter?'

'How should I know?'

A golden glow was now spreading like a halo behind the tallest of the peaks that rose above them. The drums quickened still more.

'As Somerset told Ivan, there was no fear of scandal. On the contrary, there was the promise of pleasure and amusement, and plenty of money to make the very most of the situation. So Somerset was pleased, tickled pink, before he went. And yet, when he came back ... where did he go, Peter? Where did this woman live?'

'I asked that, *and* the woman's name; but Ivan didn't know because Somerset hadn't told him, and it hadn't occurred to Ivan to ask. It would have been most impolite.'

'Oh, bloody hell,' said Detterling. 'There must be some connexion between that journey and Somerset's suicide. Somerset wasn't afraid of scandal or blackmail, nothing like that, but some connexion between all this and Somerset's death there just must be. If we could find that woman ...'

'I've told you all I know, Detterling. You might find out about her from Somerset's old House at school. After all, she was employed there.'

'Yes,' grouched Detterling; 'in 1945, twenty-seven years ago. How can I possibly hope that she'll still be re—'

He broke off to give a long, deep sigh of pleasure. For the golden glow behind the peak had suddenly turned into a full round moon, which now sailed out to illumine the plain below and the re-entrant which led from it to the

grove. Up the re-entrant a procession was coming, in single
file along the right-hand bank of the stream. The procession
was still distant; but a faint beat of drums could be heard
from it, which was now answered by the drums in the
grove. After three or four tattoos had been given and answered in this way, the members of the procession began to
chant; and as they came closer, Detterling could distinguish
the words:

> 'Dies irae, dies illa,
> Solvet saeclum in favilla
> Teste David cum Sibylla ...

A stripling boy set large glasses of cognac before Detterling and Peter; he was followed by a girl, who placed
wreaths of rose petals on their heads.

> 'Day of wrath and doom impending,
> David's word with Sibyl's blending,
> Heaven and earth in ashes ending ...'

The procession was much nearer now. By the light of
the torches which some of its members carried Detterling
began to make them out more plainly; they wore white
cowls and their faces were bowed and invisible in their
hoods.

> 'Quantus tremor est futurus
> Quando Judex est venturus
> Cuncta stricte discussurus ...'

The procession wound out of sight as the re-entrant nar-
rowed and turned steeper. They'll be in the dead ground
beneath the lip of the grove, thought Detterling, making
the final ascent up here. The sound of their voices is nearer
every second. But these are only shadows on a wall, he
thought: they can never reach us. Wrong. Over the brow
of the hill they came, flesh and blood, still chanting:

'The dead are risen from the tomb,
Lo at last the Judge is come,
To unseal the Book of Doom.'

Then silence, absolute silence.

As the single file of white monks threaded its way through the grove, the nymphs and satyrs rose up out of the nooks and bushes to greet them. Swiftly the two parties paired off, one nymph or satyr to each monk, and two by two they advanced towards the diners, then swung right or left to pass round them, then took up stations in front of the cave-mouth and behind the couch on which the skeleton reclined. Still an unbroken silence except for the slight swish of the monks' habits.

'What now?' whispered Peter to Detterling in a troubled voice.

Several of the monks were carrying the drums which had been heard beating down in the valley. One of these now played a brief roll, and then, after a pause, gave a single sharp beat. As at a signal all the monks raised their bowed heads. Another beat, and they swept back their hoods.

'Oh, Christ,' said Peter.

The faces were representative of disease. There was the chalk-white and wasted face of tuberculosis, the drooping mouth and wall eye of the incurable stroke, and the wild, slobbering grin of sheer idiocy; there were cheekbones laid raw by leprosy, noses flattened by the pox, and chins so eaten with cancer that they appeared to have been freshly carded by nails. There were lolling tongues, black buboes, and huge wet open ulcers where there should have been lips; there were goitres hanging like bunches of grapes and eyes running with pus.

'Christ,' Peter said again.

But the nymphs and satyrs raised a howl of happy laughter. They pranced and capered with glee, nudging each other and pointing to particularly succulent deformities, running hither and thither to relish each exhibit, pressing their bodies up against the monks to peer even more closely at their sores and carbuncles. A lively tune sprang up, and they began to dance.

'Hey nonny no,' they sang, 'hey nonny nonny no.'
Round and round the monks they danced.

> 'It's a splendid thing to laugh and sing
> When the bells of death do ring
> And turn upon the toe
> And cry "Hey nonny no,
> Hey nonny nonny no".'

And the monks began to dance with the nymphs and satyrs. At first reluctantly, then faster and more warmly, then lewdly. As they danced they sang and laughed and gibbered. As before, the two parties paired off, one monk to each nymph or satyr. The little servants, the boys and girls, danced too. Some of them partnered each other, some of them attached themselves as satellites to adult couples, some of them danced singly, leaping up and down for the joy of it. The dance spread, came swirling among the couches. Bottles and dainties were seized from the marble table; bumpers were drunk, food torn and gobbled.

'Hey nonny no; hey nonny nonny no.'

The monks ripped away their habits, revealing petticoats and pantaloons of tainted linen, and bodies as deformed and festering as were their faces. The nymphs and satyrs laughed the louder and sang and danced the faster.

> 'Oh-ho-ho, a splendid thing
> When the bells of death do ring
> To dance and drink
> And laugh and stink
> And turn upon the toe
> And cry "Hey nonny no".'

And couple by couple, group by group, child by child, they danced past Death, saluting him, as they went, with

blown kisses or arms outstretched in gratitude, and away
into the cave. One by one the stars began to go out, and the
moon failed. Pitch darkness. And from the cave, wild,
piercing laughter; unquenchable; peal after peal; the laughter of those who are about to sink, madly, foully, irre-
claimably, into an oblivion of lust.

'Lights,' called the Marquis Canteloupe: 'LIGHTS.'

The laughter stopped as if it had been switched off.
Some bright bare bulbs lit up round walls which had been
daubed with crude patches of paint and hung about with
pieces of gauze and sacking and tissue paper. There was a
gutter where the stream had been; gaps between squares of
turf; pots showing through the paper foliage at the base of
the trees. Here and there Detterling saw half-hidden pro-
jectors which were trained on to some part of the wall. At
the end of the grove the top of a step-ladder protruded
above a slab of green cardboard. Four or five tired and
middle-aged midgets, their faces running with grease paint,
came out of a nasty gash in one wall and started to help
themselves to the broken meats on the table, wiping their
fingers, from time to time, on knee-length smocks of coarse
and grubby cotton.

'Though it was only a cardboard moon,' sang Jonathan
Gamp,

> Sailing over a painted sea,
> Though it was only make-believe
> It was paradise to me.

Congratulations, Canteloupe. A very pretty show. I only
hope Oliver doesn't charge too much.'

'Very animated,' observed Peter Morrison, 'but what did
it all add up to?'

'Easy,' said Maisie: 'old Somerset rises up out of his
watery grave and becomes the Genius of the Shore, like the
poet says. This bit of shore' – she waved towards where
the sea had been – 'and so he lives in this wood in the
mountains overlooking it. Right?'

'Right,' said Detterling.

'But of course anywhere old Somerset lives there's bound to be goings-on, and so this is where all the monks and that sort come up for a nice secret dirty.'

'But why such horrible monks?' said Carton Weir. 'Dropping to bits they were.'

'White monks,' said Gregory Stern tentatively: 'White Friars. They once had a monastery in Fleet Street and gave their name to the district. Diseased White Friars from Fleet Street equal journalists – the corrupt and filthy priests of our own age who also parade themselves in shining white. Somerset, himself once a journalist and later an editor, becomes the patron saint of the whole rabble. Am I right?' he said to Canteloupe.

'Ingenious,' said Canteloupe, 'but a bit too specialized. You could say those whited monks were the entire modern establishment, the whole rotten, greedy, envious, trendy mob, not only of journalists, but of politicians and lawyers and dons and businessmen – the lot. And there's one thing more. Those nymphs and whatever. They were the creatures of Somerset's grove, and they were prepared to give those filthy old monks a good time, taking great pleasure, as you saw, in what they were doing and without any apparent fear that they themselves might be infected. What does that suggest to you?'

There was a long silence.

'That Somerset enjoyed playing with dirt?' said Detterling at last.

'And also that he was immune from it. It never stuck to him long enough,' said Canteloupe, 'to get under his skin. Or you might say he was like a scientist – examining all kinds of disgusting microbes but never getting bitten. His was the pure spirit of investigation.'

'He certainly knew how to investigate,' said Maisie fondly.

'But something got him in the end,' said Detterling. 'One of those microbes got through his rubber gloves. You're sure,' he said aside to Peter, 'that Ivan didn't know that woman's name? Or where she lives with the boy?'

'Quite sure.'

'Because if only we could find them...'

'I've told you. Try his old House at school. They may have records of their employees.'

'What's all this muttering?' said Canteloupe.

'Peter has been telling me about the very last investigation which Somerset undertook. It could be the one that proved fatal.'

'Ah well,' said Canteloupe softly, 'even *his* luck had to run out some time. "Weep no more, woeful shepherds, weep no more." He had a fucking good ride for his money.'

'Such goings-on,' said Percival the next morning, after Detterling had rendered an account of the dinner. 'And one big dividend. Now we know where he went on his last day.'

'Correction. We know his errand. We do not know where it took him, and we do not know the name of the people he went to see.'

'Well, Morrison was quite right about that: we must go to Somerset's House at your old school. They have long memories in places like that.'

'The Housemaster will have changed at least twice since that woman left in 1945,' said Detterling; 'and the man that had the House in Somerset's time is dead.'

'Never mind. There'll be others who could remember. Let's be off, Detterling.'

Detterling rang a bell.

'I keep asking myself,' he said, 'what could have happened on that journey to make Somerset do what he did. He was pleased with the woman's letter, he was reassured by the manner of her approach, he was looking forward to his visit...'

'The journey may have nothing to do with his death,' said Percival. 'We are not entitled to make any assumptions. We just follow where the arrow points – and at the moment it points to your old school. Going to wear the tie, are you?'

'No,' said Detterling crossly; 'it looks like the flag of a banana republic. I shall wear the one I have on. Hamilton's Horse.'

'Yes, I remember the crest,' said Percival, looking at it closely: 'the skull and coronet. Really rather appropriate – in our present line of business as well. But someone did tell me once that crested ties were common.'

'That depends on the crest. Corporal,' said Detterling to his manservant, who was now standing to attention in answer to the bell, 'please have the car round in ten minutes.'

'Order of dress, sir?'

'Summer order: light tunic and overall trousers.'

'Sir,' said the manservant.

'Do you go back to the old place often?' said Percival, as the Mercedes ran past Virginia Water.

'About once a year. Usually to watch the Eleven in the summer.'

'Were you happy there?'

'I suppose so. I managed to be quite important towards the end of my time. Senior cricket colour next to the Captain, second Monitor in my House. But it wasn't a very good school, you know, not in the '30s, when I was there. Narrow, with a priggish Headmaster. Mind you, a good man took over in 1935 – but that was after I'd left. There was only one of the beaks I had any time for – the Senior Usher, "the old man", as we called him. He taught the Sixth Classical.'

'But I suppose you were in the army class?'

'No. That was run by a little brute called Morris. I read the classics, and punched up enough stuff for Sandhurst on the side. You couldn't fail Sandhurst in those days unless your head was made of teak.'

'Why did you go into the army, Detterling? Family tradition?'

'No. My family don't run to traditions. We're just

money, Leonard – very old money by now, so we pass as
belonging to the old gang, but in fact we don't because
none of us has ever served the country. We've just taken
and spent.'

'You served in the army.'

'You should have a fair idea after what I've told you,
Leonard, of the quality of my service.'

'Well … let's just say, I don't think that *au fond* you
were suited to the army. Which brings me back to my
question : what sent you to Sandhurst in the first place?'

'I *wanted* to serve, Leonard. I wanted to be unlike my
family and serve my King and country as a gentleman
should. The trouble was … I just couldn't.' Detterling
winced. 'But by the time I found that out, it was too late.
I couldn't resign because the war was coming. There I was,
stuck with my regular commission.'

'But you quite enjoyed the life, and you liked your regiment?'

'Oh, yes.'

'Then why couldn't you serve it?'

'Because they took our horses away. That was one thing.
Up till 1939 we had horses, and I liked what I was doing,
and I understood it, and I valued it. But then … tanks.'
Detterling shuddered. 'But it wasn't just that, Leonard. It
wasn't just the tanks that turned me into such a putrid soldier. It was something inside myself – something that's
always been inside us Detterlings – a kind of rock-hard
egotism that dictates, always and everywhere, *Detterling
first*; Detterling before honour, before service, before
friends, before love, before truth; Detterling before his
regiment – before his sovereign, his country or his God.
Although one side of me longed to serve faithfully, to be a
loyal officer and lead my men with courage and skill, something else in me, the Detterling curse you might call it,
dictated that if ever my life or my body, or even just my
comfort, was at risk, I should immediately place my convenience before my obligations and contrive to bilk my

duty in order to preserve my skin. Since I did this very cleverly, very plausibly, I was never finally disgraced; not even in my own eyes, because the Detterling curse carries complacency along with it.'

'It's on record,' said Percival, 'that you rejoined your regiment for the Suez expedition in '56 – though you'd resigned some years previously. That seems very quixotic behaviour and refutes what you say of yourself.'

'I had to go, as far as I remember. Even though I'd resigned, I had to stay on the Reserve for a time. RARO Class I. They called us back for the Suez rumpus, and that was that.'

'You could have excused yourself as an M.P.'

'I dare say. I suppose,' said Detterling, 'that the chivalrous side of me was strong enough to make me answer the trumpet. But the Detterling strain saw to it that I never got within range of a bullet. Graceful and ingenious shirking – that's what we Detterlings are bred to.'

'You're a distant cousin of Canteloupe's. Would you say the same kind of thing about him?'

'No. The Sarums – that's his family name – the Sarums, like the Detterlings, started as money. But they got beyond it. They have served. Canteloupe himself has served. If you ask him what he did in the war, he'll tell you he liaised with the Free French, and set up a chain of brothels for the allied troops during the invasion of Europe. What he might also tell you, but won't, is that he led the remnants of a smashed battalion clean through the German lines and into Dunkirk in time to get a ship out. He should have had at least a D.S.O. for it, but the Army Council wasn't in a very giving frame of mind just then.'

'Come to that, Canteloupe still serves, as a Minister of the Crown. And so do you, Detterling, as a member of Parliament.'

'Thank you for trying to defend me, Leonard, but I'm bogus on that count too. My seat in Parliament is like my commission in Hamilton's Horse; I wanted it and so it was got for me. But neither before or afterwards did I do anything to earn or deserve it. Whereas Canteloupe, in his maverick way, is quite genuine: he deserves his place, Leonard; he believes in what he's doing and he does it with all his might.'

'Well, at least you've done one thing: you've helped me – and I mean *helped*, Detterling – in a necessary and perhaps important enquiry.'

'Thank you, Leonard. But even here my motives are private: curiosity about an old friend. Detterlings do not serve. It might be our family motto.'

For some time the Mercedes had been climbing a steep hill. Now the car took a very sharp turn to the right, and after a hundred yards turned right again, over a bridge that crossed the road by which they had ascended. At the far end of the bridge was a gatehouse, of modern but not unseemly design, having a broad arch at its centre through which they presently passed. On their left were now lawns and a somewhat officious twentieth-century chapel; while in front of them and to their right was a messy sprawl of late Victorian buildings, from among which protruded several capped and rebarbative towers. Yet the whole was not displeasing. The buildings, ugly in themselves, had settled down together in their place; they knew their business here.

'*Alma mater*,' said Detterling in a mocking voice, 'and welcome to it.'

But even as he spoke he felt his eyes prick, as they always did when he came back.

'Well, well, well,' said Percival, his glasses glinting in the sun. 'So this is where you all grew up. You, and then Somerset and Morrison ... and Fielding Gray. Can you see your own ghost?'

'Yes,' said Detterling. He pointed to some trees that stood beyond the far end of the chapel, and to a green field which lay on the other side of them. 'On that field,' he said; 'batting in the middle of it.'

'We must go and meet him later. But first,' said Percival, 'we have work to do. Where do we begin?'

They began with the Housemaster of Somerset's old House. He and his wife had been there since 1967. There were no records of domestic staff, they said, which went back further than 1965. The House Matron, who had been there since 1964, deposed that the House Butler, who went back to 1955, might be able to help. The House Butler remarked, irrelevantly, that the office of Boys' Maid had been abolished in 1960, in accordance with the social scruples of the egalitarian Housemaster then incumbent. However, the gentlemen might be interested to know that lists of all employees together with their personal particulars were sent in by every House, once a year, to the Comptroller of the School Burse, or Bursar for short, who was responsible for making a statistical return to the Ministry of Labour. It was at least possible that this system had its origins in wartime regulations and therefore that the woman they sought would be on record in the Bursar's office.

· Indeed she should be, the Bursar agreed ... if his secretary could only find the back records. If they would care to come back that afternoon ... no, it was his secretary's half-day off ... tomorrow ... no, he himself had to be in London for a Committee meeting ... the next day, perhaps? At this stage Leonard Percival rose to his feet, went to a shelf and took down a box-file which was clearly labelled *Menial Employees: 1942–47*. The Bursar, deprived of the pleasures of obstruction, went puce with self-righteous fury, began to say something about 'presumption', was silenced by a quick look from Percival (a look which Detterling hadn't seen before and hoped not to see again), and consented to turn up the year 1945.

The returning date had been March 1; and the Boys' Maid in Somerset's House at that time had been 'ATWELL, Mrs Albert (Enid Silvia), of 22 Blixom Cottages, Nashley, Nr Guildford, age 63 yrs and 7 mns.' A pencilled note beneath the entry stated that Mrs Atwell had died suddenly the following April, and that notification would be received when her successor was appointed; as indeed it had been – but not until September 20 of 1945, against which date a new Boys' Maid was listed as 'TOMPKINS, Mrs Ethel (widow)' etc., etc. In short, the woman who had done the job during the Summer Quarter, Somerset's woman, had slipped through the system unnoticed.

'Bloody hell,' said Detterling.

'What?' said the Bursar.

'Shit,' hissed Detterling.

'Come on, old man,' said Percival; and then insincerely to the Bursar, 'Thank you, sir, for being so helpful.'

When Detterling had calmed down a bit, Leonard Percival suggested a soothing walk on the cricket field which his friend had earlier pointed out. On the way there they passed groups of boys who had just been released from their class-rooms, and Detterling started once more to be angry. The boys mostly had longish hair, which, he explained, he could tolerate, but several of them had taken their ties off and, worst of all, one wore sandals.

Detterling gave this one a particularly fierce look, and was grinned at in return.

'All right,' the boy said, 'I don't like you either.'

But luckily the cricket field was now in sight. They walked along a broad terrace, then down some steps and on to the grass.

'Ah,' said Detterling; 'there's Joe. We'll go and have a word.'

'Who's Joe?'

'The groundsman. Mowing the square in the middle.'

'He looks rather old to be mowing.'

'Groundsmen live to a great age ... as long as they're allowed to go on being groundsmen. 'Morning, Joe,' called Detterling.

''Morning, Mr Detterling,' said Joe. 'Getting any runs this season?'

'I've given up, Joe.'

'Pity. It was a handy 200 you made some years back.'

'Nearly forty years back, Joe.'

'As long as that, is it? Ah well. This here's the only lad,' said Joe to Percival, 'who's made a double century in a school match. I doubt you'd get as many just now,' he said to Detterling. 'I was off poorly this April, and young bastard rolled bugger wrong. Didn't listen to what I told him. Knew best, young bastard did. Two balls in three go flying round their lug-holes and the third slips through flat as an adder. Who's he then?' said Joe, pointing to Percival as if now seeing him for the first time.

'Friend of mine. Mr Percival.'

'Bat does he, or bowl?'

'Neither. But he's all right.'

'If you say so, Mr Detterling . . .'

Joe extended a hand to Percival.

'How do you do,' said Percival as he shook it.

'Not so fine.' Joe turned back to Detterling. 'Retiring next year,' he said.

'Surely not.'

'They say it's time for young bastard to take over.'

'Well, perhaps you could do with a rest.'

'I'll be resting for good soon enough. Young bastard. So idle he is he won't push mower. Has to have one with a motor, dripping petrol all over bloody wicket. Here he comes now for a gossip, lazy young sod.'

A venerable gentleman perhaps five years younger than Joe was walking across to them.

'How do, Mr Detterling? How do, Mr D's friend? You've heard what happened to the wicket then? Joe put down soot last autumn, thinking it were the new weed-killer. Whole thing's full of clinkers.'

'Clinkers my arse.'

'I dare say, Joe. Now Mr D,' said young bastard, 'what about Mr Lloyd-James, now, doing away with himself? He was here well after you was, I reckon, but you must have known him, being in Parliament along with him.'

'Never played cricket so's you'd notice,' said Joe; 'used to watch a lot, though.'

'Did to the end,' said Detterling.

'Played other games,' said young bastard, and winked.

'Let's have respect,' said Joe, 'respect for a dead man even if he weren't a cricketer. He did watch to the end, Mr Detterling said.'

'Oh, I respect him all right, dead or alive. Best of luck to him. Head of the School he was, so I remember. And the best of luck.'

'Then stop making insinuendos.'

'We know what we know, Joe.'

'We only know what Meriel told us.'

'She never told lies. A straight girl, Meriel.'

'Straight enough.'

'What is all this?' said Detterling.

'Just a summer's tale, Mr D. Can't matter if you hear it. Not now. Eh, Joe?'

'Suppose not,' said Joe. 'Not now.'

'What did Meriel tell you? Who was she?'

'Nice girl,' said Joe, rather gruffly. 'They were mostly old hags with gristly tits and legs like bean-poles – because that was in the war, see, or not long after, and all the young ones were off wagging their butts about in uniform. But there was this Meriel, nice, young girl, had something wrong with her feet, so was excused any war service. Here only a few months she was, and used to come down to The Chequers of an evening. Boys' skiv, in one of the Houses.'

'Mr Lloyd-James's House,' said young bastard. 'It was the summer the war ended. They had some plan for doing up the insides of the Houses, which they hadn't been allowed before, because of the war regulations. So they kept Meriel on through August, after the boys had gone, to help with the rough; she was glad of the extra money, she said. And most nights that August she'd be down at The Chequers, never overdid it, not really – till one night she got good and plastered, with the drink running out of her eyeballs. "Bloody hell," she said, "do you know what? I've gone and got a bun in the oven".'

' "Gone and got myself lumbered," ' took up Joe. ' "Who

was it?" we asked her. "One of the boys." "Go on with you." "One of the bleeding boys, I tell you. That Mr Lloyd-James," she says, "with the fancy Christian name. I got hot for him one morning when there was nobody about, and I was that excited I never put a rubber on his john. Lovely job we did," she said; "I come off like a cartload of crackers, I'm telling you that. But now you see what's come of it. Up the spout." '

'So I says,' said the young bastard, pushing himself forward again, 'that Mr Lloyd-James's people are well-to-do and perhaps they'd see to it all if she told them.'

'Nosey, interfering bugger like you always was, knowing everything,' said Joe. 'But she says no, that'd get him into trouble with his parents and probably with the School as well, and she'd heard he's to be Head Boy some time next year, and she wouldn't want to spoil it for him. "Not after that bit of fun we had together," she says; "it makes me wet to think of it, and I'll not do the dirty on him now. It was my fault; I should have put a rubber on his john." Kind girl she was, you see; generous.'

'So then I says,' insisted young bastard, 'that there's Jim Weekes over in the public, what's always liked her. "He's a bit soft," I says, "that's why they wouldn't have him for a soldier, but he's good-hearted and hard-working. If you go and offer him a bit, he'll grab it, and then you can tell him it's his baby on the way, and he's so soft he'll believe it and marry you." '

'Interfering bugger,' said Joe.

' "Well," she says, "I wouldn't mind settling down, and that's the truth, but it seems a bit of a mean trick to play on poor Jim." Generous girl, even if Joe did say it first. "Go on," I says; "he'd marry you anyway for twopence." "Maybe he would. But palming him off with Lloyd-James's get," she says, "it's a bit of a mean trick." "Well, it's now or never," I tells her: "you leave it too long, and even Jim Weekes will know it can't be his, what's cooking." And there and then she's off and into the public, and the next thing we hear, Jim Weekes has up and married her.'

'Where did they live, Mr and Mrs Weekes?' said Detterling.

'I saw her just after the marriage,' said Joe. ' "I'm off,"
she tells me. "Weekes and me are going to live the other
side of Guildford." '

'Where?'

' "I mean to make him a good husband," she tells me
"to make up for you know what, and if we stayed round
here, I'd be hanging about that school all day, hoping
Lloyd-James would come out for a turn in the bushes. No
good for me, now I'm married, and none for him either. So
Weekes and me are going off the other side of Guildford." '

'WHERE?'

' "I don't want Lloyd-James to have no trouble," she said,
"so you keep your mouth shut. It might have been your
brat or young bastard's," she said, "though I know it's not
because of when I started missing, and if it had of been,
you wouldn't have wanted no trouble with the school any
more than he does. So for the sake of the good times we've
all had together—" "—Say no more," I says, "not a word
shall pass these lips." Nor it has, nor young bastard's either.
You can rely on him for some things, I'll say that. But now,
well, since the poor gentleman's gone and there's no harm
talking of it, it's fun to remember. A summer's tale, like
young bastard says, and there won't come another summer
like it.'

'Joe. It is very important that Mr Percival and I should
know where the Weekeses went to.'

'Why?'

'We want to help Mrs Weekes. Her husband is dead.'

'So you knew the whole story?' said young bastard.

'Yes. No. From another angle. I can't explain just now.
The thing is, we must know where to find Mrs Weekes.'

'To see her right?'

'Yes.'

'Sorry Jim Weekes has gone. I never knew. Soft, but you
couldn't help liking him. What happened to him, Mr Detterling?'

'I don't know. Only that he's dead. Please, Joe: where did they go to live?'

'Sorry, Mr Detterling. I've been out of touch with them since they left. It's a long way, the other side of Guildford. Like I say, I didn't even hear that Jim was dead.'

' "The other side of Guildford ..." Surely she must have said where?'

But both Joe and young bastard shook their heads.

'She didn't mean we should meet again. She was going off to start fresh. And now, Mr D and friend, it's time for Joe and me to have our lunch; so if you'll be so kind as to excuse us ...'

Both old gentlemen removed their caps, sweeping them down to their navels. Then they replaced them, turned together, and walked slowly away across the grass.

'Never mind,' said Percival. 'We know the name: Weekes. Somerset House – how appropriate – will have a birth certificate for the child. The certificate will carry the parents' address at the time of the child's birth.'

'There could be thousands of Weekeses.'

'But not all of them born round-about – let's see – April to May of 1946. Anyway, my department is entitled to special assistance in finding such documents. They'll turn it up for us quick enough.'

' "Signature, description and residence of informant," ' read Percival from the birth certificate: ' "Meriel Weekes, mother. 134 Long Lane, Engelfield Green, Surrey." That's it.'

'If she still lives there,' said Detterling. 'What did they call the child?'

'Born on May 1, 1946 ... "Name, if any",' read Percival: ' "James".'

'After the putative father, Jim Weekes. But also, unknown to Weekes, commemorating the real father.'

'No doubt. And now at last,' said Percival, 'it is time to call on Mrs Weekes and James Weekes, junior.'

And once again the deep red Mercedes was summoned, to carry them out of London, through Staines and Egham, to Engelfield Green.

Long Lane was a narrow street, mainly but not entirely residential, winding down a hill. No. 134 was a toy shop, a small old-fashioned toy shop, with a magic lantern in the window and a display of slides, these being arranged in front of a row of torch bulbs and showing, in rich primary colours, knights and princes on horseback, as they rode through deep forests in which lurked ogres and magicians. As Detterling and Percival went through the door, a little bell sounded. A stooping middle-aged woman came through a curtain of raffia and stood behind the counter. Detterling took a deep breath.

'Mrs Meriel Weekes?' he said.

'The same, sir.'

Detterling breathed out again.

'My name is Captain Detterling,' he said, 'and this is my friend, Mr Percival. Let me now try to explain why we've come. I'll suggest, if I may, that unless you have an assistant it might be as well to close the shop. We don't want to be interrupted.'

'Don't you worry, sir. No one else will come.'

'Then perhaps we can go through?'

Detterling indicated the raffia curtain.

'We'll stay in here.'

'Very well.' And Detterling, standing on one side of the counter, started to explain himself to the woman on the other, while Percival examined a row of hand-made dolls and a model railway engine that had been built to run on steam.

'So you think,' said Meriel Weekes when Detterling had finished, 'that Mr Lloyd-James's suicide might have to do with something that happened when he came here?'

'All we know,' said Detterling, 'is that he left London, apparently in good spirits, in order to come here; that he returned to London; and that late that night he killed himself.'

'So can you help us,' said Percival, turning from the model railway engine, 'to fill in the gap?'

'He came here all right,' said Meriel Weekes.

'And of course you were expecting him?'

'Yes. He'd written some days before.'

'Mrs Weekes ... what happened while he was here?'

'He stood there, where you're standing. And I told him.'

'Told him what?'

'Everything that had happened since ... since we last met. About this shop, for a start. How it belonged to an uncle of Weekes's who took him on in 1945. He heard we wanted to move from where we were, and he invited us to come and live here. Weekes was good with his hands, see, and his uncle was getting too old to make things. His sight was going. So he taught Weekes.' She pointed to one of the shelves. 'Those wooden soldiers there: the ones in kilts were made by Weekes's uncle. But the ones in the middle, on horses, were made by Weekes. He took to it. He was ... a simple man, Weekes, but very clever with his fingers.'

'I can see that,' said Detterling, looking up at the beautifully carved and appointed horsemen. 'One of them is from my regiment. I should rather like to buy it, if I may.'

'So time went on,' said Mrs Weekes, ignoring Detterling's request; 'little Jim was born; and Weekes's uncle died three years later, leaving us the shop and four thousand pounds in savings. It was a good time, that, though we were sad when the old man died. There was a decent living in the shop, then, because the people who lived round about were interested. Rich people, who liked the fine and pretty things that Weekes could make. But now all the big houses have gone, and they've built rows of bungalows over the fields, all the way to Runnymede. Another sort has come here now ...

'But then ... then was a good time. Little Jim was growing up nicely, and though we couldn't have no more we didn't mind very much, as long as we had Jim. Weekes never dreamt that Jim wasn't his own, so he was happy; and I was happy if he was, because he was a good, kind husband, and he deserved to be. So we all three lived behind the shop, and good money came in, and everything was as it should be. It wasn't till 1960, even later, that we started to go wrong.'

She paused, went to the raffia curtain, peered through it, and then returned to the counter.

'And all this,' she said, 'I told to Mr Lloyd-James when he came here that day, just as I'm telling you. And then I told him how we went wrong. Like this it was. Little Jim left school in 1961, when he was fifteen, and Weekes wanted him to learn the trade and help him make things to sell in the shop. But little Jim had other ideas. To begin with, he wasn't much use with his hands, having taken after his real father in that. And then he could see, as could I, that already this neighbourhood was changing, and there wasn't the trade which there had been. Even as long ago as that, we were starting to nibble at Weekes's uncle's savings which we'd been left. Not much, not just yet, but nibbling we were. So little Jim said, and I supported him, that the days for this kind of thing' – she jerked her head at the shelves – 'were coming to an end, and that he'd sooner learn some other trade. He fancied something in business or commerce. So the end of it was he got himself a job as an office boy in London, and went up and down every day.'

'Nothing so bad in any of that,' said Percival.

'Not at first, no. Only he'd hurt his father – hurt Weekes, I mean. Weekes had hoped for them to carry on together, father and son (as he thought), and it hurt him that little Jim thought himself too good for the shop. "Don't be silly," I used to tell Weekes, "it isn't that. It's just that he wants something different. And anyway," I said, "it's no bad thing, just now, to have his extra money coming in." But Weekes wouldn't see it. He was a simple man, as I've said, and he didn't realize what was happening in the shop. As long as he could go on modelling soldiers or making dolls, he was happy – or would have been, if he'd had

little Jim doing it along of him. So about this time there was
feeling between the two of them: Weekes being hurt with
Jim and Jim thinking that Weekes wanted to tie him down
to the shop and spoil his chances. And things got worse,
because little Jim started feeling his oats and took to going
with girls – London girls he met at his office. He was still
only young, sixteen or so, but like his father he had a way
with him. Although he was ugly, the dead spit of Somerset,
he had a better skin and a fresher look, and since he put
that same sexy feel into the air that Somerset used to, he
had no trouble getting girls. But he had to treat them and
so on, and he started getting late with the money he paid
me for his board. I didn't tell Weekes that, but Weekes was
angry just the same, because little Jim would stay up in
London till late at night, and Weekes thought a boy's place
was back at home in the evenings and he liked us all three
to be together.

'And then, one night, little Jim didn't come home at all.
We were worried. We went down the road to the telephone
box and rang up the local police. "How old is he?" they
said. "Sixteen, nearly seventeen." "We can't chase after
sixteen-year-olds who stay out late." "But something may
have happened. You see, he always comes home, even if it's
a late train. But now there'll be no more trains tonight.
He's never done this before." "There has to be a first time
for everything, madam; he'll turn up." And so he did; in a
London police court the next morning; charged with breaking and entering. He'd needed the money, he said, to take
out one of those girls; he'd promised her a weekend in a
posh hotel.

'In the end they put him away for six months. So that
was the end of his job, and it made it almost impossible for
him to get another when he came out – except as a common labourer, and he didn't fancy that. So now he had to
work at home here with Weekes. And hated it. And hated
us for it, though it wasn't our fault. Miserable we all were
together. The shop was doing worse and worse, there was
no extra money coming in from Jim's job any more,

Weekes's uncle's savings were going faster and faster, and Jim and Weekes were quarrelling all day long. "Sell the shop," said Jim. "Where would we go?" said Weekes. "Australia, where no one knows about me being put away." "A man's place is in his own country." "Some bloody country." And so on.

'And all this time Jim was still going with girls. Local ones, but not nice ones, they wouldn't have anything to do with him; low girls from Staines, whores more or less, they fancied him, you see, they gave him some of the money they made. So now he took to spending the day away from the shop, in pubs and cafés, pimping for these girls, or befriending them as he tried to call it when the police came. We hadn't known about it, not really, till then: only when the police came and charged him with living off immoral earnings did we realize what he'd been up to. I thought it would have killed Weekes. This time it was two years before we saw Jim again.'

'I don't suppose,' said Percival, 'that Somerset much enjoyed hearing all this about his son.'

'He was quite calm. Calm and quiet, Somerset was. "Go on," he said to me: "what happened when Jim came out again?" Well, by then it was 1967, and Jim was twenty-one. Weekes suggested the army – it was the only thing he could think of – but of course Jim wouldn't go. He'd learnt a trick worth five of that, he said, this last time in prison. He was going to be a courier. "A what?" we asked. A courier, a man who delivered messages, and other things. Easy money, lots of money. He'd met a bloke inside who'd fix him up as soon as he came out himself. And in no time at all this man had come out and my Jim was working for him – pushing drugs. The deadly ones. Heroin, that sort. Not that I knew till later, but that's what it was.'

'How did Somerset react when he heard that?' said Detterling.

'He looked very uncomfortable. "Don't you worry," I said; "that's all over. He'll never push drugs again now." Because what happened was, the police got on to him and there was a car chase. Jim's car crashed and caught fire, but the police pulled him out just in time. And the shock of all that made a good man of Jim. It reformed him. He knows now that honesty's the best policy, he's sorry for all he's done, he's going straight for the rest of his life, I can promise you that. Pure too. No more of those filthy girls. He lives here, quiet and respectable, and he's making it up to me. He's all I've got, since Weekes died, and he's taken Weekes's place in the house, and he's redeeming his past, and I love him more now than ever I did. But we were very poor, after Weekes died, because hardly anyone came to buy things here, and all Weekes's uncle's money had gone, bar a hundred pound or so, which is why I hoped Mr Lloyd-James might do something for us. I didn't want to beg, and I hadn't any real right to anything, but it would be only natural for him to help us, once he knew about little Jim. So I wrote and told him. And he came. And he heard what you've heard. And then he met Jim. I expect you'd like to, gentlemen? I can fetch him for you if you like.'

Detterling nodded, as did Percival.

'Jim,' called Meriel Weekes, and then went through the raffia curtain. 'Jim,' Detterling heard her say, 'you're wanted.'

The curtain parted. Somerset's face, as Detterling remembered it had been when Somerset was in his late twenties, was peering at them, grinning. His shoulders followed. Left arm gone, only a stump for the right. Then the torso, on an invalid chair pushed by Meriel Weekes. No legs. The face went on grinning as though it would never stop. And of course, Detterling now understood, it would never stop. A vegetable; living purely and quietly with mother at home, going straight.

'The car crash did this?'

'Yes.'

'What ... what did Somerset say?'

'He looked very hard at Jim for a long time. Then he said, "My son," and touched Jim on the cheek. Then he turned away and muttered. But I heard.'

'What did he mutter?'

'"God is not mocked",' said Meriel Weekes.

And then, Meriel told them, Somerset had left the shop for a good hour. When he came back, he said,

'"You need never be really poor. Not with him to take care of. I've been to the Government welfare people down the road in Egham. They say you've never been near them. Why not?"

"I've got my pride," Meriel had told him.

"Sink your pride," said Somerset. "They'll come and see you tomorrow. They'll either take him off your hands—"

"—Never—"

"—Or they'll make you a special allowance. For medical appliances, special care, and so on ... quite apart from other benefits which are due to you. There should be considerable arrears to come. If they ask you why you never applied, say you didn't know you were entitled. If you have any difficulty, write to your M.P. He's a good man enough and he'll see you right. You can use my name; tell him you knew me and I advised you to approach him. That's all, I think," Somerset had said; "so I'll be going now."'

And he went.

'"God is not mocked",' said Percival to Detterling, as they drove back to London. 'What exactly did he mean? That he, the father, had been punished in the person of his son?'

'Partly. He also meant, I think, that no one ever escapes ... and that even this would not be the end of it. If this horror was what came of a casual morning's fornication twenty-seven years ago, then anything might come from anything at any time. And yet again, there was the disappointment: his only son, a petty, squalid and incompetent crook. And the comparison: Somerset himself was also a crook, on an incomparably more refined level, of course, but his moral failure had been of the same kind. Like his son, Somerset had used people as if they were things.

He had got away with it so far, but here was God reminding him that he had his eye on Somerset; reminding him, too, of the hell that lay in store for all those like Somerset and his son, which is to be loved and tended when helpless by the very people whom they have deliberately injured or exploited: the hell of being forgiven. To receive unrefusable charity bears very hard on men like Somerset. It is the curse of the Detterlings,' said Detterling, 'but in the passive form. We Detterlings cannot serve selflessly: the Somersets cannot bear to be selflessly served.'

'But suicide, Detterling? Suicide because a son was paralysed in a motor smash?'

'Somerset had bred that thing on the wheelchair.'

'But it's not as if the boy had been born like that.'

'Somerset had bred him to be such that he had reached that end. The shame was Somerset's.'

'That's sheer Calvinism.'

'Somerset was a Calvinist – or a Jansenist as they call it in his Church. But like all Calvinists he believed that he himself was exempt from the system, that God had made him special. Now God was telling him different.'

'Your friend Peter Morrison,' said Percival after a pause, 'has a son who has been turned into an idiot by meningitis. And yet no one has ever suggested that he would even for one second consider suicide.'

Detterling looked at the miniature Light Dragoon on horseback which he had purchased before leaving Meriel Weekes's shop. He held it up to eye-level to examine the detail of the sabretache.

'Peter has another son,' he said. 'He has a wife. He still has people to love him, people whom he can love. And he can still love poor ruined Nickie, because he can remember him as he was when he was whole. Perhaps Somerset, when he heard about his child, began to hope for a son to love; but he could not love that thing on the chair for what it was, and he could not love it for its past, because he never knew it when it was lovable ... if it ever was.'

Detterling smiled at the toy Dragoon.

'That boy was a chip off the old block,' he said; 'and on its underside, where it had been hewn off, Somerset could see his own maggots.'

There was another pause, during which Detterling peered very closely at the epaulettes of his Dragoon.

'As I understand your account of that Memorial Dinner,' said Percival at last, 'Canteloupe suggested that Somerset was in some sense immune from evil, that he was only experimenting with it, out of a purely objective interest.'

'Somerset may have thought that too. But it wasn't true, Leonard. He could think himself immune from evil as long as he managed to guard himself against its effects. But when something he hadn't foreseen got under his guard ... then he got a mighty shock: at last he knew he was the same as everyone else, vulnerable, Leonard, because even he could not anticipate everything. Only God could do that.'

'Back with your theory, Detterling?'

'Yes. When did he make his mistake ... the fatal mistake which he never even noticed? When he got drunk? When he drank that glass of cheap sherry? When he was sick without getting himself to the loo? When he pleasured the skivvy? No, for my money, Leonard, the fatal mistake – the mistake which started all of this off and in the end destroyed Somerset – was a typical little act of meanness, so typical that of course he didn't notice it: trying to pass off half a crown on the Boys' Maid for a job that was always rated at five shillings. If he'd left the statutory five shillings, Meriel would not have looked for him that next morning and they would not have come together as they did. James Lloyd-James (for so he should truly be called) would neither have been gotten, nor born, nor later transformed into that grinning obscenity, the horror of which possessed and killed his father.'

'All very neat and clever,' said Percival; 'but what am I going to tell them in Jermyn Street?'

'No need to labour the point,' said Detterling. 'Just tell them ... that God is not mocked, and that God pulled the rug from under Somerset.'

PRINCIPAL CHARACTERS IN
ALMS FOR OBLIVION

The *Alms for Oblivion* sequence will consist of ten novels, of which nine so far have been published. They are, in chronological order: *Fielding Gray* (FG), set in 1945; *Sound the Retreat* (SR), 1945–6; *The Sabre Squadron* (SS), 1952; *The Rich Pay Late* (RPL), 1955–6; *Friends in Low Places* (FLP), 1959; *The Judas Boy* (JB), 1962; *Places Where They Sing* (PWTS), 1967; *Come Like Shadows* (CLS), 1970; *Bring Forth the Body* (BFB), 1972.

What follows is an alphabetical list of the more important characters, showing in which of the novels they have each appeared and briefly suggesting their roles.

Balliston, Hugh: an undergraduate of Lancaster College, Cambridge, in 1967 (PWTS).

Beatty, Miss: a secretary in the firm of Salinger & Holbrook (RPL). † 1956 (RPL).

Beck, Tony: a young Fellow of Lancaster College, well known as a literary critic (PWTS).

Beyfus, The Lord (life Peer): a social scientist, Fellow of Lancaster College (PWTS).

Blakeney, Balbo: a biochemist, Fellow of Lancaster College (PWTS).

Blessington, Ivan: school friend of Fielding Gray in 1945 (FG); later a regular officer in the 49th Earl Hamilton's Light Dragoons (Hamilton's Horse); ADC to his Divisional Commander in Germany in 1952 (SS); by 1955 an attaché at the British Embassy in Washington (RPL); by 1972 retired from the army and working at high level for a prominent merchant bank (BFB).

von Bremke, Herr Doktor Aeneas: a prominent mathematician at the University of Göttingen (SS).

Brockworthy, Lieutenant-Colonel: Commanding Officer of the 1st Battalion, the Wessex Fusiliers, at Berhampore in 1946 (SR).

Bunce, Basil: Squadron Sergeant-Major of the 10th Sabre Squadron of Earl Hamilton's Light Dragoons at Göttingen in 1952 (SS), and on Santa Kytherea in 1955 (FG).

Bungay, Piers: Subaltern officer of the 10th Sabre Squadron at Göttingen in 1952 (SS).

Buttock, Mrs Tessie: owner of Buttock's Hotel in the Cromwell Road (RPL, FLP, JB, CLS), a convenient establishment much favoured by Tom Llewyllyn and Fielding Gray q.v.

Canteloupe, The Marchioness (Molly): wife of The Marquis Canteloupe (FLP, SR).

CANTELOUPE, The Most Honourable the Marquis: father of The Earl of Muscateer (SR); distant cousin of Captain Detterling q.v. and political associate of Somerset Lloyd-James q.v.; successful operator of his 'Stately Home' and in 1959 Parliamentary Secretary for the Development of British Recreational Resources (FLP); Minister of Public Relations and Popular Media in 1962 (JB); Shadow Minister of Commerce in 1967 (PWTS); Minister of Commerce in the Conservative Government of 1970 (CLS), still Minister in 1972, though under heavy pressure (BFB).

Carnavon, Angus: leading male star in Pandarus/Clytemnestra Film Production of *The Odyssey* on Corfu in 1970 (CLS).

Carnwath, Doctor: a Cambridge don and historian; an old friend of Provost Constable and a member of the Lauderdale Committee; † early 1950s (BFB).

Chead, 'Corpy': Corporal-Major (*i.e.* Colour Sergeant) of the 10th Sabre Squadron at Göttingen (SS).

Clewes, The Reverend Oliver: Chaplain to Lancaster College (PWTS).

CONSTABLE, Robert Reculver (Major): demobilized with special priority in the summer of 1945 to take up appointment as Tutor of Lancaster College, Cambridge (FG); by 1955 Vice-Chancellor of the University of Salop, and *ex officio* member of the Board of *Strix* (RPL); elected Provost of Lancaster in 1959 (FLP); still Provost in 1962

(JB) and 1967 (PWTS), and 1972 (BFB).

Corrington, Mona: an anthropologist, Fellow of Girton College, Cambridge. Chum of Lord Beyfus q.v. (PWTS).

Cruxtable, Sergeant-Major: Company Sergeant-Major of Peter Morrison's Company at the O.T.S., Bangalore, in 1945–6 (SR); 'P.T. expert' at Canteloupe's physical fitness camp in the west country (FLP).

DETTERLING, Captain: distant cousin of Lord Canteloupe; regular officer of The 49th Earl Hamilton's Light Dragoons (Hamilton's Horse) from 1937; in charge of recruiting for the Cavalry in 1945 (FG); instructor at the O.T.S., Bangalore, from late 1945 to summer 1946 (SR); by 1952 has retired from Hamilton's Horse and become a Member of Parliament (SS); still M.P. in 1955 and a political supporter of Peter Morrison q.v. (RPL); still M.P. in 1959, when he joins Gregory Stern q.v. as a partner in Stern's publishing house (FLP); still M.P. and publisher in 1962 (JB) and 1970 (CLS), and 1972, at which time he gives important assistance to those enquiring into the death of Somerset Lloyd-James (BFB).

Dexterside, Ashley: friend and employee of Donald Salinger (RPL).

Dharaparam, H.H. The Maharajah of: an Indian Prince; Patron of the Cricket Club of the O.T.S., Bangalore (SR).

Dilkes, Henry: Secretary to the Institute of Political and Economic Studies and a member of the Board of Strix (RPL, FLP).

Dixon, Alastair: Member of Parliament for safe Conservative seat in the west country; about to retire in 1959 (FLP), thus creating a vacancy coveted both by Peter Morrison and Somerset Lloyd-James q.v.

Dolly: maid of all work to Somerset Lloyd-James in his chambers in Albany (BFB).

Drew, Vanessa: v. Salinger, Donald.

Engineer, Margaret Rose: a Eurasian harlot who entertains Peter Morrison q.v. in Bangalore (SR).

de FREVILLE, Max: gambler and connoisseur of human affairs; runs big chemin-de-fer games in the London of the fifties (RPL), maintaining a private spy-ring for protection from possible welshers and also for the sheer amusement of it (FLP); later goes abroad to Venice, Hydra, Cyprus and Corfu, where he engages in various enterprises (FLP, JB, CLS), often in partnership with Lykiadopoulos *q.v.* and usually attended by Angela Tuck *q.v.* His Corfiot interests include a share in the 1970 Pandarus/Clytemnestra production of *The Odyssey* (CLS). Still active in Corfu in 1972 (BFB).

Frith, Hetta: girl friend of Hugh Balliston *q.v.* (PWTS.) † 1967 (PWTS).

Galahead, Foxe J. (Foxy): Producer for Pandarus and Clytemnestra Films of *The Odyssey* on Corfu in 1970 (CLS).

Gamp, Jonathan: a not so young man about town (RPL, FLP, BFB).

Gilzai Khan, Captain: an Indian officer (Moslem) holding the King's Commission; an instructor at the O.T.S., Bangalore, 1945–6; resigns to become a political agitator (SR). † 1946 (SR).

Glastonbury, Major Giles: an old friend of Detterling *q.v.* and regular officer of Hamilton's Horse; temporary Lieutenant-Colonel on Lord Wavell's staff in India 1945–6 (SR); officer commanding the 10th Sabre Squadron of Hamilton's Horse at Göttingen in 1952 (SS).

Grange, Lady Susan: marries Lord Philby (RPL).

Gray, John Aloysius (Jack); Fielding Gray's father (FG). † 1945.

Gray, Mrs: Fielding Gray's mother (FG). † c. 1948.

GRAY, Major Fielding: senior schoolboy in 1945 (FG) with Peter Morrison and Somerset Lloyd-James *q.v.*; scholar elect of Lancaster College, but tangles with the authorities, is deprived of his scholarship before he can take it up (FG), and becomes a regular officer of Earl Hamilton's Light Dragoons; 2 i/c and then O.C. the 10th Sabre Squadron in Göttingen in 1952 (SS) and still commanding the Squadron on Santa Kytherea in 1955 (FG); badly mutilated in Cyprus in 1958 and leaves the Army to become critic and novelist with the help of Somerset Lloyd-James (FLP); achieves minor distinction, and in 1962 is sent out to Greece and Cyprus by Tom Llewyllyn *q.v.* to investigate Cypriot affairs, past and present, for BBC Television (JB); in Greece meets Harriet Ongley *q.v.*; by 1967 has won the Joseph Conrad Prize for Fiction (PWTS); goes to Corfu in 1970 to rewrite script for Pandarus/Clytemnestra's *The Odyssey* (CLS); in 1972 is engaged on a study of Joseph Conrad, which is to be published, as part of a new series, by Gregory Stern (BFB).

Grimes, Sasha: a talented young actress playing in Pandarus/Clytemnestra's *The Odyssey* on Corfu (CLS).

The Headmaster of Fielding Gray's School (FG): a man of conscience.

Helmutt, Jacquiz: historian; research student at Lancaster College in 1952 (SS); later Fellow of Lancaster (PWTS).

Holbrook, Jude: partner of Donald Salinger *q.v.* 1949–56 (RPL); 'freelance' in 1959 (FLP); reported by Burke Lawrence *q.v.* (CLS) as having gone to live in Hong Kong in the sixties.

Holbrook, Penelope: a model; wife of Jude Holbrook (RPL); by 1959, divorced from Jude and associated with Burke Lawrence (FLP); reported by Burke Lawrence (CLS) as still living in London and receiving alimony from Jude in Hong Kong.

Holeworthy, R.S.M.: Regimental Sergeant-Major of the Wessex Fusiliers at Göttingen in 1952 (SS).

Jacobson, Jules: old hand in the film world; Director of Pandarus/Clytemnestra's *The Odyssey* on Corfu in 1970 (CLS).

James, Cornet Julian: Cambridge friend of Daniel Mond *q.v.*; in 1952 a National Service officer of the 10th Sabre Squadron at Göttingen (SS).

Joe: groundsman at Detterling's old school (BFB).

Lamprey, Jack: a subaltern officer of the 10th Sabre Squadron (SS).

La Soeur, Doctor: a confidential practitioner, physician to Fielding Gray (FG, RPL, CLS).

Lawrence, Burke: 'film director' and advertising man (RPL); from c. 1956 to 1959 teams up with Penelope Holbrook q.v. in murky 'agency' (FLP); c. 1960 leaves England for Canada, and later becomes P.R.O. to Clytemnestra Films (CLS).

Lewson, Felicity: born Contessina Felicula Maria Monteverdi; educated largely in England; wife of Mark Lewson (though several years his senior) and his assistant in his profession (RPL). † 1959 (FLP).

Lewson, Mark: a con man (RPL, FLP). † 1959 (FLP).

Lichfield, Margaret: star actress playing Penelope in the Pandarus/Clytemnestra production of The Odyssey on Corfu in 1970 (CLS).

LLEWYLLYN, Tom: a 'scholarship boy' of low Welsh origin but superior education; author, journalist and contributor to Strix (RPL); same but far more successful by 1959, when he marries Patricia Turbot q.v. (FLP); given important contract by BBC Television in 1962 to produce Today is History, and later that year appointed Namier Fellow of Lancaster College (JB); renewed as Namier Fellow in 1965 and still at Lancaster in 1967 (PWTS); later made a permanent Fellow of the College (CLS); employed by Pandarus and Clytemnestra Films as 'Literary and Historical Adviser' to their production of The Odyssey on Corfu in 1970 (CLS); still a don at Lancaster in 1972, when he is reported to be winning esteem for the first volume of his magnum opus (published by the Cambridge University Press) on the subject of Power (BFB).

Llewyllyn, Tullia: always called and known as 'Baby'; Tom and Patricia's daughter, born in 1960 (JB, PWTS, CLS, BFB).

Lloyd-James, Mrs Peregrina : widowed mother of Somerset Lloyd-James (BFB).

LLOYD-JAMES, Somerset : a senior schoolboy and friend of Fielding Gray in 1945 (FG); by 1955, Editor of *Strix*, an independent economic journal (RPL); still editor of *Strix* in 1959 (FLP) and now seeking a seat in Parliament; still editor of *Strix* in 1962 (JB), but now also a Member of Parliament and unofficial adviser to Lord Canteloupe *q.v.*; still M.P. and close associate of Canteloupe in 1967 (PWTS), and by 1970 Canteloupe's official understrapper in the House of Commons (CLS), still so employed in 1972 (BFB), with title of Parliamentary Under-Secretary of State at the Ministry of Commerce; † 1972 (BFB).

Lykiadopoulos, Stratis : a Greek gentleman, or not far off it; professional gambler and man of affairs (FLP) who has a brief liaison with Mark Lewson; friend and partner of Max de Freville *q.v.* (FLP), with whom he has business interests in Cyprus (JB) and later in Corfu (CLS).

Maisie : a whore (RPL, FLP, JB) frequented with enthusiasm by Fielding Gray, Lord Canteloupe and Somerset Lloyd-James; apparently still going strong as late as 1967 (ref. PWTS) and even 1970 (ref. CLS), and 1972 (BFB).

Mayerston : a revolutionary (PWTS).

Mond, Daniel : a mathematician; research student of Lancaster College (SS) sent to Göttingen University in 1952 to follow up his line of research, which unexpectedly turns out to have a military potential; later Fellow of Lancaster and teacher of pure mathematics (PWTS).

Morrison, Helen : Peter Morrison's wife (RPL, FLP, BFB).

MORRISON, Peter : senior schoolboy with Fielding Gray and Somerset Lloyd-James *q.v.* in 1945 (FG); an officer cadet at the O.T.S., Bangalore, from late 1945 to summer 1946 (SR) and then commissioned as a Second Lieutenant in the Wessex Fusiliers, whom he joins at Berhampore; by 1952 has inherited substantial estates in East Anglia and by 1955 is a Member of Parliament (RPL) where he leads 'the Young England Group'; but in 1956 applies for Chiltern Hundreds (RPL); tries and fails to return to Parliament in 1959 (FLP); reported by Lord Canteloupe (CLS) as having finally got a seat again after a by-election in 1968 and as having retained it at the General Election in 1970; in 1972 appointed Parliamentary Under-Secretary of State at the Ministry of Commerce on the demise of Somerset Lloyd-James (BFB).

Morrison, 'Squire': Peter's father (FG), owner of a fancied racehorse (Tiberius). † c. 1950.

Mortleman, Alister: an officer cadet at the O.T.S., Bangalore, 1945–6, later commissioned into the Wessex Fusiliers (SR).

Motley, Mick: Lieutenant of the R.A.M.C., attached to the Wessex Fusiliers at Göttingen in 1952 (SS).

Murphy, 'Wanker': an officer cadet at the O.T.S., Bangalore, 1945–6; later commissioned as Captain in the Education Corps, then promoted to be Major and Galloper to the Viceroy of India (SR). † 1946 (SR).

Muscateer, Earl of: son of Lord and Lady Canteloupe q.v.; an officer cadet at the O.T.S., Bangalore, 1945–6 (SR). † 1946 (SR).

Nicos: a Greek boy who picks up Fielding Gray (JB).

Ogden, The Reverend Andrew: Dean of the Chapel of Lancaster College (PWTS).

Ongley, Mrs Harriet: rich American widow; Fielding Gray's mistress and benefactress from 1962 onwards (JB, PWTS, CLS), but has left him by 1972 (BFB).

Pappenheim, Herr: German ex-officer of World War II; in 1952 about to rejoin new West German Army as a senior staff officer (SS).

Percival, Leonard: cloak-and-dagger man; in 1952 nominally a Lieutenant of the Wessex Fusiliers at Göttingen (SS), but by 1962 working strictly in plain clothes (JB); friend of Max de Freville, with whom he occasionally exchanges information to their mutual amusement (JB);

transferred to a domestic department ('Jermyn Street') of the secret service and rated 'Home enquiries only', because of stomach ulcers in 1972, when he investigates, in association with Detterling, the death of Somerset Lloyd-James (BFB).

Percival, Rupert: a small-town lawyer in the west country (FLP), prominent among local Conservatives and a friend of Alastair Dixon q.v.; Leonard Percival's uncle (JB).

Philby, The Lord: proprietor of Strix (RPL, FLP) which he has inherited along with his title from his father, 'old' Philby.

Pough (pronounced Pew), The Honourable Grantchester Fitz-Margrave: Senior Fellow of Lancaster College, Professor Emeritus of Oriental Geography, at one time celebrated as a mountainer; a dietary fadist (PWTS).

Pulcher, Detective Sergeant: assistant to Detective Superintendent Stupples, q.v. (BFB).

Restarick, Earle: American cloak-and-dagger man; in 1952 apparently a student at Göttingen University (SS) but in fact taking an unwholesome interest in the mathematical researches of Daniel Mond q.v.; later active in Cyprus (JB) and in Greece (CLS).

Roland, Christopher: a special school friend of Fielding Gray (FG). † 1945 (FG).

Salinger, Donald: senior partner of Salinger & Holbrook, a printing firm (RPL); in 1956 marries Vanessa Drew (RPL); is deserted by Jude Holbrook q.v. in the summer of 1956 (RPL) but in 1959 is still printing (FLP), and still married to Vanessa; in 1972 is reported as having broken down mentally and retired to a private Nursing Home in consequence of Vanessa's death by drowning (BFB).

Schottgatt, Doctor Emile: of Montana University, Head of the 'Creative Authentication Committee' of the Oglander-Finckelstein Trust, which visits Corfu in 1970 (CLS) to assess the merits of the Pandarus/Clytemnestra production of The Odyssey.

Schroeder, Alfie: a reporter employed by the Billingsgate Press (RPL, FLP, SS); by 1967 promoted to columnist (PWTS).

Sheath, Aloysius: a scholar on the staff of the American School of Greek Studies in Athens, but also assistant to Earle Restarick q.v. (JB, CLS).

Stern, Gregory: publisher (RPL), later in partnership with Captain Detterling q.v. (FLP); publishes Tom Llewyllyn and Fielding Gray q.v. (RPL, FLP, JB, PWTS, CLS); married to Isobel Turbot (FLP).

Strange, Barry: an officer cadet at the O.T.S. Bangalore, 1945–6, later commissioned into the Wessex Fusiliers, with whom he has strong family connexions (SR).

Stupples, Detective Superintendent: policeman initially responsible for enquiries into the death of Somerset Lloyd-James in 1972 (BFB).

Tuck: a tea-planter in India; marries Angela, the daughter of a disgraced officer, and brings her back to England in 1945 (FG); later disappears, but turns up as an official of the Control Commission in Germany in 1952 (SS). † 1956 (RPL).

TUCK, Mrs Angela: daughter of a Colonel in the Indian Army Pay Corps, with whom she lives in Southern India (JB, FLP) until early 1945, when her father is dismissed the Service for malversation; being then *in extremis* marries Tuck the tea-planter, and returns with him to England in the summer of 1945 (FG); briefly mistress to the adolescent Somerset Lloyd-James q.v., and to 'Jack' Gray (Fielding's father); despite this a trusted friend of Fielding's mother (FG); by 1955 is long separated from Tuck and now mistress to Jude Holbrook (RPL); in 1956 inherits small fortune from the intestate Tuck, from whom she has never been actually divorced *pace* her bibulous and misleading soliloquies on the subject in the text (RPL); in 1959 living in Menton and occasional companion of Max de Freville q.v. (FLP); later Max's constant companion (JB, CLS). † 1970 (CLS).

Turbot, The Right Honourable Sir Edwin, P.C., ... tician; in 1946 ex-Minister of wartime coalition ac... panying all-party delegation of M.P.s to India (SR); b, 1959 long since a Minister once more, and 'Grand Vizier' of the Conservative Party (FLP); father of Patricia, who marries Tom Llewyllyn (FLP), and of Isobel, who marries Gregory Stern (FLP); by 1962 reported as badly deteriorating and as having passed some of his fortune over to his daughters (JB). † by 1967 (PWTS), having left more money to his daughters.

Turbot, Isobel : v. Turbot, Sir Edwin, and Stern, Gregory.

Turbot, Patricia : v. Turbot, Sir Edwin, and Llewyllyn, Tom. Also v. Llewyllyn, Tullia. Has brief walk-out with Hugh Balliston q.v. (PWTS) and is disobliging to Tom about money (JB, PWTS, CLS). In 1972 is reported by Jonathan Gamp to be indulging curious if not criminal sexual preferences (BFB).

Weekes, James : bastard son of Somerset Lloyd-James, born in 1945 (BFB).

Weekes, Mrs Meriel : *quondam* and random associate of Somerset Lloyd-James, and mother of his bastard son (BFB).

Weir, Carton : Member of Parliament and political associate of Peter Morrison (RPL); later official aide to Lord Canteloupe (FLP, JB). P.P.S. to Canteloupe at Ministry of Commerce in 1972 (BFB).

Winstanley, Ivor : a distinguished Latinist, Fellow of Lancaster College (PWTS).

'Young bastard' : assistant groundsman at Detterling's old school (BFB).

Zaccharias : an officer cadet at the O.T.S., Bangalore, 1945–6; commissioned into a dowdy regiment of the line (SR).